RUNAWAY BRIDE

Jennifer had just turned back from the little wicket gate that led out on to the open down when a sound behind her made her turn. As she did so, her arms were caught from behind and a heavy cloth bound over her face, making speech or sight impossible. Struggling frantically, but to no avail, she felt herself pushed along by her captors and heard the click of the wicket gate behind her. For a moment, wild visions of romantic terror darted through her mind, of foreign villains and castle dungeons. Then she remembered how her brothers had laughed at such horrors.

So, when she was half pushed, half pulled into a waiting carriage, and the bandages ungently removed from her eyes, she greeted her uncle, sitting there to receive her, with a calm that surprised him. 'What now, Uncle?'

'Why, that's the girl.' Her uncle made no attempt to conceal his pleased surprise at her meek acceptance of defeat. 'You and I may deal admirably together yet.'

Runaway Bride

Jane Aiken Hodge

CORONET BOOKS
Hodder and Stoughton.

© 1975 by Jane Aiken Hodge

First published 1975 by Fawcett
Publications Inc., New York

Coronet edition 1976
Second impression 1978

Printed and bound in Great Britain for
Hodder and Stoughton Paperbacks, a
division of Hodder and Stoughton Ltd.,
Mill Road, Dunton Green, Sevenoaks,
Kent (Editorial Office: 47 Bedford
Square, London, WC1 3DP) by
Richard Clay (The Chaucer Press), Ltd.,
Bungay, Suffolk

ISBN 0 340 19862 1

CHAPTER I

'Mark my words, George, you must marry – and quickly.' The Duchess hitched up her auburn wig which had, as usual, slid down over one bejewelled ear.

'I fear you are right, ma'am,' said her grandson gloomily as he bent down to offer her his enamelled snuff-box. The Honourable George Ferris – or, to give him his baptismal due, George Frederick William Edward Ernest Augustus Adolphus Ferris – was having a bad half-hour with his grandmother. According to his friends at Brooks' Club there were only two people in the world that this formidable young man feared: one was the Duke of Wellington, the other, the Duchess of Lewes. Friend of Dr Johnson and confidante of Fox, she was indeed a grandmother to make a man tremble, particularly as he himself was set on a political career. It was she, of course, who had insisted on his being named after all the deplorable Royal Dukes, sons of George III, and had browbeaten them into resolving their differences for long enough to stand godfathers together at his christening. It was not, as she frequently pointed out, her fault that his royal godfathers had in fact done so little to advance his career.

The younger son of a duke's spendthrift heir, George Ferris had his own way to make in the world. While his older brother made the Grand Tour as best he might in the intervals of the long war with France, George had been given his father's un-enthusiastic blessing, a small and spasmodic allowance, and introductions to Beau Brummell and Brooks' Club. Luckily for him, his erratic old grandfather the Duke had finally gone mad in Trafalgar year and the Duchess had lost no time in immur-ing her husband in one of his smaller and more remote castles and taking control of his fortune. One of her first actions had been to buy a commission in the Blues for George, whom she much preferred to his dissolute elder brother.

George had thanked her warmly, packed his few possessions and joined his regiment in the Peninsula. Handsome in a blue-eyed, black-browed, frowning way; short-tempered, dare-devil, a judge of horses and men, he had soon made his mark in the field and had been rebuked by the Duke himself for putting up his umbrella to keep off the rain while waiting to charge at Salamanca. Once noticed, he was not easily forgotten. Soon afterwards, he was taken on to the Duke's staff where he distinguished himself by capturing an Eagle in the intervals of carrying despatches at Waterloo.

With peace at last secure, the army's attractions had dwindled. He had sold out and persuaded his father to send him to Parliament as member for the family's pocket borough of Cuckhaven. Once admitted to the House he had delighted that staunch old Whig his grandmother by the point and ferocity of his attacks on the Government, and was already being talked of as a rival to the colourless Ponsonby for the leadership of the Party.

'But depend upon it, George,' continued his astute grand-mamma, taking a pinch of snuff and sneezing with gusto, 'Bachelor's chambers are a damned awkward rallying ground for a coterie. A political leader must have a house, and a house must have a mistress. With the right wife, you can put them all in the shade. Marry now, marry well and, above all, marry richly and who knows where you may find yourself when the King finally dies and Prinny's friends come into their own at last. There's not a leader among them: Ponsonby, Tierney . . . bah, you're worth six of them. But marry, George, only marry . . .'

He looked down at her ruefully. 'You're mighty insistent, ma'am.'

'I am mighty correct.' The fierce old eyes softened as they gazed up at him. 'George, it cannot be that you still wear the willow for that Ponsonby chit?'

He drew himself up and for a moment his eyes flashed, fierce as hers: 'Lady Caroline Lamb will always have my heart.'

The old lady sighed. 'To add to her collection? Or to offer, among other things, to Lord Byron? No, no,' she put a delicate restraining hand on his arm, 'I'll not tease you, George, but if you have no heart to give, you still have a hand, and there's many an heiress will take it, and glad to. What do you think of one of the Markham girls?'

'As little as I can, ma'am, I assure you. Now spare me, I beg, the catalogue of this year's possible misses, for I have a mind that if marry I must it shall be a girl of my own choosing.'

She sparkled up at him, arch as the brilliant girl who had once charmed Dr Johnson. 'George, I declare you have someone in mind. Tell me quick, who is she? What is she like? Do I know her?'

He smiled down at her. 'No, ma'am, she is, I apprehend, something of a country mouse, nor, to deal plainly with you, do I know her myself, but of her, I think, enough . . .'

'More and more romantic,' she twinkled at him. 'Who is this paragon you would marry unseen?'

'She is a Miss Purchas, ma'am. Jennifer Purchas.'

'Hmmm,' the old lady considered it. 'A pretty name, for what that is worth. Let me see, Purchas . . . Ah, I have it: the Cornish Purchases, I collect. Bought the Sussex estate with their profits out of the South Sea Bubble. There's an American branch – they spell it differently I believe. A good old Whig family and shrewd as well. He married . . . now let me see, there was something of a breeze over it: yes, of course, not a Miss Butts, but some other banker's daughter. But she was produceable enough, I always understood. Died in childbirth, did she not?'

'Ma'am you amaze me as always, and, as always, you are entirely in the right of it. Jennifer – it is a pretty name, is it not? – Jennifer was the child. She grew up under the guardianship of her father and his sister, and much the companion of my friends, her older brothers.'

'Oh, there are brothers are there? I had quite forgot.'

'Were, ma'am, not are. Both her brothers, and her father, were killed at Waterloo.'

She considered it, quiet for a moment. 'They were always a military family, but, surely, George, that was excessive?'

'Indeed, yes. Her father rejoined the army when his wife

3

died. The sons must needs follow him – and now Jennifer is alone.'

'George, I declare, you are in love with her name!'

'So much the better if I am, for, I must tell you, I feel in honour bound to marry her.'

'In honour bound? What absurdity is this?'

'No absurdity, ma'am, but a very real duty. Let me explain. I was, as doubtless you recall, at Waterloo myself, attached to the Duke.'

The old eyes softened. 'Strangely enough, George, I remember it very well. It was you who took the pains, on the very day of the battle, to send me news by the messenger who announced the victory to Lord Harrowby. But we were fortunate . . . most fortunate. All three Purchases were killed, you say?'

'Yes, and worse than that.'

'Worse?'

'Yes, I apprehend, for Jennifer. It was this way, ma'am. Francis, the eldest, died in the first charge. "Damme," said the Duke, "there goes one of my best young men."'

''Twas a terrible day. I think I have grown too old for wars. But tell me of the other two.'

'Her father was killed rallying his men at Hougomont. I came there with the Duke's orders that they hold the farm if it cost every man of them. Purchas smiled at me. "Someone else will have to hold it," he said, "but never fear, they will." And died.'

He paused. 'Well?' she asked. 'Naturally I am aware that Hougomont was held. But what of the third?'

'Richard.' His voice was quiet. 'Richard was on the Duke's staff with me, and many a night we made of it together.'

'A wild young man?'

'Wild enough for me. But not that day. I had to tell him of his father's and brother's deaths. "Damn," he said, "that's bad, George." But we were interrupted. The Duke rode up. It was midday and he had had no news of Blücher. He looked at us both. I had my wound by then; it was a nothing, a scratch, but it bled most confoundedly.'

She raised her eyebrows. 'Such language to a lady?'

'I ask your pardon, ma'am. It is sometimes hard to remember you are a lady.'

She laughed outright. 'I find it hard enough myself. But to your story. Your wound was bleeding . . .'

'Yes. A damned awkward place . . . The Duke looked at me. "You have got yourself deucedly knocked up, Ferris, and your horse is blown. Purchas shall bring me news of Blücher. It should be a lively ride." Richard saluted, finished his bottle and rode away. After that, we were busy for a time. It was some hours before I observed that Richard had not returned from his lively ride. The Duke had noticed it too. Our men were being badly mauled: he called me to his side and looked me over: "So," he said, "you are presentable again. Very good. You will ride after Purchas and bring me news of Blücher without fail. Of Purchas, too, if you can do so without overmuch delay. Do not you get yourself killed. Good men are growing damnably scarce."

'I found Richard not half a mile away, under a hedge. There was nothing I could do for him. A cannon ball had done its business. He could just speak: "Finishing my errand, George? I wish you may speed better than I have. But I'll not delay you. Only, George; one kindness," he paused for breath, then went on: "My little sister, Jenny, George. She will be all alone. Father's will cannot stand, since Francis died before him . . . No protection for Jenny," he was gasping for breath now, "an heiress, and a damned bad hat of an uncle. Look after her, George."

'I promised, filled my flask with water for him, and left him.'

'And you found Blücher?'

'Naturally, ma'am, since I am here today. I would scarce have faced the Duke without. As for Blücher, he embraced me on both cheeks, and nearly suffocated me with his stink of gin and rhubarb.'

'A barbarous concoction. And now, you would tell me that, because of your promise to a dying man, you feel in honour bound to marry this Jenny?'

'How else can I look after her, ma'am?'

She smiled. 'It is indeed a difficult task for a young man of thirty, is it not?'

'Thirty-five,' he corrected her.

'Time indeed that you thought of marriage. But, forgive me, George, you do not seem to have hurried yourself overmuch. It is a year now since Waterloo. Who, pray, has been protecting your Jennifer?'

'Not I, more shame to me. But you well know that I have only these last few days got my affairs into some sort of order. And she is but a child, seventeen at most.'

'At seventeen, George, I was your father's mother. I think you would do well to bestir yourself. Besides, what of the wicked uncle? Is he not in all likelihood at this very moment making ducks and drakes of her fortune?'

'I earnestly hope not, ma'am. But if he is, I am informed he is well able to make restitution. He is her mother's brother, a Gurning, one of the banker lot, as rich as Rothschild.'

'What makes you think, then, that he'll marry his rich ward to a younger son with, forgive me George, no prospects but of his own making and a certain something in expectation from a long-lived, bad-tempered old grandmother?'

The dark eyes, so like her own, flashed down on her. 'A duke's grandson, ma'am. Don't forget my connections. The man's not such a fool. He has, I am told, a puppy of a ward he's mad to get into Parliament and some such ambition on his own part too. My father has three boroughs at his disposal. I expect no difficulty.'

'You think, then, that your father will back you in this enterprise?'

'I know it. No need to beat about the bush with you. My father is damned nearly in Queer Street since the peace and now with my brother's debts to be paid before he can marry he'll think himself advantaged if he can get me a fortune in exchange for one of the family seats.'

She sighed. 'Indeed Henry has been most imprudent. A few thousands of debt are merely to be expected in an elder son but he, I collect, has not been so modest.'

'Modesty, ma'am, was never Henry's forte, as you well know.

6

I can only regret that he has not chosen to have a few inexpensive vices.'

She frowned. 'George, he is your elder brother.'

'Yes, deeply to my chagrin, he is. No, no,' he put a hand on hers, 'do not think I grudge him the title, but his opportunities . . . and to see them so wasted.'

Once more she sighed. 'Yes, I know it is hard. I told your father he gravely mistook when he made such a difference between you two boys, but he was always set on his own opinions, and so it was Oxford and the Grand Tour for Henry . . .'

'And nothing for me,' he interrupted her, 'if you had not stepped into the breach and paid my shot at Cambridge. I'll never forget it, nor the gift of my commission. All I am I owe to you.'

She smiled at him fondly. 'And a most satisfactory hobby you have proved. But never thank me till you are First Minister. I shall dearly love to be grandmother to the power before the throne.'

He laughed. 'I might have known you had your own axe to grind. Well, let me but make this marriage, set up my London house, and we shall see . . .'

She looked at him thoughtfully. 'And the girl, George, what of her? Perhaps she may have a mind to wed someone else.'

He showed his surprise. 'The girl, ma'am? I hope she knows a man when she sees one.'

She smiled her wise old smile: 'So do I, George, so do I . . .'

7

CHAPTER II

But down in Sussex, some ten days later, Jennifer Purchas
stamped her foot on its Waterloo heel and glared up at her
Uncle Gurning.

'I'll not have him, Uncle, were he the Czar of all the Russias.'
She had just returned from a gallop on the Downs. Her cheeks
were flushed, her auburn hair glowed against the dark green of
her habit.

'But Jenny my dear, only consider,' bland, placating, he
loomed over her, a red-faced monster of a man.

'Don't "Jenny" me.' The foot stamped again. A year's pent-
up rebellion had exploded in a day when her uncle had announced, with odious certainty, that she was to marry George
Ferris. The bitterness had been growing within her since that
sun-drenched June day when her Uncle Gurning, the banker,
had arrived from London with the news that she was alone in
the world. 'But my dear Jenny, never trouble yourself, I will
take care of you . . .' He had failed to conceal his pleasure in the
prospect and she had never forgiven him.

But there had been no escaping his control. Only sixteen, she
had been unable to prevent him from moving his household
into the big house near Denton that was, she supposed, now
hers. Her father's sister, kind Aunt Julia, had protested feebly,
then, routed by the patronising takeover of Uncle Gurning's
city wife, had packed her trunks and fled to cousins in Yorkshire.

Since then, a year has passed. A wretched year in which
Jennifer had watched her uncle's penny-pinching ways on the
estate and fought skirmish after skirmish with her aunt. Loathing both of them, she had grown reluctantly fond of their
daughter Elizabeth, a year her junior, and even of their ward,
bumbling, good-hearted Edmund Butts.

But here was the last straw. Marry to please her uncle she

would not. Nor did she believe his claim that the man who asked her hand did it as her brother's friend; she had known her uncle's shifts too well for that. She gave him one of the straight looks that still reminded him uncomfortably of her father: 'If he's Richard's friend, why has he waited so long to come to me? It was last year I lacked a friend.' Unspoken between them lay the truth of this.

But he tried to shrug it off. 'Nevertheless, he claims much knowledge of Richard – and Francis too.'

She could not bear to hear him speak her brothers' names. 'No doubt he had drunk with them often enough; they were never over nice in their choice of acquaintance. But a friend, Uncle, would have come sooner. No,' she shook off the damp hand that fell placatingly on her wrist, 'I have no doubt you have reasons to wish for the match, but I'll hear no more of it.' With a swirl of skirts, she broke from him. In a minute she would be in tears, and she had never let her uncle see her cry.

Running up the house's wide central stairway to her own room, she dug furiously in a cupboard to find the precious bundles of her brothers' letters. Yes, there it was, in a letter from Richard: 'Rather bosky last night, I fear,' he had written not long before Waterloo, 'but who could help it with Ferris passing the bottle? He has taken me regularly in hand since I joined the Beau's staff. The other fellows say I'm damned lucky to have such a friend. He's a regular Corinthian; older than me, of course. He was with the Beau right through Spain. A friend of Brummell's too . . . and, oh Jenny, you should just see his cravats.'

Tears filled her eyes at the boyishness of the phrases. Already, after a year of grief and trouble, she felt older than her brothers would ever be. And as for this rakehelly boon companion of theirs, who had doubtless been the reason for the pile of debts her uncle had paid with such intolerable grumbling after their deaths . . . she would show him what their sister thought of him.

There was a discreet tapping at the door.

'Yes,' she called impatiently. Was there to be no end of this persecution?

But it was only Soames, the butler, to say with unspoken sympathy that Mr Gurning wished her company in his study.

His study, she thought to herself, fanning her anger to keep up her courage. Her father's study turned into a banker's office. For her Uncle Gurning still kept up his city business and spent several days of each week in London. The house that had once been headquarters for the Whig élite of the county had degenerated into little better than a banker's office. Only her best friends still came to see her and they did so apologetically, almost surreptitiously, by appointment, picking hours when her uncle was away in London and doing their best to avoid her aunt's ostentatious hospitality.

As she went reluctantly downstairs again, she considered these friends. To whom could she turn for support in this crisis? There was Aunt Julia, of course, but she had proved herself a broken reed at the first onslaught of the Gurnings. Even at sixteen, Jennifer had wished to hold her own, to treat them as guests, to defer still to Aunt Julia as the chaperon in whose charge her father had left her. Aunt Julia had failed her then; hopeless to expect more of her now – and, besides, she was hundreds of miles away, with those unknown cousins in Yorkshire. Useless to appeal to her. Only Lucy Faversham remained. Lucy was her best and oldest friend, whose governess she had shared for years, and the daughter of her father's staunch political associate, General Hugo Faversham. But Lucy was only eighteen, and motherless like herself. And though the General made no secret of his dislike for Uncle Gurning, Jennifer much doubted whether he would support her in open revolt. His radical politics hardly included rebellious young women. Indeed, she had long recognised him for the kind of man who would always prefer words to deeds . . .

But she had reached the study door. Entering, she found her uncle busy at the desk that looked so out of place among her father's sporting prints.

'Ah, Jenny, my dear.' The bland tone told her he was going to pretend nothing untoward had happened between them. She knew this gambit of old and steeled herself to resist.

'We were discussing the question of your betrothal,' he

went on, 'and I believe I may have failed to make my position in the matter quite clear. There will be no question, naturally, of an early marriage. Your aunt and I would not lightly part with our dear niece . . .' he paused, every inch the loving uncle.

'No,' said Jennifer, but, wisely she finished the sentence to herself: nor with her fortune neither.

'Indeed,' continued her uncle, 'your aunt and I had been busy only the other day with plans for your début which, as you are well aware, has of necessity been postponed until you should be out of black gloves. We have been seriously considering how best we might proceed, for, as you know, your Aunt Gurning is not, most unfortunately, in a position to present you to society.'

Reluctantly, Jennifer found herself admiring the man. It was not everyone who would have the courage so to face his wife's social unacceptability. But what in the world was to follow? She had heard no talk of a début before, and had resigned herself to the belief that her chance of this, with so much else that was more important, had been lost with her father. Did Uncle Gurning perhaps think that Aunt Julia could be persuaded to return and chaperon her? For herself, she doubted it strongly. The breach between Aunt Julia and the Gurnings had gone too deep to be easily bridged. And it would, she told herself, be foolish to imagine that the Gurnings would loosen their hold on her – and her fortune. They had no other produceable connection, she was sure, or she would have heard of it.

But her uncle, who had paused to shuffle the papers into place on his desk, was talking again. 'Now,' he said blandly, 'we have hit on a most eligible solution for this difficulty. The Honourable George Ferris, as you may perhaps not be aware, is the grandson of a duchess, and, I apprehend, for, believe me, my dear, I have not been idle in my enquiries on your behalf since I received his application for your hand . . .' he paused, lost for once in his own parenthesis, while Jennifer commented angrily to herself on his love of a title. But he had found his thread: "As I was saying, his grandmother, the Duchess, is said to be devoted to Mr Ferris, for all that he is nothing but a younger son; and has done much, they say, to make his career. Now I propose, in answering this letter and accepting Mr Ferris's very flattering proposal, to suggest that your position in society would be best secured if you were to make your début as his affianced bride under the protection of his grandmother. No, do not be alarmed; we would not quite abandon you: your cousin Elizabeth might, I believe, very suitably go with you to keep you company and your aunt and I would never be far away.'

No, she said to herself, I dare swear you would not. The prospect of being foisted in this way upon Mr Ferris's reluctant family was, if possible, more unpleasant even than that of marriage with him. Brought up in the realistic male society of her father and brothers, she saw nothing out of the way in Ferris's proposal for her hand. Doubtless he was pressed for money, as her brothers had always been, and was prepared to swallow her aunt and uncle for the sake of her fortune . . . But to have to take her into his family even before marriage had given him control of his prize . . . that, surely, he would find the outside of enough. For a moment she wondered whether she dared accede to her uncle's proposals in the hope that they would prove so galling to her suitor that he would cry off from the match himself. But it was too great a chance to take, too extreme a sacrifice of her pride. She turned seriously to the task of persuading her uncle that she was resolute against the match.

But her arguments were wasted. She had never seen Mr Gurning so determined, and soon suspected that there must be much more of advantage to him in the scheme than he had so far admitted to her. Gradually, as he grew angry, it came out that George Ferris had hinted in his letter at the possibility of a seat in Parliament for young Edmund Butts and even, perhaps, for her uncle himself. She had long been aware of her uncle's intense ambition to get his stupid, biddable ward into Parliament, where he hoped, no doubt, to use him as a mouthpiece for his own interests. Her heart sank. The snare was well baited indeed. Driven to panicky anger by a sense of her own helplessness, she protested so vehemently that Gurning in his turn grew angry. He had expected her to jump at what seemed to him a most eligible connection and in the surprise of her refusal had himself less well in hand than usual. 'Very well, miss,' he concluded, 'we shall see who is to be master in this house. Get to your room and stay there.'

'Master, indeed,' she flared back at him. 'You forget, I think, Uncle, that this is my house and you and your family my guests. You should think shame to batten on my hospitality and use me thus. I'll not have it: a set of cadging cits,' she stopped, appalled at what she had said. But it was too late: the words were out. She hung her head, shamed into silence by thoughts of what her father or her courteous Aunt Julia would have said to such a breach of manners.

Her uncle was quick to recognise and pursue his advantage. 'Yes, miss, I should think you would hang your head. Now, to your room, and there you shall stay till you have recollected yourself and made amends by accepting this offer which is so much more than your ill breeding merits.'

Speechless with mortification, she turned and left the room. But outside she paused. She had thrown away the hand, but need she lose the whole game? If she went meekly to her room now, she knew she was lost. She had seen too often how her uncle made his word good with his recalcitrant ward to have much confidence in her own capacity to stand out against him. She looked around her. To demonstrate, no doubt, his certainty of triumph, he had made no move to see that she obeyed him and went to her room. And the front door stood invitingly open. Escape. Could she? Dared she? She knew it was now or never. Automatically, she smoothed the folds of her riding habit. Yes, that settled it; she was dressed for the venture. She would ride to Lucy Faversham's house and throw herself on the General's mercy. Surely he could not refuse at least to send her safely to Aunt Julia in Yorkshire?

She hurried round the side of the house to the stables, keeping well away from the study windows and half scorning herself for the cowardly precaution. If only she had the courage to stand up to her uncle and tell him she was leaving. For the first time she found herself sympathising with Aunt Julia's flight;

Uncle Gurning had a most uncomfortable gift for putting one in the wrong . . .

Old Thomas, the groom who had taught her and her brothers to ride, and picked her out of more hedges than she cared to remember, looked dubious when she told him to saddle her horse, Starlight, for her again.

'Again, Miss Jenny? I doubt he's not half blown yet. You'd best take one of the others.'

'I'll do no such thing.' Impossible to explain to old Thomas that since her uncle had reorganised the stables Starlight was the only one of the horses she felt was really hers. Besides, she was well aware that his protest referred not at all to the horse's condition but to the fact that it wanted but half an hour of the family luncheon. 'Come,' she put on her best air of determination, 'saddle me Starlight and no more of your grumbling.'

'You sound for all the world like your father, Miss.' It was capitulation, but he still muttered to himself as he obeyed her, his old hands working with maddening deliberation while she waited impatiently, her ear cocked for sounds of pursuit. But none came. Her uncle must have assumed implicit obedience to his commands. Soon she was safe away, free and happy as she always was on horseback, riding across the Downs to Lucy's house, five miles away. The sun shone, a lark sang high above her, she let the reins lie loose on Starlight's neck and rode slowly along, dreaming of liberty . . .

But at Faversham Hall, disappointment awaited her. Lucy was delighted to see her, as always, but it came out at once that her father was away in London, where he would stay for the better part of a week. Jennifer received the news in so white a silence that her friend was alarmed. 'But, my love, what ails you? Why so desperate for my father? Nothing is amiss, I trust?'

Jennifer laughed bitterly. 'Amiss? All's amiss, love. I'm blown up, Lucy, capoted, sunk. In short, I'm a runaway. I doubt you should not receive me in your father's absence.'

'A runaway? My dearest creature, what madness is this? But, come, calm yourself, drink a glass of wine and tell me all from the beginning.'

She punctuated Jennifer's story with a soothing chorus of horrified exclamations, but when, at the end, Jennifer turned to her with a pleading: 'What else could I do then, but throw myself on your mercy and your father's?' she looked grave.

'You well know I would walk to Brighton barefoot if it would profit you, my love, but do but consider for a moment. Are you not letting your dislike of your uncle blind you to the eligibility of this connection? I have heard my father speak of Mr George Ferris and indeed he cites him as quite the coming man of the Party. I have always thought that with your looks and your spirit you were born to preside in a political house. And I confess I am hard put to it to find what grounds you have for taking such a dislike to Mr Ferris. Your brothers' friend, Jenny?'

'Friend, Lucy? What kind of a friend was it who left Richard to die at Waterloo? I have it from his servant who found him ... Small wonder it took him a year to summon up courage to face me. A year ago perhaps he could have explained ... told me something of Richard's last moments ... brought me some message. But now? It is but too plain that he seeks me only to repair his fortune.'

'I never heard that he was spendthrift.' Lucy considered it. 'And indeed marriages have been made for worse reasons than that. He is a younger son, it is true, and no doubt his wings do want feathering a trifle. But what disgrace is there in that? It is not as if he was his elder brother who has, I apprehend, lost a fortune at play ... And, forgive me, Jennifer, but circumstanced as you are, it may be difficult for you to make another match.'

'I'd rather set up for an old maid at seventeen than have it said I stooped to a catch-match. No, do not laugh at me, Lucy, and indeed you are wrong about Ferris. It was he, I know, who introduced Francis and Richard to all the gaming hells in Brussels. You remember what a potheration my Uncle Gurning made over their debts.'

'The more fool he. All young men play and run into debt, Jenny, it's the nature of the beasts. Nor would you want a tame pigeon if I know you. But, come, I'll stop teasing you. I only wish I could fathom why you are so deeply incensed against this man. His only crime seems to be his wish to marry you.'

'Oh, Lucy,' exclaimed her friend, 'if you had but seen his letter you would understand. My uncle showed it to me. He thought it was "most proper". I tell you, I might as well have been a parcel of merchandise of which my lord proposed to take delivery at my uncle's convenience and on such and such a date. Small wonder my uncle was pleased with it; it was just such a letter as they write on "Change". If there had been but one word for me, myself, one thought of the boys ... but nothing, Lucy, nothing. I am the camel that's to bring him riches, the necessary conveyance, nothing more. I'll not bear it, I tell you. And besides, my quarrel with my uncle is gone too far now for drawing back. You'll not fail me, Lucy. I cannot go back and eat humble pie with him. I will not. If you'll not help, I'll ... I'll go for a governess.'

Lucy laughed. It was indeed a desperate threat. But she soon sobered. 'Indeed, I do not know how to counsel you for the best. You know I will always stand your friend, but your uncle is sure to look for you here, and how can I protect you with my father away? And to deal plainly with you, I much misdoubt me but that if he were here the General would think it his duty to send you back to your uncle. They are fellow magistrates, you know, and though he cannot like the man, I believe he has a considerable respect for him. Only the other day he told me that Gurning could hit a haystack better than most, and you know that is high praise from my father. Oh, if only your father had left a valid will and appointed you another guardian, Jenny ... But as things stand I much fear you are in Mr Gurning's power until you are twenty-one.'

'I was in his power,' said Jennifer, rising to her feet, 'but as you see, I have escaped. I am sorry you do not feel able to assist me, Lucy, but since it is so, I must e'en bid you farewell.'

She was preparing to sweep out of the room when Lucy stopped her. 'Come, come, Jenny, you know me better than that. Spare me your tragedy queen, I beg. I've done preaching. If you are really bent on revolt, I'm your friend. But what can we do? Impossible to conceal you here; it would be all over the neighbourhood in three days.'

'I had wondered,' said Jennifer seating herself again by her friend, 'whether your father might not be prevailed upon to send me to my Aunt Julia in Yorkshire. She was always kind to me and surely would prevail upon our cousins to take me in.'

Lucy looked doubtful. 'I think you are deluding yourself, my love. Only consider Aunt Julia a little – Mistress Mouse we used to call her, did we not, and I fear she has the spirit of one. No, depend upon it, Jenny, if she did not send you posting back to your uncle, she would deliver you up to him at his first demand.'

Jennifer nodded gloomily. It was all too accurate a confirmation of her own unacknowledged fear. 'Then what can I do? It is but to remain hidden till I am twenty-one and my own mistress and then I'll have my Uncle Banker packing soon enough. But four years are a long time . . .'

'A very long time.' Suddenly Lucy jumped up and ran across the room to her writing desk. 'I believe I have it.' She dug excitedly among her papers and returned with a lavender sheet of much-crossed, highly scented writing paper. 'My cousin Lavinia,' she explained to Jennifer, 'I had the letter from her only yesterday. What you said of going for a governess put me in mind of it. But would you truly dare, Jenny?'

'I'd dare anything rather than knuckle under to Uncle Gurning and his Lombard Street lover. But what do you mean? What's your plan?'

Lucy was intently deciphering the spidery handwriting. 'Dear Cousin Lavinia's letters are mighty hard to read and often, I confess, since she writes purest nothing, I do not stay to finish them, but something I am sure she said of the governess. Yes, here we have it: ". . . in despair, my dearest Lucy, Miss Milward (that's the governess) has had the effrontery to elope with the curate . . ." something indecipherable here, poor Cousin Lavinia is clearly distracted . . . What's this . . . "the vapours." Yes, I am sure she has them . . . "the children beyond all control . . ."' She put down the letter. 'Poor Cousin Lavinia. The silliest woman, my dear Jennifer, it has ever been my good fortune to meet with, and no more control over her children than a hen with a brood of ducklings. Her husband died several years ago and Miss Milward has been her right hand ever since. I cannot conceive of that household without Milly, as they all called her. But I apprehend that she has grown tired of being the general dame of all work, *femme de compagnie*, governess, bottle-holder, philosopher and friend to my foolish cousin and has found it better to make her party good with the curate. I fear they will have but an uncomfortable time of it if Cousin Lavinia proves unforgiving . . . But, to the point; now do you smoke my plan?'

'I collect that I am to take the place of the estimable Miss Milward. But tell me more of my charges. Are they so very shatter-brained a parcel of children?'

'No, no, not the least in the world. They always minded Milly perfectly. It is only their mother who cannot control them. I am positive they will have a most healthy respect for you, Jenny, if only for your seat on a horse.'

Jenny laughed. 'An unusual recommendation for a governess, surely?'

'An unusual family. I never met Lavinia's husband: he was always off at the wars when I visited her, but I believe he was fonder of his horses than of wife or children. Even you will find nothing to fault in the stables at Teyning Park.'

'They live at Teyning, then?'

'Yes. A fine house on the edge of the Downs. Not unlike your own in some ways. I truly believe you might be happy enough there if you could but come to terms with Cousin Lavinia and the children. There will be but three that concern you. Lord Laverstoke, the eldest son, is a man grown now, and is away, I apprehend, at Oxford. After him come twin boys, Edward and Jeremy, who must be rising nine, and my pet and god-daughter Lucinda who is seven and the most adorable little imp you can imagine.'

But Jennifer interrupted her. 'Boys of nine! But my dearest love, consider, that means Latin and Greek. French, music and the use of the globes I can easily compass, but as for Greek declensions and *Propria Quae Maribus*: alas, I should be quite at a nonplus.'

Lucy laughed. 'Never trouble yourself for that. Since their doting mother would not let them go to school, their studies have been in the curate's hands these three years past. That must be how he contrived to make his party good with Milly. Small wonder poor Lavinia is in a puzzle: it is indeed a sad blow to lose tutor and governess in one elopement. But all the more reason why she will be delighted to see you and will not, I hope, look too closely at your recommendations.'

'Lord, Lucy, how shall we contrive for those?'

'Nothing to that. We will write you a most elegant testimonial, and your Aunt Julia shall do you the kindness of signing it. You recollect I used to take pleasure in imitating that spidery old lady's hand of hers.'

Jennifer laughed. 'Yes, it is but poetic justice that she should help me so. But, Lucy, what of my wardrobe? I have nothing but what I stand up in.'

Lucy looked her over. 'And that, though it becomes you *à merveille* is hardly the thing for a very respectable governess. But I have already taken thought for that. Do you not recollect that poor dear Miss Martindale, who bore with our schoolroom vagaries so patiently, took the fever some years past and died here?'

'Of course I do, but what's that to the question?'

'Only that her one relative – a brother who always neglected her – would not put himself to the trouble of taking away her box. It is still here in the attic somewhere and from it we will outfit you as the most respectable dowd who ever straightened a back or rapped a knuckle.'

Jennifer pulled a face. 'Miss Martindale's clothes? Oh, Lucy, must I?'

Her friend was adamant. 'It is that or George Ferris. As for me, to deal plainly with you, Jenny, I'd marry ten times before I went for a governess. Come, it's not too late to reconsider. Ride back, ask your uncle's pardon and have him. After all, a husband's a husband be he never so younger a son.'

'No.' Jennifer's little chin went up. 'I'll not have him, were he Prince Leopold himself. Have at your clothes, Lucy, there's no time to be lost if I'm to reach Teyning tonight.'

So they adjourned to the attic, where, with many a giggle from Lucy and long face from Jennifer, they outfitted her from the deceased Miss Martindale's outmoded crêpes and bombazines. At last the shabby box was repacked and Jenny decked protestingly forth in a dove grey travelling dress whose unfashionably high waist and small sleeves proclaimed its ancient vintage.

'There,' said Lucy triumphantly, "tis but to take issue with those modish curls of yours and cover all with this calash and you will be every inch a reliable frump. No, never trouble yourself with protesting; Cousin Lavinia is too much the faded beauty to tolerate anything in her house as handsome as you in your natural state. Once get her accustomed to you and I promise you she'll never see you. Then you may make your own modifications on poor Miss Martindale's toilette. But for the first impression you must be ruled by me.'

Jennifer reluctantly conceded the wisdom of this and resigned herself to a penance of frumpery, though she did insist on packing her own green riding habit among the limp and crumpled garments in Miss Martindale's box. They then composed a letter from Aunt Julia commending 'Miss Jenny Fairbank' as a clergyman's impoverished daughter of impeccable reliability, refinement and – to Jennifer's disgust – sobriety. 'Indeed, my love, it is quite necessary,' explained Lucy. 'Poor Cousin Lavinia once had a governess who grew tipsy on her ratafia. She has never forgotten it.'

'I look forward to meeting your Cousin Lavinia,' said Jennifer, heroically settling the maroon calash at a still more unbecoming angle on her auburn hair, whose curls Lucy had forced into the fashion of 1810. She turned to consider herself in the looking-glass. 'Will I do?'

'Admirably. I would never have thought you could look so reliable, Jenny.'

She swept a curtsy. 'Thank you, my love. Oh, one more favour. Tell your groom to turn Starlight loose. He'll find his own way home and my uncle can spend a happy night thinking I'm dead in some stone quarry, and he my heir. Then, to-morrow, send him this letter by your new man – he's never been to our house, I fancy, and so cannot be recognised as connected with you. I have told my uncle that I choose to live by my own devices until I am twenty-one, when I shall expect a strict accounting of my estates. Uncle Gurning's a knave, but no fool. So left, he'll not dare risk his name by robbing me. And now, Lucy, good-bye. Write to me as Miss Fairbank sometimes and tell me how the world goes with you.'

CHAPTER III

Fortunately for the success of the girls' scheme, the Faver-shams' coachman had been in their service since Lucy could remember and was devoted both to her and to Jennifer. His expression, when he first saw the latter in her borrowed bomba-zine, was almost too much for the girls' composure, but he listened without protest, though with an extremely disapprov-ing expression, to Lucy's instructions that he was to say noth-ing about Jennifer to Lady Laverstoke's servants. Pursing up his lips in affront at the very suggestion that he might gossip, he however obeyed his instructions heroically and, by speedy driving, got Jenny to Teyning before the last light had ebbed from the sky.

Laverstoke House, which stood in wooded parkland under the shoulder of the Downs below Chanctonbury Ring, looked large and gloomy in the dusk. No lights showed. At the door, Jennifer had a moment of unwonted fright. Suppose Lady Laverstoke was away? Or refused to receive her? What then? But whatever happened, retreat was now impossible. Muster-ing up her courage, she was relieved to see a glimmering light develop behind the high windows on each side of the front door. It opened, revealing a surprised footman whose livery jacket showed every sign of having been donned at speed. He looked Jennifer up and down with haughty distaste. Schooling herself into the timidity her new position in life demanded, she swallowed her anger and handed him Lucy's letter with a muttered, half comprehensible explanation. Told, haughtily, to wait inside, she gave one last glance at the friendly coachman at the horses' heads and scurried indoors with a mixture of real and affected fright.

The wait, in the chilly little salon, seemed endless. My lady, the footman had informed her, was still drinking her tea. It was doubtful whether this ceremony would be interrupted for anything so trivial as the announcement of a new governess. Jennifer was pacing nervously up and down the room, trying to compose her thoughts, when she heard a peal of childish laughter in the hall outside. Suddenly, the door of the room was thrown open and a little girl rushed in, black curls flying, closely pursued by two rather older boys. Not noticing Jennifer, who had retired to a window, they seized the girl, whose hands were full of sugarplums, and began to twist her arms to make her let them go, ignoring her shrieks and the protests of an aproned maid who had followed them into the room and stood ineffectually appealing to Master Edward and Master Jeremy to 'be good boys and give over do'. Laughing and defending herself at first, the little girl soon began to cry in good earnest and Jennifer thought it time to intervene. Coming briskly forward, she removed a boy with either hand, and, holding them at arm's length, looked them over.

'What cads' game is this?' she asked. 'Fight each other, if you wish, but think shame to attack a girl – and smaller than yourselves, too.'

'But she always gets the best of everything,' protested the taller of the twins, whom Jennifer had already identified, from the maid's cries, as Edward.

'Then she should share with you.'

So it was that Lady Laverstoke, appearing somewhat dubiously to interview the new governess her cousin had sent, was surprised by an animated scene.

Kneeling on the floor, Jennifer was surrounded by the three children. 'And one for Lucinda' she was saying, 'one for Edward, one for Jeremy, and here is one over which shall go to whoever is first to bed. There,' she handed it to the maid. 'You shall make the award.'

'Huzza,' shouted Jeremy. 'I shall beat, I'm positive. Lucinda cannot undo buttons and Edward always forgets his prayers.' With these words, the three children rushed from the room, followed, more sedately, by the maid, who gave a glance of deep gratitude to Jennifer and one full of meaning to her mistress, whom Jennifer now noticed for the first time.

'Oh,' she found no need to pretend embarrassment, 'I beg

your pardon. I had not observed . . .' she rose guiltily to her feet and made her second best curtsy. Did governesses curtsy, she wondered. Best be on the safe side . . .

It seemed to be well taken. Lady Laverstoke shook out her crimson skirts and settled herself on a sofa, every inch the beauty. Considering her blonde, fragile and well cared for prettiness, Jennifer did a quick female calculation and put her age at forty. Her manner, however, had never passed its thirtieth birthday. 'How do you do, Miss Fairbank.' It was a beauty's sighing air. 'You look very young,' she went on reproachfully, 'my cousin hardly prepared me for such a girl. But,' the appraising glance took in Miss Martindale's outmoded calash and darned mittens, 'you appear to have a way with children.'

'I like them, my lady,' said Jennifer with truth.

'Oh . . . liking,' said the beauty, 'as to that . . . I dote on them, but it does not make them mind me. If you can contrive to do so . . . why, perhaps your being young is no such bad thing after all. But we must be practical . . .' And she proceeded to put Jennifer through a surprisingly competent cross-examination as to her qualifications and experience, thus giving her a very harassing quarter hour of improvisation. At last, she gave a sigh of satisfaction. 'I really believe you will do. Pray ring the bell. Hawkins shall show you to your room. Mary has been looking after your charges and will, I am sure, be delighted to tell you all you need to know.'

So easily, relieved, Jennifer found herself mistress of a tiny room which, she was glad to find, she did not have to share with the children, and the expectation of ten pounds per annum. Not bad, she told herself, for an heiress's first earnings.

Nor, indeed, did she find the life a bad one. Her charges, though deplorably spoiled by their mother, recognised her firm hand with respect and, she thought, relief. Children do not like to be spoiled. They settled down gratefully to a placid routine of lessons and walks in the park. The rector consented to supervise the boys' classical studies in default of his errant curate and Jennifer was relieved to find that the relics of her own education were amply sufficient for Lucinda, who never seemed to have been taught anything at all. Lady Laverstoke explained this by remarking languidly one day that book learning was a dead bore and a sad waste of time for a female, and Jennifer soon learned that in the children's unregulated lives, only appointments with singing and dancing masters were held to be of any real importance.

It was different for the boys, sighed Lady Laverstoke. Their guardian, a tyrant, with strong views about education, was apt to make unexpected descents on Laverstoke Hall and insist on hearing them their Latin declensions. 'He wishes them sent to school,' wailed their doting if inattentive mamma, 'to that barbarous Eton to be bullied to death. I do not know how I shall endure it.'

The boys told a different tale. Uncle George, it seemed, was a trump, a Trojan, a Corinthian. They ransacked their school-boy vocabularies for epithets worthy of him. As for Lucinda, he had once brought her a doll with real hair and a silk dress all the way from Paris: she was his for ever. Jennifer found herself looking forward with somewhat mixed emotions to the next appearance of this paragon. She had, she felt, made her part good with Lady Laverstoke almost too easily: would the peremptory guardian be so readily satisfied?

But, meanwhile, time passed peacefully enough between the pianoforte and the globes. Jennifer found herself increasingly contented in this strange new life. It had not occurred to her before that perhaps the worst of what she had suffered under her uncle's unwelcome guardianship had been boredom. She had had far too little to do and, worse still, no one to care for. Now her case was altered indeed. Lady Laverstoke, who habitually lay in bed till after midday, was quite satisfied if she saw her children for a decorative half-hour's doting after dinner. Any more of their company was sure to bring on a fit of the vapours. So, inevitably, their lives revolved round Jennifer.

And she, in her turn, was soon devoted to them. She came to enjoy their constant demands on her time and patience, whether to settle a quarrel, mend a broken toy, or merely act as audience for an account of their exploits. Their company changed from a task to a pleasure. And, besides, it was positive happiness, she found, to be away from her uncle and aunt. A letter from Lucy told her that it had been given out that she was in Italy for her health. There had been no general alarm or search for her. The Gurnings were making the best of a bad business and – no doubt – enjoying her estate in the meanwhile. Of George Ferris, there had been, Lucy said, no sign. Jennifer wondered what story he had been told.

Summer slipped blandly into autumn. Jennifer tried a more becoming hair style and nobody noticed except Lucinda. Lucy had been right. Once they are used to them, people do not look at their governesses any more than they do at the pictures on their walls. She began to think she might safely pass her time here till her twenty-first birthday.

Then, one bright October morning, Lucinda did not appear at her usual hour for her lessons. At first, Jennifer was not perturbed. The child had been very well behaved of late. No doubt the temptation of the fine morning had been too much for her and she had run over to the rectory with her brothers. She would be back soon enough. Though she did her best to conceal it, Jennifer knew she enjoyed her lessons.

But time passed and the child did not appear. Jennifer rang the schoolroom bell and questioned the footman. After various experiments in effrontery, even the upper servants had, by now, acquired a healthy respect for the new governess, recognising the determination under her quiet manner. No, he answered her civilly, he had not seen the children, but would make enquiries. He returned shortly with alarming news. The new stable boy admitted having saddled the children's ponies at Jeremy's orders. The hunt, explained the footman, was meeting in the long meadow.

'The hunt?' Jennifer was out of her chair in an instant. 'Lucinda? A child of seven? Madness.' Running downstairs, she hurried by the back way out to the stables. She had not ridden since her arrival, but knew her way well enough. It was here that the children were most often to be found, talking to the old groom, Charlie. But today the place was oddly quiet. There was no sign of Charlie. A hoof stamped in a loose box, doves cooed on the rooftop. The only sign of life was Harry, the new stable boy, who was walking a big grey hunter up and down in the yard. Its splendid proportions drew a sigh of admiration from Jennifer. It was none of Lady Laverstoke's, who would ride only the mildest of ladies' mounts. It was just, Jennifer realised, what she needed.

'Quick,' she ordered the boy. 'Put me Lady Laverstoke's side-saddle on him.'

'On this one,' the boy opened a half-wit mouth in protest. 'I doubt my master . . .'

'A fiddle for your master.' For a moment, she was Miss Purchas again. 'Saddle him this instant. 'Tis a matter of life and death.'

Unwilling, but quick-handed, he did as she bade him, casting critical glances at her house dress the while. She, too, spared a moment's thought for her unsuitable garb – a moment, but no more. Then she was up, delightedly feeling the hunter's powerful movement under her as she took him down the back drive, out of the gates and over the slope of the Downs towards the long meadow. Already she could hear the yelp of the hounds, the shrill of the huntsman's horn clear in the morning air. No time to be lost . . . The boys rode well enough to follow the hunt, though it was something their timid mother would never allow, but little Lucinda was still far from steady in the saddle. Putting the big horse to the gallop, Jennifer let herself hope that some neighbour would have recognised and stopped the child. But she knew the hope for a forlorn one; people noticed little in the excitement of a meet.

As she approached the long meadow she knew that she was too late. The hounds' voices rose in a crescendo; they were away . . . Guessing their direction from the sounds, she turned aside into a narrow white lane that led over the shoulder of the hill. From this angle she had a good chance of catching up at least with the stragglers of the hunt. She well knew that Lucinda's plump little pony would not be to the fore.

But when she came over the side of the hill and caught sight of the hunt streaming over the far slope at an angle to her, she caught her breath in dismay. Jeremy and Edward, with

Lucinda's fat pony between them, were alarmingly well forward. Setting her teeth, she put her willing horse again to the gallop. She would need all his power. Her headlong course was taking her down the side of the hill as the hunt streamed away over the next one. She had been observed by now. Uncaring, she half noticed the nudging comments that her wild appearance drew from the hunt's stragglers. Passing them, still at a gallop, she took a short cut across a field, only to see at the last moment – for this was country she did not know – that it was bounded on the far side by a deep, sunken lane. No time to find a way across. She put the big grey at it and cleared it with a sigh of satisfaction that he was indeed the magnificent jumper she had expected.

She was almost up with the hunt at last and could see Lucinda's small figure jogging along a little behind her brothers. Perhaps all would be well after all. Then she saw that hounds and huntsmen had disappeared into a copse. What would happen, there, to Lucinda who had never ridden except on the open grass of Laverstoke Park? For the first time in her life, Jennifer wished she had spurs, but a dig of the heels and a word of encouragement brought a new spurt of speed from the grey. Absurdly, in this moment of crisis, she found herself wondering what his name was.

She was close to the children, who were now among the outlying trees of the copse, when she saw a branch disturbed by Jeremy's mount lash back across Lucinda's pony, which she had let follow too close behind her brothers. With a snort of terror, it darted away, entirely out of control, along the side of the wood. Riding now like one possessed, Jennifer was after it ... alongside ... then, leaning down, she had a hand over Lucinda's fat ones which still clutched desperately at the reins. For a few seconds the big grey and the pony raced side by side, while Jennifer prayed that Lucinda would hang on. Then, as the grey slowed at her command, she felt, with relief, that the cob was doing likewise, steadied by the presence of the big horse. Stopping at last, Jennifer jumped to the ground and put her arms round Lucinda, who was sobbing with fright. 'All's safe now, my precious, I've got you,' she soothed.

'I say,' it was Edward's voice behind her. 'Can't you just ride, Miss Fairbank. You're a Trojan and no mistake.'

Looking round, over the head of the still sobbing Lucinda, she was relieved to see that both boys had followed her. So, too, had various of the less devoted followers of the hunt, who had allowed their curiosity at the strange figure she cut to overmaster the excitement of the chase. Uncomfortably aware that she presented an odd enough spectacle, Jennifer delivered a swift but stinging rebuke to the boys, ordered them to follow her home, and got herself once more into the saddle with the assistance of the chastened Edward. Then, reassuring herself with one anxious glance that none of the busy-bodies gathered round knew her as anything but 'Miss Fairbank' she took a firmer grasp on Lucinda's reins and started for home.

Lucinda was still much shaken and Jennifer decided to take the long way round by road rather than risk another fright in the rough short cut across the fields. Thoroughly subdued, the boys followed meekly behind, exchanging, *sotto voce*, awed reminiscences of her cross-country gallop. She was far too busy trying to keep up little Lucinda's spirits to pay much attention to them. When they reached the front lodge of Laverstoke Park she hesitated for a moment. Should she risk taking this odd little cortège up the front drive? But no one was ever about at this hour in the morning. She had never known Lady Laverstoke to appear before one o'clock at the earliest. And Lucinda was obviously exhausted and shivering with delayed shock. She turned boldly in at the gate, which had meanwhile been opened, with an expression of some astonishment and much disapproval, by plump Mrs Meggs, the lodge keeper's wife.

As they rode up the winding, tree-lined drive, Jeremy pushed his pony up beside her. 'I say, Miss Fairbank, you won't tell, will you? Mamma would be in such a taking.' He looked anxiously up at her, a deep appeal behind the casual seeming words.

She recognised it: 'No, I'll not tell this time, Jeremy. But no more hunts, 'pon honour.'

'Honour bright,' he began, then interrupted himself with a gasp: 'Scuppered, by Jupiter!'

She would have rebuked him for the exclamation, but, looking ahead, saw what had caused it and gasped in her turn. They had rounded the last curve of the drive and now found themselves on the carriage sweep in front of the house. And on top of the shelving steps that led up to the front door was a formidable tableau. Lady Laverstoke, astonishingly up and dressed at this unfashionable hour, was half-swooning on the arm of a tall man whose deep mourning seemed to accentuate an air of black rage about him. Jennifer had only time to take in fierce blue eyes under astonishing black brows before he advanced upon her, with Lady Laverstoke still clinging, tearful and apparently beyond speech, to his arm.

'So.' The furious eyes looked Jennifer up and down. 'This, I conclude, is your paragon of a governess, Lavinia. You did not tell me that she acted also as groom to the children. Nor do I entirely comprehend why she should have done me the honour of borrowing my horse.'

'Oh, Lord Mainwaring, I am distracted,' began Lady Laverstoke, while Jennifer dismounted in a furious bound, careless of Miss Martindale's crumpled muslin, and turned to the stranger, a stinging rebuke on her lips. No one had ever, in the course of her short life, looked at her with such insolence. Then – she remembered. This was how governesses were treated. Swallowing her fury, she turned towards Lady Laverstoke: 'Indeed, my lady, I must beg a thousand pardons.' She was beginning to force out the words when Jeremy interrupted her: 'But Mamma, Uncle George: – you do not properly understand. Miss Fairbank is a hero – I mean a heroine. She is a perfect Trojan and saved silly Lucinda's life when her pony ran away with her. Indeed she does not deserve a scold, and, oh, Uncle George, you should just have seen her ride. She jumped Lightning over the sunken lane by the ten acre field.'

'I am much obliged to her then for bringing him back unhurt,' said the black-browed gentleman. 'Though I am yet to learn that horseback riding is part of a governess's duties. But come, Lavinia, you will be taking cold and so will Lightning here. We will hear more of this strange business indoors.'

30

'Is his name Lightning?' Jennifer forgot herself for a moment. 'Indeed, it suits him.'

'I am happy that it meets with your approval.'

Reddening at his ironic tone, she turned, with another murmured apology to Lady Laverstoke and led the big grey and Lucinda's pony towards the stables.

'Be so good,' the odious voice pursued her, 'as to hand Lightning directly to the groom for a rub down.'

Intolerable insult: to make her a bearer of messages to the groom. For the first time she found herself bitterly hating her subservient position. What would she not give to turn on this odious stranger in her own character as Miss Purchas of Denton Hall. But she must not do it. She could not throw away the security she had gained for a moment's satisfaction. Inwardly fuming, she listened with half an ear to the children's rejoicings – which she found herself unable to share – at the arrival of their Uncle George.

'He is not really our uncle,' explained Jeremy, 'but our father's cousin and dearest friend. They served together in the Peninsula and father left him our guardian.'

'Yes,' chimed in Edward, 'and Mamma was furious and said it was an insult to make someone so young our guardian, but Milly said she would soon be reconciled to it.'

'Yes,' added little Lucinda, now somewhat recovered, 'and Milly said she thought Mamma had a good mind to marry him for his pains. I heard her telling Mr Peasegood.'

Jennifer was about to rebuke her for this tale-bearing when she was stopped by Jeremy's next remark: 'I doubt Uncle George is come to see if you are a fit governess for us, Miss Fairbank. He says Mother has no more judgement than a pea-hen.'

Jennifer was so appalled by the realisation that the odious stranger would in some sort control her destiny that she forgot to reprimand Jeremy for his remarks about his mother, and listened absent-mindedly while Edward chimed in: 'By Jupiter, it was worth six whippings to see his face at sight of Miss Fairbank on Lightning. Lord, he will not even let Laverstoke ride him.'

They were in the stable yard by now and he interrupted himself to exclaim: 'Look, there's Quicksilver. Laverstoke must be here too. Huzza!'

And indeed when they entered the house, they found all in a bustle. Lord Mainwaring had arrived unexpectedly, bringing with him Charles Laverstoke, who it seemed was in some small disgrace at Oxford over a matter of a performing monkey let loose in divinity class. Lucinda told Jennifer all about it as she wriggled her way into her best sprigged muslin in preparation for a hoped-for summons to join the party at dessert.

Jennifer, on the other hand, was praying inwardly that the summons would not come. She had seen enough of the governess's martyrdom on such occasions to wish very heartily that she might be spared it. And, besides, there was something intolerable about the idea of another encounter with Lord Mainwaring's arrogant blue eyes, particularly when she had no stronger defence than Miss Martindale's best dress of sober brown watered silk.

As Lucinda prattled away about her beloved elder brother, and kind Uncle George who might or might not have brought her a present, Jennifer cast a gloomy glance at her own reflection in the big looking glass before which she was arranging Lucinda's curls. Intolerable to have to face Lord Mainwaring in Miss Martindale's drooping finery.

But Lucinda, catching her eye in the glass, smiled at her lovingly: 'How well you look, Miss Fairbank. That dress becomes you excessively.'

Smiling at the child's parroting of her mother's phrases, Jennifer gratefully conceded that there was something in what she said. An impatient but successful needlewoman, she had spent several evenings improving the fit and style of the dress, and it was true that its russet brown did indeed set off her auburn hair. When the dreaded summons came, she followed the children with the comfortable thought that Lord Mainwaring must surely find her much changed from the tousled hoyden who had confronted him that afternoon.

But, deep in conversation with Lady Laverstoke, Lord Mainwaring spared her hardly a glance beyond what the barest civility demanded. For the first time, as she watched his black head bent so close to Lady Laverstoke's blonde ringlets, she wondered if there had perhaps been some truth in Milly's gossip. Well, heaven help Lady Laverstoke if she should marry him: his was no temper to bear with a beauty's faded foibles.

Her charges, meanwhile, had clustered eagerly round their elder brother, clamouring for sips of his wine and details of his exploit with the monkey. A fair, open-faced, very young man, he was obviously in considerable awe of his cousin and guardian whose elegance of dress and manner he tried hopefully to imitate. Tonight his colour was high and his speech rapid. Jennifer suspected that he had drowned the memory of his mother's plaintive reproaches in a great deal of claret. To her dismay, he paid her so many compliments on her prowess as a horsewoman, about which his brothers had told him, that she found it necessary to withdraw, with her recalcitrant but obedient charges, at the earliest possible moment.

CHAPTER IV

Now began an era of unwonted gaiety at Laverstoke Hall. The big public rooms were unswathed from their voluminous dust sheets, candelabra were polished, candles bought by the gross and two extra girls hired from the village to polish up the enormous stretches of untrodden parquet – in short, Lady Laverstoke was at home to the county.

She grumbled a good deal in her languid way about the exertion this entailed, but it was obvious to Jennifer that she enjoyed every minute of it, feeling herself freed from the restrictions of her long and monotonous widowhood by the presence of Lord Mainwaring and her grown-up son. At first, Jennifer was surprised at the willingness with which Lord Mainwaring lent himself to these junketings, for he had not struck her as at all a sociable man, and indeed made little attempt at concealing his relief when some particularly tedious band of local talkers had finally taken their leave. It was, incidentally, on these occasions, when half a dozen dull worthies from the neighbouring houses had descended upon her, that Lady Laverstoke was most apt to ring and summon her children to join her and her friends. Many a prosy dowager and many a faithful companion did Jennifer accompany round the rose garden or chaperon dutifully through the glass houses.

She was, at these times, increasingly sorry that she had not been able to seek asylum a little further from home. When each new set of morning callers arrived, she felt fresh terror lest there should be some of her own acquaintance among them, consoling herself, however, with the thought that she had in fact moved so little in society since the fatal news of Waterloo that this was unlikely.

Besides, she was soon aware of a particular character in the company that now frequented Laverstoke Hall, and realised, when she did so, what lay behind Lord Mainwaring's amazing

34

affability. He was, in fact, hard at work keeping up his interest in his neighbouring constituency. Jennifer heard enough scraps of conversation on the occasions when she took the children down for dessert, to realise that he was finding it heavy enough going. Evening after evening, as the ladies rose and the gentlemen gathered over their wine, she heard the attack begin. Mainwaring, it seemed, had shocked his country constituents by the length to which he carried his radical views. Every evening he was under fire, sometimes even before the ladies left the table, for his friendship with Burdett and Hunt, whose meetings and petitions were, in the opinion of his attackers, at the bottom of all the country's present discontents. 'Split the party', 'Out of office long enough already', 'Dissolution', 'Going to the dogs', these and other gloomy phrases echoed through the halls of Laverstoke when, very much later, the gentlemen joined the ladies for tea and scandal.

Unwillingly, Jennifer found herself compelled to admire the masterly ease with which Mainwaring handled his critics. With an unfailing courtesy that amazed her, he bore with his attackers, turned their arguments, and at last managed, somehow, to convince them that they had been on his side all the time, or he on theirs. Scorning their gullibility, she had, reluctantly, to concede his skill in argument.

For the children it was a time of ecstasy. Schoolroom discipline was increasingly hard to maintain. The boys had to be driven almost by main force over to the rectory for their morning lessons, while Lucinda, too, was hard to settle at her tasks, and seized every opportunity to reconnoitre at the big door that separated the children's apartments from the main stairway.

One morning, after there had been unwontedly early activity downstairs, Lucinda returned from this point of vantage with a disappointed face. 'It is too shabby; they are gone out in the chaise and never even thought of taking me.'

Sorry for the child, Jennifer exerted herself to be entertaining, but Lucinda drooped and moped until the nursery lunch hour brought the boys shouting back from the rectory. They were in high feather. They had met their brother in the stable yard and he had invited the nursery party to drive out with him that afternoon. Jennifer had noticed for some time past that Charles Laverstoke found Lord Mainwaring's politics as little to his liking as his mother's gossip, and was increasingly apt to turn to the nursery for a society more certainly admiring and less demanding of thought or of punctilio. The children were entranced at the invitation, Jennifer more dubious.

"Tis only in the carriage,' said Edward regretfully. 'Uncle George has taken the chaise.'

'But I thought Lord Laverstoke was gone out already,' said Jennifer, temporising. Was this an outing to be permitted? What would Miss Martindale have done in such circumstances? 'No, no,' Jeremy explained. 'It is but mamma and Uncle George who are gone out. Doubtless they are gone to pay their respects at Petworth House. Uncle George always visits Lord Egremont when he comes here; they are famous cronies.'

Lucinda pouted. 'I wish they would have taken me. I dote upon those children. Only think, Miss Fairbank, they have marchpane every day.'

'Never fret yourself for that, Lucinda,' comforted Edward, 'it will be a deal more entertaining to drive out with Charles. He is a deuce of a whip, Miss Fairbank.'

'But nothing like Uncle George. He is a real Corinthian,' said his brother.

'Yes, but what use is that with Mamma in the carriage? He will let the coachman drive, I wager. You know Mamma cannot bear to go above a snail's pace. The last time Charles took her out she vowed she would never drive with him again.'

Jennifer, half listening to this discussion, was still debating the propriety of the proposed expedition and the feasibility of preventing it, when Lord Laverstoke bounced into the nursery.

'How do you do, Miss Fairbank,' he swept the hat from his blonde curls, looking quite a man in his many-caped greatcoat, 'are these imps ready to come driving with me?'

'Yes, yes, quite ready,' shouted Jeremy as he and Edward snatched up their own coats, while Lucinda, quicker than they to recognise Jennifer's hesitation, looked up at her appealingly:

'I may go, may I not, Miss Fairbank?'

'Of course you may, Puss.' Laverstoke tossed her up on to his shoulder. 'And Miss Fairbank shall come too to see that you conduct yourself like a lady. Is that a bargain, Miss Fairbank? We'll proceed most properly, I promise you, though, I warrant,' an admiring glance swept her up and down, 'that you'd handle the ribbons as well as you do the reins.'

To turn the subject, for she was heartily sick of references to her exploit at the hunt, Jennifer busied herself with preparing Lucinda for the drive, debating with herself, as she did so, whether or not to accompany them. In the end, she decided reluctantly that it was the lesser evil. It was all too likely that her lively charges would get into some mischief if allowed out with no weightier companion than their brother and she did not feel sufficiently sure of her ground to forbid the outing altogether. So she compromised by stipulating that it should be only a brief turn up over the Downs, and they all piled gleefully into the carriage, Jennifer congratulating herself that Laverstoke had chosen to drive and would therefore have no opportunity for the flattering speeches and speaking looks with which he seemed to think it necessary to distinguish her.

She gave a sigh of pure pleasure as the big carriage swung up the road that led over the Downs. Except for church on Sunday and her brief and anxious outing on Lightning on the day of the hunt, this was the first time she had left Laverstoke Park since her arrival. It was good to smell the damp woodland air, even qualified by the musty interior of the carriage, and then, as the road climbed higher, to catch a glimpse of the sea, sparkling in the autumn sunlight. The children, too, were in ecstasies, as their brother whipped up his horses and they bowled down the long slope of the hill.

But once on the flat, he did not turn back as he had promised. The boys were delighted, but not surprised. They had evidently never believed he would. 'He's a devil when he gets the ribbons in his hands,' confided Jeremy. 'I wonder where he's taking us.'

Anxious, but hardly liking to protest, Jennifer sat still, looking out of the window at the brown and fallow fields. Time passed, Lucinda became restless and the boys noisy, and still Lord Laverstoke showed no sign of turning back. Presently, to her horror, Jennifer recognised the outskirts of Brighton and, while she rapped fruitlessly on the glass, saw Lord Laverstoke give a triumphant flourish of his whip as he turned his horses into the Steine. At last, with Edward's help, she contrived to lower the stiff glass and leant out to expostulate with Laverstoke, when, to her horror, she saw advancing down the other side of the street two banker friends of her Uncle Gurning's who were frequent visitors at Denton Hall. She popped her head back into the carriage and bent solicitously over Lucinda until they were safely past them, then leaned out again and expostulated with Laverstoke to such effect that he turned sheepishly homeward and whipped up his horses.

It was growing dark when he finally drew up in the stable yard and Jennifer helped the weary and grumbling children to alight. She was beginning an angry expostulation with their brother when Lord Mainwaring appeared at the entrance of Lightning's loose-box and surveyed the scene with raised eyebrows. There seemed, suddenly, nothing to be said. Picking up the now tearful Lucinda, she called the boys sharply to heel and took them all up to the nursery where she distinguished herself, for the rest of the evening, by an unwonted outbreak of bad temper.

To her relief, the children were not summoned downstairs for dessert. Like her, they were jaded from the long drive and yielded with only a formal protest to her decree of early bed. Then, at last, came what she sometimes thought the best moment of her day. A shawl over the unnecessary brown silk, she settled by the schoolroom fire, feet snug on the fender, to read another chapter in the boys' Latin Grammar over which she had found it necessary to supplement the labours of the aged and somnolent rector.

She was busy in the fourth declension when the schoolroom door burst open and Lord Laverstoke appeared. One look at his flushed face and tousled curls told her that he was more than a little intoxicated. Wondering quickly whether, on such occasions, he became gloomy, like her father, or riotous, like

38

both her brothers, she rose to her feet and made him her stiffest curtsy. The schoolroom suddenly seemed unpleasantly isolated in the big house. But she had dealt with her brothers often enough when they were bosky. She would soon freeze him out.

'To what am I indebted for this honour?' she asked frigidly.

He advanced upon her, staggering ever so slightly: 'Come to make my apologies,' he said. 'Damned ungentlemanly touch this afternoon. Mainwaring says so. I say so. Took you to Brighton when you didn't want to go. Damned caddish thing to do. Came to apologise.' He paused for breath and his eye lit on her book, in which her finger still hopefully kept her place. 'And now I've interrupted you at your reading. Damned shame for a dasher like you to be sitting up here reading. Should be living romance, not reading it.' He held out his hand for the book, swaying slightly as he did so.

'No romance, my lord, but a Latin Grammar.' She handed it to him.

His hand closed over hers. 'A damned shame. Fero, ferre – hic – I beg your pardon – latum. Waste of a pretty girl's time. Much better things for a smasher like you to be doing. And don't "my lord" me either. Call me Charles. Everybody does. Call me Curly. They all do. And give me a kiss, for the most beautiful redheaded governess of them all.' He pulled her towards him. Resisting, she was aware of the strong smell of port and snuff, of the hard line of his jacket buttons against her breast. Then a hand closed on his shoulder and he reeled away.

'Go to your room, Charles,' said Lord Mainwaring.

For a moment, Jennifer thought Laverstoke was going to resist, then, with a muttered 'Damned inconvenient ... damned shame ... Servant, Miss Fairbank,' he left the room.

Mainwaring looked down at her in silence, as she picked up her book and settled its ruffled pages. What could she say? Intolerable that he should have found her in yet another compromising situation.

'Well, Miss Fairbank?' There was no charity in the steel-blue eyes. He echoed her thoughts: 'What am I to think?'

'Think what you please, my lord.' It was Jennifer Purchas who spoke. Then she recollected Miss Fairbank. 'Only, I beg, do not think that this encounter was any of my choosing. Had I known of Lord Laverstoke's purpose I would assuredly have bolted the door.'

He turned, gravely, to consider it. 'Alas for your good intentions. I note that the bolt is lacking. Were you to continue in your post, I collect it would be necessary to provide one.'

'Were I?' she seized upon his use of the word. 'Oh, my lord, you cannot advise Lady Laverstoke to dismiss me!'

'Cannot?' The black eyebrows rose.

'I mean – I beg your pardon – I meant.' She stopped in confusion, then collected herself together and began again: 'My lord, I beg of you, let me continue here. I am sure Lady Laverstoke will speak for my success with the children. I fear you have seen me in but an unhappy light, but, indeed, my lord, we have gone on famously so far.'

'So I apprehend from Lady Laverstoke who speaks for you as well as you could wish. But I cannot feel it right for so young a girl to hold a position of such trust.'

It was too much. 'Indeed,' she flared up at him, 'I am sorry that I am not older, but time will doubtless amend it. And in the meanwhile I am hard put to it to see what it has to do with the business.'

'You are very ignorant of the world, Miss Fairbank, if you think so. I find myself compelled to allude to your recent scrapes. It is no part of a governess's duties to be seen disporting herself in a gentleman's carriage, nor yet riding to hounds.'

'It would, I apprehend, have been more suitable to let Lucinda be killed?'

'It would have been better to have seen that the occasion did not arise.'

She was silent at the mixture of reason and injustice in this, and he continued: 'Indeed, I am at a loss to imagine how Miss Faversham came to recommend you.'

'She recommended me because she cared for me and knew how desperately I needed the position.' She was suddenly near to tears at the truth of her own words.

'I am sorry to hear it.' He turned away, apparently considering the conversation finished.

She nerved herself to a last effort: 'And so I am to go? And, what, pray, is to become of the children – and Lady Laverstoke? Governesses – even old ones – do not grow on every tree. This house was in revolution when I arrived, and Lady Laverstoke near hysterics. The children have just learned to feel safe with me; I'll not be answerable for the consequences if you send me away.'

'Fine talk, Miss Fairbank, but you will not find threats avail you. I am sorry if it proves inconvenient to you, but I must urge Lady Laverstoke to lose no time in finding someone less unsuitable.'

The door burst open behind him and Mary, the under parlour-maid, hurried in. 'Oh, Miss Fairbank, Miss Lucinda's had the nightmare and is calling for you. You must come at once.'

Curtsying swiftly to Lord Mainwaring, Jennifer hurried to Lucinda's room. She was used to these nightmares of hers now and had discovered how to deal with them when she learned their origin. Some previous nurse had used Boney as a bugbear to such good effect that Lucinda, if overtired, would wake, screaming, convinced that she was about to be handed over to the French monster. Treating her fears seriously, Jennifer had promised her she would never allow this to happen, and Lucinda, who believed her new governess to be capable of anything, need only be reminded of her protection to forget her fears. So, now, Jennifer, bent over her:

'It's all right, precious, I'm here; I won't let him get you.'

The child clutched her hand in a feverish grip: 'He had me in the carriage: he was carrying me off . . .' Her sobs threatened to break out anew.

'Nothing of the kind,' said Jennifer briskly. 'You know he has been on St Helena this age; now hush your crying and I will tell you a story.'

Ten minutes later, she laid the child down, heavy with sleep, and was about to steal away when Lucinda caught her hand: 'Promise you'll not leave me – ever.'

'Of course I'll not leave you,' Jennifer hedged, 'I am coming back directly to spend the night on the sofa.'

Satisfied, the child settled down in bed, half asleep already. Jennifer, rising, was startled to see Lord Mainwaring at the door. How long had he been there? But Lucinda came first:

'Shh . . .' She laid a finger on her lips, tiptoed out and closed the door. 'I will fetch my things and then spend the night on the sofa in her room. I should have known she would have one of her bad nights after such a day.'

He looked down at her. 'So, it seems, you win, Miss Fairbank.'

'I win?' Busy calming the child, she had forgotten what had passed before. Now it all came back to her. 'Oh. You mean I may stay?'

'You appear to have made yourself indispensable. Yes, you shall stay. And I will take young Laverstoke away tomorrow.'

She curtsied. 'It will be mighty good of you, sir.'

But the house seemed strangely dull and quiet without them. Lucinda moped openly, and so, Jennifer suspected, did her mother, in secret. The weather broke, and several days of drenching rain reduced schoolroom tempers to breaking point. At last, the wind changed, the sun came out and frost sparkled on the trees of the park. Lucinda had a cold and was in bed, snuffling plaintively over barley water and Dr James's powders. After the schoolroom lunch, Jennifer settled her down for a sleep, forced the reluctant boys to their classical studies, confiding them to the care of the devoted Mary, and put on her bonnet and pattens for her daily indulgence – sadly missed of late – of a walk in the park.

Breathing deeply of the crisp, cold air, she walked quickly across the frost-hard lawn to the shelter of the shrubbery. Lady Laverstoke had never said in so many words that she disapproved of this daily walk, so contrary to her own sedentary habit, but she had sedulously hinted her dislike. Blandly ignoring these suggestions, Jennifer did, however, do her best to make it as inconspicuous as possible, taking her exercise in swift perambulation of the long, concealed walk that lay among the rhododendrons. Today she was determined to cut it short; Lucinda might wake and cry for her.

She had just turned back from the little wicket gate that led out on to the open Down when a sound behind her made her turn. As she did so, her arms were caught from behind and a heavy cloth bound over her face, making speech or sight impossible. Struggling frantically, but to no avail, she felt herself pushed along by her captors and heard the click of the wicket-gate behind her. For a moment, wild visions of romantic terror darted through her mind, of foreign villains and castle dungeons. Then she remembered how her brothers had laughed at Mrs Radcliffe's horrors. Simultaneously, she recollected her encounter with her uncle's friends in the Steine. They must have seen her and told him. This was the result.

So, when she was half-pushed, half-pulled into a waiting carriage, and the bandages ungently removed from her eyes, she greeted her uncle, sitting there to receive her, with a calm that surprised him.

'You are setting up in the brigandage business, I see, Uncle.' Shaking out her crumpled skirts, she looked him over with a dislike which he returned in good measure.

'You should be grateful to me, Niece,' he said as the carriage began to roll forward, 'for taking so discreet a means to recover you. It would hardly have suited either of our books if I had ridden up to Laverstoke House and demanded the return of my errant ward.'

'No ward of yours, Uncle Gurning, as you well know.' By this bit of defiance she did her best to conceal her horrid recognition of the truth of what he said. Now he had found her, she was helpless in his hands. And, oh, she thought to herself, what of poor little Lucinda, waking from her snuffling slumbers and calling for her beloved Miss Fairbank? What would happen to her? And what would Lady Laverstoke – and Lord Mainwaring – think? But she had no time now for such self-tormentings. With her usual strong common sense she swallowed salt despair and applied herself to discovering her uncle's plans for her. The sooner she knew what he intended, the better she would be prepared to circumvent him. And he had certainly not gone to these uncharacteristic lengths to reclaim her without strong reasons of his own.

Sinking back into the corner of the carriage, she feigned a

hopeless compliance she was all too near to feeling: 'What now, Uncle?'

'Why, that's the girl.' He made no attempt to conceal his pleased surprise at her meek acceptance of defeat. 'You and I may deal admirably together yet. Particularly since I must tell you that this mad start of yours – together with some other circumstances – has quite put an end to any hope of the match that was proposed for you. Only think, niece, Mr Ferris's father and brother have been killed in a carriage accident. If you had only taken him when he offered, you would have been in a fair way to being a duchess. But he will fly higher now than a country miss, I warrant. Never fret, though, I have a capital scheme in hand for you; I am only puzzled I had not hit upon it sooner. You are to marry Edmund, my dear. The bans are called, the parson willing, the licence ready and tomorrow is the happy day!'

Now he had indeed surprised her. 'Edmund? Tomorrow? Impossible!' She had always been fond enough of her uncle's puppyish ward, but the idea of marrying him was beneath ridicule. Her uncle could not be serious. One look at his face undeceived her. He was never more so.

He cut short the protests into which he had surprised her. 'Spare me your tantrums. It is you who have brought yourself to this, with your jauntings about the countryside. Your aunt and I have done everything in our power to stifle the tittle-tattle it has given rise to, but in the face of the report that you had been seen driving down the Steine with a young nobleman of so very unsteady a reputation, there was nothing we could do but announce your engagement forthwith. You should be grateful that Edmund is prepared to take you with so tarnished a name.'

Despair bit cold into her. There was too much truth in what he said. Useless to protest the innocence of that drive, her helplessness, the presence of the children. If the report had got about, her reputation was indeed tarnished. But marriage with Edmund . . . that was a desperate remedy.

CHAPTER V

Jennifer had never imagined the sight of her home could be so depressing. Her uncle handed her out of the carriage with an affected gallantry that sickened her, and Soames, the butler, who opened the door, gave her a look in which sympathy and curiosity were disconcertingly blended. Was she, from henceforth, to find herself the target of such looks? Intolerable thought. She almost persuaded herself that she had best marry Edmund and be done with it. Doubtless he would prove a complaisant enough husband, and marriage would give them both control of their fortunes. But the idea was sickening. She did not want a complaisant husband. She wanted a man who would stand no nonsense, someone older than herself, settled in the world, fit to be her master. In short, a man . . .

Her uncle led her into his study. 'I will send Edmund to you,' he said. 'You will have much to say to each other. But remember, miss, tomorrow is the day.'

Leaving the room, he locked the door behind him. It was a foretaste of what she could expect. She paced up and down the room, thinking, contriving, planning . . . All depended, now, upon Edmund. Would she be able to manage him?

Her uncle opened the door to let him in. 'I will leave you two love-birds alone together.' His coyness was odious. 'But I'll not be far away.'

It was at once a warning and a threat. Jennifer, who had had wild ideas of rushing out into the house and throwing herself upon the loyalty of her father's old and trusted servants, thought again. It would merely lead to a painful scene and achieve nothing.

She faced the blushing Edmund. 'Well?' she said.

'Well Jenny?' His attempt at nonchalance was pitiful. 'What do you think of this scheme of our uncle's?'

'I abominate it,' she answered him fiercely. 'Surely, Edmund, you cannot be willing to submit?'

45

He looked uncomfortable. 'To deal plainly with you, Jenny, I did not take to it too kindly at first, but you will find it grows upon you. We are old friends, are we not? And, only think, Jenny, we will be free, able to control our own fortunes. We'll have a house in London, and our own stables in the country, and go to all the races – and you shall have your own box at the opera. I promise you, I'll not meddle with you more than you wish. You go your way – I go mine – and the freedom, Jenny, only think of the freedom.'

'Freedom? You call it freedom to be tied for life to someone you do not love?'

'Oh, as for love, Jenny, I have had my dream of that too, but who marries for it these days? You and I will deal well enough together, I promise you. And, remember your smirched name; in truth, our uncle is right, you should be grateful to me for granting you the protection of mine.'

She turned on him in a fury. 'I'd not take it, were you the last man on earth. I know you think to do well enough supporting your racehorses out of my fortune, but I'll not be a party to it. I'll make such a scene tomorrow that the parson shall refuse to marry us.'

He smiled at her knowingly. 'I collect you are not aware who the parson is to be. It is Dean Gurning.'

She had forgotten her uncle's brother the Dean, whose plural livings caused less scandal than his many mistresses. Dependent, she suspected, for many of his luxuries on his brother's help and financial advice, he would be a willing tool. No hope of help from him. Almost, she began to be frightened. Surely this could not really be going to happen?

She made another effort. 'I promise you, Edmund, I'd lead you such a life you'd wish you had never seen me.'

'No use to fly out at me, Jenny. If you mean to act the termagant it will have to be separate establishments, that's all. Your fortune, I apprehend, will be enough for both. No need to call on mine.'

'You dispose mighty freely of my fortune.' She was becoming really angry now.

'I shall be able to. My uncle's lawyers are drawing up the

settlements today.'

'I'll never sign them.'

'I warrant you will, if Uncle Gurning intends you should.'

It gave her coldly to pause. How far would her uncle go? She changed her tone. 'Edmund, we are old friends. Only help me in this and I'll do anything for you. The half of my fortune – anything.'

'How should I help you? Believe me, you are beyond help. But compose yourself and make the best of it. I promise I'll not be a demanding husband. Indeed,' he reddened, 'separate chambers will suit me vastly well.'

Absurdly, the fact that he did not even want her was the last straw. She broke into furious tears and might even have flown at him if her uncle had not appeared. He must, she realized, have been listening outside the door.

'Well, well,' he rubbed his hands. 'Enough of your billing and cooing. Time for that tomorrow.' His voice hardened. 'To your room, miss, and do not think to leave it again tonight.'

Hope dwindled. 'But shall I not see Elizabeth?' She had always been fond of her cousin.

'Time enough for that tomorrow. Promise you'll do nothing to shock her and she shall act as your bride's maid.'

It was defeat. In numb despair, she heard the key of her room turn in the lock, then started, ceaselessly, to pace up and down. Below, she heard the sound of carriages driving up. So her uncle was entertaining tonight. No doubt he felt he had cause for celebration. The settlements she and Edmund were to sign tomorrow would conceal for ever his depredations upon both their fortunes.

To and fro she paced, to and fro. What did she care for her fortune if she could only save herself? She went to the window and looked out. The front drive lay far below her, clear in the moonlight. A cord of knotted sheets? But if she could make one long enough, where would she go? Lucy Faversham's house was five miles away; the stables were securely locked at night. No matter for that. She would walk. Systematically, she removed the sheets from her bed, rejoicing that they were the finest of strong cambric, and set to work. But the rope, she soon saw, would not be nearly long enough.

Again, she was facing despair, when she heard a tiny scratching at her door. She hurried to it.

'Who's there?' she whispered.

'It's I, Elizabeth. Oh, Jenny, what are they doing to you?'

Hope sprang, unreasoning. Here, perhaps, was an ally.

'Lizzy, my love, I am in despair. Your father means that I shall marry Edmund tomorrow.'

'Marry Edmund?' There was a catch in the whispered breath, and suddenly Jennifer saw it all. Edmund's detachment, the despair in Elizabeth's voice . . . Here, indeed, was an ally.

'Lizzy,' she whispered urgently. 'We cannot talk like this. Run quick to the servants' quarters. The key of the housekeeper's room fits mine. The boys discovered it years ago. Then we can talk in safety. But be sure my uncle does not see you.'

'Never fear for Father,' came the whisper, 'he is entertaining the Whig Committee. They are safe for hours. And Mother is retired with one of her megrims. Wait, Jenny, I'll fetch the key.'

Pacing, more hopefully now, up and down the room as she waited, Jennifer considered what was best to do next. When Elizabeth returned and, breathlessly, unlocked the door and slid inside, she was ready with her plan. There was no time to be lost. At any moment her uncle might come to make sure his captive was safe. Urgently, she whispered her instructions to Elizabeth. The stable door must be left unlocked. Then, when the house was quiet, she would let herself out of her room with the housekeeper's key (which would never be missed) leaving the knotted sheets hanging from the window to make her uncle think she had escaped that way, without help from the house.

'But, Jenny,' asked Elizabeth, 'where will you go then?'

'Where but to the Favershams? I am confident the General will stand my friend against such a piece of tyranny as this. Why, what's the matter?'

'Matter enough I fear. The Favershams left for their London house last Friday sennight.'

This was a blow indeed. For a moment, Jennifer was silent,

then she brightened. 'Nothing for it but to follow them then. And, indeed, I shall be safer in London than five miles away. Faversham Hall is the first place my uncle will look for me.'

'But how will you go to London?'

'By the stage coach, you goose. Do you think I'm too fine a lady to ride in it?'

'I think you'd do anything, Jenny,' said Elizabeth with fervent admiration. 'But take the stage coach tomorrow you cannot. It is three weeks past that they discontinued all but the Tuesday and Friday coaches for the winter.'

Jennifer's face fell. 'That is indeed a facer. But no doubt I could hire a chaise in Petworth. How much money can you lend me, Lizzy? You see I do not ask whether you are willing to lend it me.'

'Nor need you, my love, but alas, I fear I am in low water. My father sent me to Chichester only the other day with a host of commissions and my pockets are sadly to let. Will three guineas be of any use to you?'

Wondering if this unusual shopping expedition was an unhappy chance, or yet another instance of her uncle's providence for evil, Jennifer counted her own money, which amounted to still less. 'No use,' she said at last. 'Even with your three guineas, for which I thank you with all my heart, I shall not have enough. No help for it. I shall have to ride all the way. No, never look so cast down, Lizzy, you well know it is something I have always longed to do.'

Elizabeth did indeed look horrified at the idea. 'But, Jenny, you, a young lady, to ride all that way unattended? Only think of the scandal.'

'Too late for me to be troubling myself about scandal, I fear, but you are right for all that. I shall not ride as a lady. Do you recollect last Christmas when we acted Mr Garrick's *Irish Widow* and I took the part of Mrs Brady and had to masquerade as a lieutenant? Everyone said I made an admirable boy. Well, I shall do it again. I still have the old green coat of poor Richard's that I wore, and the breeches I made to wear with it. With a greatcoat over all and,' she looked wistfully at her reflection in the glass, 'something of an execution upon my hair, I shall pass for an excellent young sprig on exeat from Eton.'

'But what will the General say when you reach Great Peter Street so habited?'

Jennifer pulled a face. 'My love, I dare not even consider it. No time for terrors now; run, quick and fetch me the money. Even uncle's hard drinking politicos will go home at last. And you must help me crop my hair before you go. What an excellent thing it is that it is become modish to wear it short. I will be quite the thing, I promise you.'

Which did not prevent kind-hearted Elizabeth from bursting into tears as the auburn curls floated to the floor. 'Oh, Jenny, I cannot bear to have you go away. I love you so dearly. Far better than Papa.'

Jennifer smiled at her fondly. 'And are proving it, my love. But, remember, if I stay, I must marry Edmund and I do not believe that would suit either of our books.'

Elizabeth went so fiery red that Jennifer kindly said no more, but urged her to get safely back to her room before the party downstairs broke up. With a last, tearful kiss Elizabeth left her. Alone, Jennifer found the time pass slowly. She did not dare lie down on her bed for fear of falling asleep. She must make her escape as soon as the house was quiet, so as to be as far forward as possible on the road to London when her escape was discovered and pursuit began.

To give herself a little more time, she sat down and composed a note to her uncle. The ink-well in her little writing desk had nearly dried in her absence, so it had, perforce, to be brief:

'Uncle: I shall risk my life climbing from my window rather than submit to your odious plan. Do not seek for me again. I am not gone back to Laverstoke. Believe this and spare yourself the embarrassment of making enquiries there. Believe, too, that I do not intend to be found.'

Here the ink ran out and she did not even sign the note. It should, she hoped, protect Elizabeth. She hoped, too, that her uncle would believe her pockets well enough lined to permit her hiring a chaise, which would take her to London before he had any chance of catching her. He would, of course, be informed that Starlight was missing, but must, she hoped, assume that she had ridden him only as far as one of the neighbouring towns where she might hire a chaise. If her luck held, he would lose some time enquiring whether she had indeed done so. Most of all, she found herself passionately hoping that he would believe her statement and not seek her at Laverstoke Hall. The idea of his confronting Lord Mainwaring and demanding her as his errant ward was somehow intolerable. Then she caught herself up: why should she assume that Lord Mainwaring would interest himself in her disappearance? When he heard of it, he would merely shrug it off, convinced of the justice of his original doubts of her.

A tear trickled down her cheek. But this was no time for despairing. She pulled herself together and went briskly to the big closet where she had sadly packed away such of her brothers' clothes as she could not bear to part with. When she had dressed, she considered herself carefully in her looking-glass. Yes, with the greatcoat's shower of capes which added much-needed width to her shoulders, she would do well enough. If possible she must not take it off. Just as well it was winter.

A sudden burst of merriment from below told her that her uncle's party was breaking up at last. A sudden thought struck her. What if he should pay her a late visit? Quick as a flash, she hid the knotted sheets, coat and greatcoat in her closet and climbed into bed, pulling the clothes well up around her chin. Surely he would not intrude upon her bedroom, but it was best to play safe.

A few minutes later, as the carriages rolled away from the sweep below, there came a knock on her door.

'Who's there?' she called sleepily, blowing out her candle.

'It is I, your aunt. I came to see if you want for anything, Jenny?'

Not for the first time, Jennifer acknowledged in her uncle a worthy adversary, as she heard the key turn in the lock of her door. Her aunt entered in her violet négligé, her candle throwing odd shadows about the room as she looked round, clearly under orders to make sure that all was as usual. Then she approached the bed and put a cold hand on Jennifer's forehead. 'Do not attempt to fight your uncle any more, Jenny my dear.

You only waste your time. He always wins. Act a complaisant part tomorrow and it shall be the better for you.'

Terrified lest her aunt should notice that she had on one of her brothers' shirts, Jennifer buried herself still deeper in the bedclothes, pretending a sleepy obstinacy.

'Oh, very well.' Her aunt's tired figure drooped still more as she turned away. 'I just hoped to make things easier for you, Jenny.'

'Thank you, Aunt, I know you mean it kindly.'

At last she was gone, but still Jennifer forced herself to lie quiet, her eyes fiercely open, staring into the darkness, until the last sound of movement died away in the old house. She knew all its noises by heart and could tell when Soames came up the back stairs, creaking heavily on the third step from the top, and then, last of all the servants, went on up to his room above. Then she heard her uncle climb the front stairs, whistling *Jenny Sutton* to himself. How like him, she thought angrily, to take no thought for others who might already be asleep. He paused for a moment outside her door and gently tried its lock. Then she heard him slam the door of what she still remembered as her father's room, next to hers. She waited until she heard his familiar, detested snore before she slipped out of bed. She had no means of relighting her candle, but fortunately the moon shone brilliantly in at her window. By its light she finished her few remaining preparations. She made a sad botch of tying her brother's cravat, remembering, as she struggled furiously with it, the jokes and laughter that had accompanied similar struggles last time she did so. No time, now, for such memories. She pulled the greatcoat close round her, slipped the few guineas she and Elizabeth had been able to muster into her purse, then felt her way along the dark side of her room to the secret drawer of her desk. Fumbling with the well-known catch, she got it open and took out her pearls, the one piece of her jewellery that her uncle had not discovered and impounded while she was away. If the worst came to the worst they would provide her with the means to supplement her scanty resources. Then, breathlessly, she crossed to the door, turned the house-keeper's key in the lock and pulled it gently open.

CHAPTER VI

Moonlight lay cold and clear across the stable yard. Somewhere in the park, an owl hooted; nearer at hand, a horse stamped restlessly in its loose box. Jennifer moved cautiously towards Starlight's stall. She knew only too well how lightly Thomas, the head groom, slept in his room over the stables, how quickly he would wake up at any unfamiliar sound.

But Starlight greeted her with a quiet whicker of affection and showed only polite surprise when instead of the side saddle to which he was accustomed, she set an old one of her brothers' across his back, congratulating herself as she did so on memories of her tomboy days when she had scandalised Aunt Julia by riding astride with them. Whispering encouragements, she led Starlight as noiselessly as possible out of the yard and a little way down the back drive. Then, happily free in her unwonted costume, she was up, softly urging Starlight to a canter as she guided him on to the grass verge of the drive which would deaden the sound of his hooves. How furious her father would have been at the resultant marks on the smooth grass . . . But all that was long ago. She clenched her teeth against memory and urged Starlight to a gallop. The park gates were locked at night, but this was not the first time she and Starlight had jumped them.

Once on the open road, she breathed more easily. Her main anxiety now was lest she lose the road to London. To have to enquire the way might prove fatal. Luckily, she knew the first part of it so well that there was no chance of a mistake, even by the deceptive light of the moon. A quick hard ride through silent fields brought her to her first hazard, the outlying houses of Petworth town. Suppose, by an impossible bit of bad luck, she should meet some night-wandering friend of her uncle's? But why should he recognise her? With one hand she turned the big collar of her brother's greatcoat higher about her face and pulled his hat down over the vivid betrayal of her hair. Petworth must be faced. She dared not risk the delay involved in riding round the outskirts of the town.

To her anxious ear, Starlight's hooves echoed with appalling noise down the moonlit street. At every moment, she expected a window to fly open, a question to be asked . . . But, she soothed herself, this was a main road. Night traffic along it must be fairly frequent. It was only to her tense nerves that her presence there, guiding Starlight across the well-known market square, seemed so dangerous, so extraordinary as to compel comment. Now, at last, they were skirting the high walls of Petworth House. A light – the first she had seen – burned in the window of the lodge. Suppose she should ring there and throw herself on the mercy of Lord Egremont? He had long been a patron of her father's and had often chucked her under the chin in happier days. For a moment, the idea was tempting. But her uncle was too securely entrenched in the county to be braved here, so near home, and Lord Egremont too busy with his affairs of state and art to care much for the fate of one almost unknown young woman. Besides, she remembered her costume. Impossible to present herself at Petworth House so garbed. Her arrival at Lucy's was going to be difficult enough.

Her mind made up, she urged on Starlight who had sensed her hesitation and paused in his stride. Soon they were out of the town, following the long wall of Petworth Park. Relieved for the first time from immediate apprehension, with the moonlit road unwinding itself before her, Jennifer had time to feel how tired she was. Soon, she must sleep. And yet, dared she? How long could she reckon before her uncle found she was gone? What if he should bully the truth out of Elizabeth and come straight after her, instead of losing time, as she hoped, in enquiries at the livery stables in Petworth and even, perhaps, Chichester?

Arguing this way and that with herself, she rode determinedly on, swaying, sometimes, a little in the saddle, increasingly grateful for the familiar steadiness of Starlight's gait. After what seemed a very long time, a lightening of the air, the occasional chirp of a bird, and, ahead of her, a rousing chorus of cocks, told her the dawn was coming. Starlight pricked up his ears, houses lay ahead; they had reached the outskirts of Billingshurst. Wondering to herself how much Starlight had been exercised the day before and whether he, too, was tired, she remembered, suddenly, a little tavern in Billingshurst, not the regular coaching inn, but an insignificant little place in a side road upon which she and her brothers had happened once after a long day's hunting. She remembered the landlady's kind red face and her hearty welcome, still more, the admirable ham and eggs she had produced with profuse apologies for insulting the gentry with such simple fare. There, surely, she might bait Starlight and sleep in safety for an hour or so? Instantly decided, she turned down the remembered side road and was soon rapping in authoritative imitation of her brothers at the door of the little house.

It was opened, after a nerve-racking delay, by the very red-faced woman of her memory. Too civil to show her surprise at the early visit, the woman – elderly now and stooping, but loquacious and obliging as ever – begged many pardons for her delay. She had been out at the back feeding the hens – had had no idea – was very sorry. She punctuated this incoherent speech with strident calls for 'John, John, where is the boy . . .'

He appeared, a half-grown lad, still rumpled from bed and rubbing sleep from his eyes, but roused himself at the sight of Starlight, took the bridle from Jennifer and promised him the best of care. His mother, meanwhile, was busy blowing up the reluctant fire, apologising for the lack of service and promising, in the same breath, a grilled chicken, and the best chamber to the strange young gentleman who looked so tired and must, she thought, be ill, since he kept his greatcoat close round him even indoors.

Jennifer, murmuring something half-intelligible from fatigue, about illness and great haste, asked to be shown at once to a room and ordered the grilled chicken and hot water to rouse her two hours later. The old lady protested: only two hours rest, lord save us, the young gentleman would kill himself and his horse, too. But Jennifer took no notice. Two hours was the most she dared allow herself.

The room over the taproom was small and snug, warmed by the main chimney of the house. The sheets smelt of lavender. Jennifer longed to undress and go fully to sleep, but dared not. Relaxed against the hard pillow, she promised herself she would be up again before the two hours were over. It was a long way, still, to London . . . a long way . . . a long way still . . .

She was roused by someone's shaking her arm, and sprang fully awake in an instant. Bright winter sunlight flooded the room. The landlady stood beside her, looking frightened, apologising harder than ever. Jennifer's first question, 'What is't o'clock?' brought forth a perfect torrent of words. Indeed, she said, she had meant no harm, but the young gentleman slept so sound, there was no waking him and in truth she was very sorry, but she thought it must be near noon, for Farmer Giles had driven his cows back to the farm some time past.

Jennifer interrupted her. Easy now to assume her brothers' autocratic air. Urgency lent unwonted firmness to her voice as she commanded food, her horse, the reckoning, all on the instant. Still muttering apologies, the landlady hurried to obey.

Appalled at the length of her sleep, Jennifer was almost tempted to forego the meal she longed for, but decided she did not dare to do without food; she would never stand up to the long ride to London. So she waited, bore the landlady's contrite speeches with the best grace she could muster, and was rewarded by a meal of the most delicious tough old fowl she thought she had ever tasted.

As she ate, the landlady bustled to and fro, supplying her every need, visibly suppressing curiosity. At last, fidgeting with a pewter tankard, she spoke.

'Begging your worship's pardon,' she said, 'but you would not be concerned about an eloping young lady, I suppose . . .' She let the sentence die away, alarmed at her own effrontery.

'An eloping young lady?' Jenniffer was proud of her tone of supercilious surprise.

'Indeed, yes, and an heiress to boot. I ran over, not ten minutes since, to borrow some French mustard (for indeed I know the Quality's tastes, though I serve them but seldom, having gone as housemaid at Petworth when I was little more than a child and married the head footman there, lord rest his soul, a hard husband he was to me, and dead these fifteen years or more) but,' she observed Jennifer's impatience, 'to come to the point, as I was saying I did but run over to my cousin Susan who is married to Sam Crompton, landlord of the Swan – a good inn, too, I must own, for those who like the hurly-burly and helter-skelter of a coaching inn, which some, I am glad to say, have more sense than . . .'

Lost in her own verbosity, she paused for a moment and Jennifer did her anxious best to steer her back to her subject: 'But the heiress, ma'am, what of her?'

'Oh, never fear for me, I was just coming to her. For I found my cousin Sam (for he is my cousin, too, through our grand-mother) – I found him in one of his passions, red as a turkey-cock, hot as a fire at Christmastide, and poor cousin Susan trying her best to soothe him – for indeed these passions of his do him much harm – and all along of a young lady, or rather of a gentleman that had come enquiring for a young lady and had so angered him with his questions and his cross questions that he was neither to hold nor to bind. To be called a liar in his own house is what Sam never would stomach and nothing would satisfy this fine gentleman but he must search every chamber in the inn himself for fear his ward lay hid there.

'For it is his ward who is run off to join her lover, and good luck go with her, say I, and so says Sam, too, and confusion to her guardian, who rode off at last, with not so much as a thank you or a glass of ale ordered, and Sam so angry he could hardly speak. And a blessing that was, too, for Susan told me the last thing of all the gentleman asked if there was any other inn in town. Sam, he was silent with rage, and Susan, she said nothing being a good friend of mine and not wanting my house turned topsy-turvy as hers had been. And so the long and the short of it is that the gentleman has rode fuming off down the London road, none the wiser for all his questions.'

Pausing in her flood of talk, she considered Jennifer with a bright, enquiring, kindly eye. Clearly she suspected something, but how much? Rapidly deciding what to do, Jennifer plunged into explanation: 'And all the better for me, ma'am, since, as you seem to suspect, the young lady is my betrothed, stolen away to meet and marry me against her cross-grained guardian's will. But it seems by some mischance I have missed her and must now make all haste to her aunt's in London, where I have no doubt she awaits me, that we may be safely wed before her guardian finds her.'

Much delighted at this confidence, and at finding herself playing so important a part in smoothing the course of true love, the landlady bustled about harder than ever, produced her modest reckoning, shouted to John for the gentleman's horse, assured Jennifer that her guardian was doubtless half-way to Horsham by now and offered her John's services to guide her by a country short-cut which should not only avoid her pursuer but give her a chance to pass him on the road and reach London before him. 'For he will doubtless be making his enquiries and turning every inn in Horsham topsy-turvy too and while he is doing so you may, with John's help, show him a clean pair of heels.'

Jennifer gratefully accepted this offer, after a rapid mental calculation as to the extent of the vails such a service would require. She could just manage it, she thought, and still leave herself enough money for emergencies . . . So, after a friendly farewell to her kind landlady, she set forward again with John, on a shaggy pony, as her silent companion. He led her along by-ways and bridle-paths that took them through no town of any size until they hit the London road again near Dorking. Here he bade her farewell, suddenly loquacious as he pocketed her tip and bade her, 'Ride fast, and you'll beat them to London yet,' leaving her wondering what tale of highwaymen or Bow Street Runners his mother had thought fit to tell him.

She rode on thoughtfully, wondering whether she had indeed distanced her uncle by this manoeuvre, or whether he would be in London – and perhaps at Lucy's – before her. One encouraging thing she had learned from the landlady's story. Elizabeth had not betrayed her. Uncle Gurning clearly did not know that she was dressed as a man.

This, she told herself, riding confidently through Dorking, was a great point gained. Her uncle was searching for a young lady in a hired carriage, not a young gentleman on horseback. She was also pleased that her friend the landlady had showed no signs of suspecting her real identity. So she rode on for a while in jaunty imitation of her brothers, whistling a few bars of *Lillibulero*. But a chill in the air brought soberer thoughts. The light was beginning to ebb from the top of the Downs; it would be dark long before she reached London. It was not a pleasant thought, and she silently cursed the landlady's negligence in not arousing her sooner. Visions of highwaymen haunted her, but she cheered herself as best she might with the thought that the road would certainly grow more clearly marked, and more frequented, as she neared London, and that at least, if her uncle should, by unhappy chance, overtake her on the way, the chances of his seeing through her disguise by the uncertain light of evening were slight indeed.

So she rode doggedly on, squaring her shoulders inside the greatcoat when a rare carriage overtook her, letting wise Starlight set his own pace, fighting off the fatigue that began, again, to overwhelm her. Incoherent thoughts, near to dreams, flickered in and out of her mind. What was happening at Laverstoke Hall which she had left – how strange it seemed – only yesterday . . .? How much did the children miss her? What, if anything, was Lady Laverstoke doing about her disappearance? Had she perhaps sent for Lord Mainwaring? Intolerable thought. The sound of a carriage behind her roused her from her half sleep. Where was her uncle now? In this very carriage, perhaps?

But it rattled past, its four horses whipped on by a young elegant who bestowed hardly a passing glance on the solitary horseman plodding so wearily along. The rhythm of Starlight's gait was broken, now, by fatigue; they went on slowly, so slowly that the journey had the quality of one of those, in a nightmare, that will never end. It was quite dark, and the moon had risen, when they passed, at last, through Lambeth village, past the Archbishop's palace and so to her first view of the Thames, lying silver and quiet in the moonlight, with beyond it the lights of London. She paused for a moment, breathtaken, despite her weariness, by the magic of the scene, then urged Starlight on to the bridge, noticing, with surprise, the number of people who were still about. But of course by London reckoning the night was young yet. She passionately hoped that Lucy would be at home in her house in Great Peter Street and not gone to some rout or other. What had Elizabeth said? They had been in London a whole week; Lucy would be well launched on the social tide by now. Vaguely anxious, Jennifer wished she had questioned Elizabeth more closely as to what had brought Lucy and her father, the General, to London at this odd time of year. Something to do with his duties at the House of Commons perhaps? She remembered a conversation between Lord Mainwaring and young Laverstoke about the present disturbances in London. They had spoken anxiously and yet, somehow, with excitement about massed meetings and petitions presented to Parliament. Would these perhaps have affected General Faversham? If only she knew what precisely he did, but it was certainly connected with Parliament, and carried with it the comfortable house in Great Peter Street where she had once stayed with Lucy for an intoxicating breath of the London season.

Reaching the north bank of the river, she was surprised to find the bridge's approaches crowded with people, who stood about in little groups, mostly quiet, some talking, some arguing, all apparently waiting for something. Was there always such a crowd when Parliament was sitting, she wondered. Surely not? As she made her way diffidently through the scattered groups, who gave way to her civilly enough, she caught scraps of conversation. One man was speaking of 'The petition', another said 'Any time now', 'Damned cold waiting', added a third.

Remembering again Lord Mainwaring's talk of bad harvests, expensive bread and resultant meetings and petitions to Parliament, she made her way as fast as she safely could through the crowd. It seemed quiet enough now, but she did not like the thought of what might happen if something should fuse together these separate, waiting groups.

The crowd was thicker still in Old Palace Yard and she had some anxious moments as she made her way, as unobtrusively as possible, towards Great Peter Street. It was a relief when she turned into its comparative quietness, but her heart sank as she saw the unlighted windows of Lucy's house. She must, indeed, be out, and her father, most likely, on duty in Westminster Hall. But Miss Milsom, Lucy's cousin and companion, would surely be there to welcome her with the inevitable exclamations. Thus reassuring herself, she tied Starlight's bridle to the gatepost, advanced boldly and rapped at the front door. A long, anxious silence followed, while she wondered more than ever at the dark quietness of the house. Then, at last, came a little glimmer of light through the window above the door. Slowly, reluctantly, the big bolts were pulled back and a wizened face peered out suspiciously at her, the door held all the time on the chain.

'Miss Faversham?' she asked impatiently.

'Miss Faversham is from home.' The old woman began to close the door.

'The General, then, or Miss Milsom?'

'All, all are from home, sir. No one's here but old Peter and me. They be all gone north for the baronet's funeral; left in a great shindig they did and won't be back these two months or more, I reckon. Staff be all gone down to the country, young sir, saving only Peter and me ... Mortal cold and lonesome it be in this great house, sir, and riot and mayhem loose outside, and now, if you please, sir ...' Slowly, remorselessly, the withered hand closed the door.

Jennifer turned away. There was nothing to be done here. This old crone could provide neither shelter nor support. Lucy's sudden trip to town was explained now; the General's ailing brother, the baronet, must have died at last in Northumberland; there was no hope of help from Lucy for some time. Her plans were all to make over again. For a moment, drooping over Starlight's bridle, she gave herself up to despair, then pulled herself together. She still had two guineas, and her pearls. Things would look better in the morning. She would go back across Westminster Bridge to a little country-looking inn she had noticed in Lambeth and pass the night there. How she wished, now, that she had yielded to temptation and stopped there in the first place. For, she confessed to herself, she did not much relish the idea of passing once more through that crowd, whose confused murmur seemed to grow as she listened. There were shouts now: 'Hunt, Hunt', she heard and then loud huzzas.

Best get it over with. She turned Starlight resolutely back into Old Palace Yard, then paused at the tumultuous scene that met her eyes. The crowd had found its focus, a man in a high white hat who was making an impassioned speech from a cart in its midst. She was too far away to hear what he was saying, but from time to time the crowd immediately around him would punctuate his speech with cries of, 'The petition' or, yet again, 'Hunt, Hunt' and 'Huzza'. Impossible, now, to go back the way she had come. The crowd had become too dense in the few minutes she had spent in the quietness of Great Peter Street. Too dense and, at the same time, somehow menacing.

As she manoeuvred to turn Starlight back into the narrow opening of Great Peter Street, a rough hand was laid on her bridle. 'Nah, then, cully,' said a cockney voice, 'this is no place for the likes of you. We eats young gentlemen, see.' It was said, apparently, with kindly, even humorous intent, and the hand on the bridle was endeavouring to guide Starlight back into Great Peter Street, but the horse, alarmed by the crowds and resenting the unfamiliar touch, reared up in sudden alarm. Exhausted as she was, Jennifer kept her seat by a miracle, and tried simultaneously to soothe the horse and the crowd, who had scattered before its lashing hooves, but now closed in on her again in a very different temper. Gone, now, was the humorous patronage of the first speaker. Instead, she found herself the target of a babel of angry voices. 'Did it a-purpose,' said one. 'Hoped to knock our brains out,' chimed in another. 'The river's the place for the likes of him,' said a third. More hands now, hot, dirty hands reached out to grasp bridle and reins. Her attempts at protest and explanation were lost in the angry hum of voices about her. 'The river, the river,' came from every side. Terrified, exhausted, her worst fear that her tormentors might discover her sex. Jennifer felt herself and the quivering Starlight pushed forward by sheer mass of numbers down a little lane leading to the river. A rude hand snatched the hat from her head and sent it spinning over the crowd towards the water. 'There,' came the exultant cry, 'young dandy, where's your titfer?' and, 'Let him go fishing for it,' came another voice.

All the time, struggling in a whirlpool of angry men, Jennifer had been half aware of a carriage that was making its slow way through the crowd in a direction at an angle to that in which she and Starlight were being pushed, its coachman, a cockney himself, persuading his way forward with inaudible blandishments. Here, surely, was help. Forcing herself to think through her terror, Jennifer did her best to guide Starlight towards the carriage. But it was no use, the human tide was sweeping her on too fast. Desperately, she rose in her stirrups and gave a wild cry for help.

As she did so, the carriage window went down with a bang, and a head leaned out and gave an order to the coachman. Breathless with hope, she saw the carriage slowly change its direction and make towards her through the crowd. Now she could hear what the coachman was saying: 'Way for Lord Mainwaring,' he cried, 'you fools, do you not know your friends?' At once, the ready crowd had a new cry: 'Mainwaring for ever, Mainwaring and the petition. Huzza!' And, with a mixture of relief and horror, Jennifer saw that it was Mainwaring himself who still leant out of the carriage window. 'That's very well,' he cried now in ringing tones that caused a sudden pool of silence round him, 'very well indeed, you'd huzza for me, would you? And what were you doing with my young friend there?'

'Friend,' a rough voice took him up, 'that's no friend of yours, nor of liberty's. Rode his horse clear into the crowd, the bastard, and might have killed a score of us.'

'Ridiculous,' said Mainwaring in his carrying voice, and, oddly, it was enough for the crowd. A dozen other voices chimed in: 'Aye, aye, true enough, 'twas accident most like,' said one, and, 'If he's Mainwaring's friend that's good enough for me,' added another. To her amazement, for she had never before encountered the volatility of a crowd, Jennifer found the very hands that had a moment before been urging her roughly towards the river and probable death, now guiding Starlight towards Mainwaring's carriage. Almost, for a moment, she would have preferred the river. But there was no help for it. He had the door open, his servant was ready to take Starlight, there was a last cry of 'Mainwaring and Hunt for ever. Huzza for Mainwaring's friend,' and she was safe inside.

CHAPTER VII

The door closed behind her. The carriage moved forward slowly through the shouting crowd. Inside, there was stony silence. Lord Mainwaring sat still in his corner, Jennifer, quick-breathing, in hers.

'Well,' he said at last, as the carriage turned into the comparative quiet of Parliament Street. 'Am I to be favoured with an explanation of this frolic, Miss Fairbank?'

'Frolic!' she caught her breath, then rallied at the mere injustice of it. 'I am happy you think it no more.'

'I trust, ma'am,' he looked at her, gravely, 'that it is no less. But, I repeat, I await your explanation.'

'It is mighty good of you to do so,' she flared out at him. 'And if it fails to satisfy you, do you propose to deliver me once more to the mob?'

He took snuff, meditatively. 'Your confidence in me is most flattering! But what, indeed, am I to do with you? You can hardly have the effrontery to suppose that I shall send you back, thus garbed, to Laverstoke House, whence, I am informed, you vanished, under mysterious circumstances, yesterday.'

She swallowed fury. 'You are well informed, sir.'

'I make a point of being so. You will find it best to tell me the truth. It may be that there is a respectable explanation of the presence of a young gentlewoman – in man's attire – however becoming,' she was aware, in the erratic light, that he sketched a mocking half bow, 'in Parliament Square at night, but what it may be I am yet to learn.' He paused.

'And if I refuse to explain?'

'I shall drive you to Piccadilly and set you down there. Then you and your horse can shift for yourselves. But, come, Miss Fairbank, recollect yourself and quit fencing with me. I promise you, if you need one, I will stand your friend. Indeed, I will go farther and cry your pardon for anything I may have said to offend you. Almost I begin to think I may have misjudged you and that there is more to this than some foolish woman's wager, as I had imagined.'

'A woman's wager?'

'My dear Miss Fairbank,' he leaned out of the window for a moment to give an order to the coachman, then turned his full attention upon her again and continued, 'your pose as a meek little governess would not do for a moment. You betrayed yourself every hour of the day. Only a rattle-pate like Lady Laverstoke would have been deceived by it for an instant. But it seemed a harmless enough deception, and no question but that the children were profiting under your care. So, I thought best to let it continue.'

'It was mighty handsome of you, sir,' she was playing for time now. How much should she tell him? How much dare she conceal?

'I am yet to learn whether it was good of me or not. But, enough of this temporising. Come, Miss Fairbank, your story. I have told the coachman to drive through the park. By then, we must have decided what is to be done with you.'

Surprisingly, this calm assumption of authority came as an immeasurable relief. Why not tell him the whole? Or almost the whole. Some things she could not bear to speak of. 'If I tell you,' she began, 'may I ask two things?'

'What are they?'

'That you will be satisfied without names or places. You are right, of course, in thinking that my name is not Fairbank, but for the time being I prefer to be known by no other.'

'Granted. And the other request?'

'Your promise of secrecy, Lord Mainwaring.'

'You are pleased to insult me, Miss Fairbank.'

She had got him, at last, on the raw, and wished she had not. It was all too much. She burst into tears. 'Indeed, I had no such intention and must beg your pardon. I have not been used to be treated with such consideration. But let me tell you the whole.' In fact, she could not bring herself to do so, and her ruthlessly abridged version sounded improbable enough, even to her own ears. Would he believe her? . . . And so, naming no names, she told him her story. At the end she paused.

But his voice now held something like respect. 'And so you are come to London, with a few guineas, a string of pearls, a suit of your brother's clothes, and a horse.'

'Yes, that I fear is the sum of my resources. But it is only until Lu – until my friend shall return to town.'

'Granted. But what are we to do with you until then?'

Again she derived extraordinary comfort from his use of the small word 'we'. Suddenly the responsibility for herself which she seemed to have shouldered for so long had been taken from her. This short-tempered, black-browed lord she had disliked so often was going to take care of her. She sighed a long sigh and leaned more easily back in her corner of the carriage.

He was silent for a few minutes, deep in thought. At last, he leaned forward and gave another order to the coachman. Then he turned to her. 'Nothing for it,' he said, 'you will have to go to my grandmother's.'

'Your grandmother? Like this?'

He laughed. 'A little late in the day to play the prude. But trust me, my grandmother has seen stranger sights than you present. I will tell her it was for a wager. She will believe me, or not, as she chooses, and you, at your leisure, may tell her as much – or as little – of the truth as you wish.'

'But will she take me in?'

'If I ask her to. And, for some reason, I find myself inclined to believe your Arabian Tale. But no more running away, mind. There has been enough of that already for three volumes folio.'

'Indeed,' she found herself suddenly fighting sleep. 'Indeed . . . I have no wish . . . to run away . . .' Her head sank back against the squab and she plunged into the deep, silent sleep of exhaustion, hardly stirring when the carriage drew up noisily outside the Duchess of Lewes's house in Grosvenor Square.

'So much the better,' said Mainwaring to himself and, as a footman opened the carriage door, he picked up the sleeping figure and remarking 'my young friend is not well', carried her indoors and straight upstairs to his grandmother's boudoir where he knew that at this time of night she would be drinking warm wine and water and writing in the diary that so terrified her contemporaries.

'George!' she looked up with pleased surprise from her writing desk. 'This is an unexpected pleasure. But what frolic is this?'

For he had put his burden carefully down on a sofa, where Jennifer stirred, put a hand to her head, then curled up, turned her head away from the light, and fell asleep again.

'Have you taken leave of your senses?' went on the old lady, reaching for her hand bell. 'Is this the place for your drinking companions to sleep off their excesses?'

His hand went out to the bell, restraining hers. 'No drinking companion. Take a closer look, ma'am.'

Her curiosity stirred, she rose heavily from her brocaded chair and waddled across the room to look down at Jennifer. 'Shame on you, George, 'tis a girl. What devilry is this?'

He laughed. 'You suspect the worst, as always, ma'am. But I assure you, for once, I am innocence itself. I find myself remarkably cast in the role of protector of virtue.'

'Virtue?' the old lady snorted. 'I never heard of virtue masquerading in greatcoat and breeches. I may be old, George, but I am not yet shatterbrained. I'll not have your bit of muslin foisted off on me. And a redhead, too, I know what that means.'

'And so you should, ma'am, having been toasted through the town as the queen of them all.'

An instinctive hand went up to settle the flaming red wig in its place. 'Ah, George, you were always a flatterer. You can twist me round your finger, as once your grandfather did. Well then, tell me the whole story of this romantic piece of virtue and we will contrive some better place for her than my sofa.'

'Alas, ma'am, the whole story is precisely what I may not tell you. I have promised my heroine that she shall herself tell you as much, or as little, as she pleases.'

'Mighty handsome of you. And in the meantime, I collect, I am to take her on trust.'

'On my word of her innocence, ma'am. Indeed, she has been

68

much misused and you would oblige me vastly if you would give her shelter for a few days. I could tell you that her strange attire was the result of a foolish girl's wager. No,' he saw that the old lady had brightened at this comprehensible explanation, 'I said I could tell you not that I would. But it will do well enough for Marsham, will it not?'

'Admirably.' The Duchess smiled a pleased, reminiscent smile. 'I recollect once I wagered Fox I'd pass for a Member in the House ... but that was long ago, and I was married, George. These frolics do well enough when one has a husband behind one. Lord,' a horrid thought struck her, 'that reminds me. What of the heiress – what was her name? Miss Purchas? She knows nothing of this, I trust.'

He laughed. 'No, ma'am. I am not, alas, as yet on such terms with Miss Purchas. Indeed there has been some delay on her uncle's part that I do not readily understand, and we are yet to meet. This is an added reason why I should be plaguily grateful if you would take Miss Fairbank off my hands. You will find her a charming, spirited girl, I promise you, but a trifle too much of the heroine for my liking.' He rose to take his leave, but his grandmother halted him with an imperious gesture.

'Come, George, am I to know no more than that she is Miss Fairbank with romantic delusions? Do you really believe I will take her in on such slight information?'

He smiled at her lovingly. 'Dear ma'am, I am sure of it, since I see your curiosity is aroused. How can you satisfy it but by giving Miss Fairbank shelter? I promise you, you will not regret it. You know you have ever been a gambler. Gamble this once for me, and I warrant Miss Fairbank will repay you richly. You have often complained of your monotonous existence, alone in this great house. You will not find life monotonous with Miss Fairbank as your guest. The first time I met her, she had taken my hunter, Lightning, without so much as a by-your-leave and ridden him to hounds. And tonight – I think I can tell you this much – I came on her alone, on horseback, dressed as you see, in the midst of a riot in Old Palace Yard.'

'A complete heroine!' The old lady smiled. 'Well, George, I see I shall have to oblige you, as usual. If I had spoiled your father as I do you, perhaps we should have ended better friends. And that reminds me, we have still to condole with each other. They were both drunk, I take it?'

'By what I can learn. And arguing about which of them should drive. My father won. At least he was killed instantly when the carriage overturned. Poor Henry lived long enough to know he was dying.'

'Losing it all. Yes, poor Henry. He counted so on being a duke. I'm sorry, George, I never could like him. I cried, not enough to make my rouge run, for your father. I have no tears for Henry. But, you, George, you're the only one now. You must marry. For my sake?'

He had never heard that pleading note from her before and it moved him as his father's and brother's deaths had failed to do. 'I mean to, ma'am. I ride to Sussex tomorrow. Since Miss Purchas's uncle does nothing but fob me off with promises and postponements, I propose to go there and press my suit in person.' Involuntarily, as he spoke, his eyes travelled to the sofa where Jennifer lay asleep, a pale cheek pillowed on her hand.

Her eyes followed his, then returned, to give him a shrewd look. 'Wisely decided. A heroine is no helpmeet for a political man. And Miss Purchas's connection in the county should prove invaluable. I only hope she can cure you of this radical folly of yours. For I warn you, I have heard many attacks on you and your wild friends these last few weeks. Only yesterday Mr Tierney came here expressly to warn me you were like to lose the confidence of all the wiser heads if you do not look about you.'

'Never fear for that,' he took her hand. 'I stand before you a man converted. I have seen enough, tonight, of Hunt and his oratory to cure me of such fancies once and for all. It is not by mob rule that we shall cure the country's ills. But I have talked enough. God bless you, ma'am, and take care of my heroine.' He raised the beringed old hand to his lips, cast one more glance at Jennifer, and left the room.

Alone, the old lady sat for a few minutes, chin in hand, gazing thoughtfully at Jennifer, then, with a sigh, she rang her bell. Her maid, Marsham, answered it so speedily that it was obvious she had been waiting outside.

'Listening again, Marsham?' said her mistress tranquilly. 'Then you will be aware that we have a visitor. Fetch me a nightgown and négligé of Miss Jane's and some more wine and water and – Marsham – before we wake her, let it be well understood, Miss Fairbank is my good friend, and Lord Mainwaring's.'

Marsham curtseyed. 'La, ma'am, no need to make heavy weather of it. I knows a lady when I sees one, even if she has chosen to dress herself somewhat oddly. If I have told you once, I have told you a thousand times we would be the better of some young life about the house, but you never would fancy one of Miss Jane's girls.'

'No, Marsham, and well you know why. Hymn singing and family prayers in this house is what I never would abide. At least Miss Fairbank does not seem like to trouble us with them. Riot and mayhem seem more probable with her for guest. But hurry, Marsham, your commissions; she begins to stir.'

Waking at last, Jennifer looked confusedly around her. She was in a large room lit by a profusion of wax candles in candelabra that glittered in their light and that of a roaring fire. Beside it, in a brocaded chair that suggested a throne, sat an old lady in a flaming red wig, heavily powdered and rouged and dressed in a puce sarsenet gown of the style of the early years of the century.

'Well, child.' She had a surprisingly deep and beautiful voice. 'You have slept long enough. Now we must talk. Yes,' she saw Jennifer's puzzled glance search the room, 'Lord Mainwaring is gone. He had business to attend to and left you in my charge. I am his grandmother, as perhaps he may have told you.'

'Yes, my lady,' Jennifer struggled to her feet and made a somewhat dizzy curtsy. 'I am most infinitely obliged to your grace for giving me shelter.'

'Fiddlestick, child, you are not obliged to me at all – and for mercy's sake sit down again. As for my sheltering you, thank Lord Mainwaring's commendation for that, or, to be plain with you, thank my curiosity which was ever my besetting sin and

71

longs to be satisfied as to what brought you here in this bizarre costume. Not but what,' she lifted her lorgnette and studied her blushing guest appraisingly, 'it becomes you vastly well. It was a more exacting costume I had to assume when I made my celebrated appearance in the House of Commons.' She laughed at Jennifer's puzzled expression. 'But enough of that for to-night. Here, if I mistake not, comes Marsham with your wine and water. Drink it up, like a good child, and she shall show you to your chamber. Tomorrow will be time enough for talk. Marsham, the blue room for Miss Fairbank. Goodnight, child, and pleasant dreams.' And the old lady turned once more to her writing desk.

Parrying Marsham's questions with as much sleepy courtesy as she could muster, and thus, unknowingly, confirming the maid her enemy, Jennifer stripped off her borrowed clothes and settled with a sigh of relief in the soft bed that awaited her. Tomorrow would indeed be time enough for talk and even for thought . . .

Waking late, she lay for a while considering her new circumstances and listening to the unfamiliar sounds of the London street. Carriages rattled by; under her window a woman cried 'Oranges, ripe oranges'; footsteps passed and repassed; scraps of conversation floated up to her. She was bone tired and would gladly have lain there all day had not Marsham appeared and, with a somewhat sour expression, offered her a blue silk négligé and told her the Duchess awaited her company for breakfast in her boudoir.

So, over toast and chocolate, she faced the sharp old eyes again. They looked her up and down. 'Blue becomes you,' were the old lady's first words, 'as it never did me. Pinks and reds were ever my colours after I had summoned up the courage to wear them. But, for you, it must be blues and greens. I think I shall enjoy this morning's work. We are going shopping,' she explained to the puzzled girl, 'you can hardly propose to appear as my *dame de compagnie* in a cravat and a pair of trousers.'

Jennifer, who had never used a less modest word than the current 'inexpressibles' found herself absurdly blushing.

'Ha,' laughed the old lady, 'so you are a mere miss for all

your adventures. There's life in me yet if I can shock George's heroine. Well, is it a match? Will you come shopping with me?'

'With the greatest of pleasure. Only,' the blush was stronger than ever, 'only I have no money nor am like to have till I come of age.'

'Which cannot be soon, I collect. But no matter for that. If it makes you easier, you shall promise to pay me then. I do not propose to die these many years yet, I find life much too entertaining. But you will be thinking me in my dotage already if I run on so, when it is you who should be telling me your whole romantic history. Mainwaring was discretion itself, he merely told me how he found you in the midst of a riot in Old Parliament Square, and left me to die of curiosity as best I might. You, I am sure, will be kinder to an old lady who has few pleasures left in life but gossip, dress and drink.' She rang her bell. 'Marsham, send for more chocolate and then go, if you please, to Miss Jane's wardrobe in the red room and look me out a walking dress that shall not shame Miss Fairbank. There,' she went on when Marsham had flounced out of the room, 'Marsham always listens if she has the opportunity, but now you are safe for this half-hour or more, if I remember Jane's closet aright. Much as she would like to, Marsham will not dare disobey me outright. So, come, your story, Scheherazade.'

So Jennifer told her story, again omitting names and places. The duchess nodded approvingly when she explained this. 'Quite right,' she said, 'quite right. You are a girl of spirit and it shall be respected. Miss Fairbank you shall remain so long as you wish it.'

She listened intently to the story, put in a question here, a sympathetic exclamation there and finally leaned back in her chair with a sigh of pure pleasure. 'George is right,' she said, 'you are indeed a heroine. It will be a pleasure to have you as my guest. I only hope your friend does not return too speedily from burying her uncle, the nameless baronet. You see how faithfully I propose to keep my word; it would, you must realise, be child's play to penetrate your secret. There cannot

73

be many baronets dead these last few weeks, nor, I apprehend, do all of them have nieces with romantic young friends. But never fear, I have promised to respect your secret and shall do so, if you will but defer to my liking for pretty clothes. Ah, here is Marsham. Help Miss Fairbank dress, Marsham, and order the carriage to be ready in half an hour. We are going shopping.'

And shop they did. Jennifer, whose wildest notion of shopping had hitherto been confined to a sedate day choosing between spotted and sprigged muslins at the linen-draper's in Chichester, found herself quite dazzled by the displays of mull and jacquonet, of gauzes and crapes, that were unrolled at the Duchess's behest. Amazing, too, was the speed with which her commands were to be executed. Returning the proud possessor of four bonnets, each one more becoming than the last, she could hardly believe that the walking dresses, the dove-coloured pelisse, the muslins and – greatest joy of all – the evening dress of figured gauze over satin were to be sent home within the week.

'Mind you.' The Duchess tapped Jennifer's cheek with her lorgnette. 'The figured gauze is perhaps a little fast for a young girl, but I am almighty tired of those insipid muslins, and when I take you to Almack's I wish you to cut a figure and make a proper stir in the world. Last season there was a chit of a girl under Lady Cowper's protection who was all the rage with her spotted and sprigged; we will see what we can do with something a little stronger. I have a great fancy to see you the toast of the town, and half measures will never achieve that. Then, when we have two or three good offers for your hand, you may snap your fingers at your banker uncle, choose the best of them and let him alone to extricate your fortune from the old skinflint's clutches.'

Jennifer had to concede the brilliance of this strategy, though she found it hard to believe that she, whose only experience of London had been one demure week spent with Lucy, might by any freak of fate or management of the Duchess, contrive to become the belle of Almack's. Besides, she reminded her patroness, they had agreed that she should rejoin Lucy (referred to as her nameless friend) as soon as she returned to London.

'True, child,' said the Duchess, sinking back against the cushions of her luxurious carriage, 'I do seem to remember something of the kind. But that was this morning and I had not properly considered what pleasure might be had in dressing you and launching you in society. Surely you cannot deny me it? To take an unknown heiress and make her the talk of Almack's, the toast of the Clubs; what a delightful occupation! I see by that pursing of your lips, you think it cannot be done, but let me alone for contriving . . . And you surely could not be so cruel as to deny me the opportunity. It will add six years to my life, terrify my daughter, and delight George.'

Jennifer laughed. 'Oh, ma'am, how can you be so kind. Nothing in this world would give me greater pleasure than to stay with you, but I have no right . . .'

'Lord, if you talk of rights,' interrupted the Duchess, 'have done. Think rather of the pleasure it will give me, consider the woeful surprise of your poor uncle when he finds you snug in my protection. Consider the sparks of St James's, sighing over your slipper, and remember that London is better conquered from Grosvenor Square than from Great Peter Street . . . In fact, consider what you please, only do, pray, oblige me by agreeing to stay.'

CHAPTER VIII

Only one shadow clouded the happiness of the ensuing days. Looking up eagerly from the muslins, the gauze, the riding habit, the bonnets and shoes that came home with such speed, Jennifer brightened each time the knocker echoed on the great front door. Surely this time it would be Lord Mainwaring, come to enquire how she did. And surely the Duchess, who insisted that she see no company until she was herself fit to be seen, would make an exception in favour of him.

But he did not come. The wise old Duchess soon saw how the land lay. 'You must wonder,' she said over their breakfast chocolate one morning, 'where my scapegrace of a grandson is all this time and why he has not come to pay his respects. The fact is, I quite forgot to tell you he is gone out of town – and on a most romantic errand.'

'Indeed?' By an effort of will, Jennifer steadied the hand that held her cup.

'Yes, I hope daily to hear news of his betrothal. It has been quite a settled thing this long time past and it is but now for the announcement to be made and the lady to name the day.' If this was not the exact truth, the Duchess told herself it was kindest so to make Jennifer aware at once of the complete impossibility of any hope in that direction.

Having administered this timely dose of information, she threw herself with more enthusiasm than ever into the game of launching Jennifer in society. And Jennifer, for her part, set her teeth and determined to succeed. The Duchess was right. Marriage for love was romantic nonsense. She would keep a cool head and settle for nothing less than a coronet to match her fortune.

The Duchess, meanwhile, had summoned her daughter, Jane, who had made, many years before, an unexceptionable match with a witless marquis and was now busily engaged in hunting a similar one for the eldest of the resultant plain Miss Beresfords. Lady Beresford was not best pleased to find herself saddled with the responsibility for her mother's all too handsome protégée. But – the Duchess was paying the expenses of Miss Beresford's season. The argument was a powerful one. Lady Beresford kissed Jennifer, declared she was 'sweetly pretty, and so vivacious' and said it would be a privilege for Pamela to share her début with so charming a girl. She also exchanged a speaking glance, behind the Duchess's back, with her old ally, Marsham. It boded no good for Jennifer.

Praising Jennifer effusively to her face – and to the Duchess – Lady Beresford lost no chance of dropping insidious doubts about her in other ears. Her grandmother was so impulsive . . . One knew so little of this latest protégée of hers . . . One hoped she would not be disappointed in her confidence . . . How odd that nobody knew anything about Miss Fairbank's family . . . And as for her fortune . . . An expressive shrug of still shapely shoulders finished the sentence. Marsham, meanwhile, was performing the same kind office below stairs. Visiting abigails were regaled with the details of Jennifer's first appearance: 'Dressed as a man and in the protection of Lord Mainwaring.' The abigails could all too easily guess what that meant.

But Jennifer was blithely unaware of this sordid undercurrent of slander. On the surface, her world was rosy indeed. Completely outfitted now as a young lady of the highest *ton*, she went everywhere with her patroness, or, when the Duchess preferred to stay at home and write in her diary, with Lady Beresford, who seemed the kindest of chaperons. Her daughter, Pamela, was a cipher of a girl, plain, dull and good-tempered, but in the first excitement of finding London at her feet, Jennifer hardly noticed this. She had conversation for two, and did not notice that in the gay little circles of young men who nightly surrounded her and Pamela, it was she who talked, while Pamela merely smiled, nodded, and listened.

Incapable of jealousy herself, Jennifer had no idea of the fury with which Lady Beresford watched all this, and innocently thought that she and Pamela were the excellent if superficial friends they seemed. So, together and yet not together, they attended balls and routs, the play and the opera, accompanied wherever they went by their little swarm of cavaliers. Of these, the conservative and cautious spirits attached themselves to Pamela, whose family and fortune were, after all, a known thing, the gay blades and gamblers dangled after Jennifer. She was not, after all, a rich Duchess's protégée for nothing . . .

Chief among these, both in rank and attentiveness, was young Lord Leatherhead, a dandy of surpassing elegance, who was said to rival even the bankrupt exile, Beau Brummell in the pains he took over his appearance. As it took him a minimum of two hours to dress for any occasion, and as he changed his costume at least three times a day, it was not surprising that his conversation was a trifle insipid. But then, as Jennifer said, his appearance was a poem in itself. It would be asking too much to expect prose too. Pamela, of course, repeated this remark to Lord Leatherhead, but unluckily for her he was too delighted with the compliment to his appearance to care about the slur on his sense. He remained Jennifer's devoted slave, to Pamela's fury, for before Jennifer's arrival on the scene, she had thought she had him safe, and had daily expected his offer. She waited, now, for some opportunity to discredit Jennifer before the fashionable world. It was but a matter of patience. Jennifer's ignorance of London etiquette was abysmal and with a little quiet help she was bound to disgrace herself sooner or later.

The season was now in full swing. At last the night came when Jennifer and Pamela were to make their first appearance at Almack's. Pamela and her mother had high hopes of this. If Jennifer could be encouraged to break one of the inexorable rules of this assembly, her social downfall was assured. Not even the Duchess of Lewes could save one who had offended the patronesses of Almack's. So, that morning, Lady Beresford paid a visit in Grosvenor Square. She talked dutifully to her mother for a few minutes, bestowed the usual false and charming smile on Jennifer, hoped that they were both in spirits for tonight's gaiety – and then retired for a word with her friend Marsham.

As a result, when the time came for the Duchess to dress for Almack's, Marsham burst into voluble protest. Her ladyship was looking quite done up; she had been out three nights this week already ... she knew she always found Almack's a dead bore. And she had not written up her diary this sennight. She would be forgetting the witty things the Duke of Wellington said to her last night at Carlton House and indeed, ma'am, they should be recorded for posterity (Marsham was pleased with that word, and repeated it). And, in short, by playing on the Duchess's valetudinarian fears and throwing in a subtle dash of flattery, Marsham contrived to persuade her that she had much better stay at home and let Jennifer go to Almack's with Lady Beresford and Pamela. It was in every way the most suitable thing, and, indeed, it was quite a pleasure, sighed Marsham, to see how devoted the young ladies were ...

So when Jennifer, who now had a maid of her own, a bouncing kindly country girl called Betty, came pirouetting to the Duchess's boudoir resplendent in the figured gauze, she was disappointed to find the old lady sitting over the fire, still in her lilac négligé.

'You see, child,' said the Duchess, 'I am to play the stay-at-home tonight. Marsham urges it; she says I have been fatiguing myself unduly. And Marsham is always right. But do you go and enjoy yourself with Lady Beresford and Pamela and mind you remember to tell me what Lady Cowper wears, and what Lady Jersey says, and who Caro Lamb is flirting with now.'

Jennifer laughed and promised to obey. It was disappointing not to have her evening enlivened by the Duchess's caustic comments and pungent character sketches of those present, but she looked forward to amusing her, on her return, with some of her own.

At first sight, she had to admit that she found the famous Almack's disappointing. The rooms were no more splendid than the Assembly Hall at Chichester. The light was good, it was true, and the room crowded with elegants, but the fact remained that she was disappointed. This was soon forgotten, however, when the musicians struck up a waltz. Pamela and her mother had left her for a moment, with a murmured, unintelligible apology. She stood alone, her foot tapping to the music, her eyes darting here and there about the room. What if

Lord Mainwaring should have returned? Surely it was time his engagement was settled. And, engaged or not, he would, she told herself, constitute a most eligible partner. But any partner would be welcome. The music called her. She longed to be dancing.

Ignorant of the sacred rule of Almack's by which no young lady might waltz before she had been approved by one of the patronesses, Jennifer was puzzled that one of her usual gallants, many of whom were present, did not request her hand for the dance. She stood impatiently, watching the graceful, swooping movements of the dancers, among whom Lady Cowper was conspicuous in black velvet, swirling about the room on the arm of Lord Palmerston.

Jennifer looked up at the approach of one of Pamela's faithful admirers, Mr Eltham, a man of small talent and considerable property in Norfolk. 'You do not dance, Miss Fairbank? May I have the honour?'

How was she to know that he came by Pamela's express command? It would be an excellent jest, she had told Mr Eltham, to get Miss Fairbank a-waltzing before she should and thus take her vanity down a peg. Mr Eltham, who had in his time suffered under Jennifer's mordant wit, was himself fresh up from the country and was unaware of the seriousness of such a flouting of the lady patronesses' authority. Glad to please Pamela, he took Jennifer's hand and led her towards the rope that separated the dancers from their audience.

But Lady Cowper, sweeping towards them on the floor, noticed their approach. 'Look,' she said to Lord Palmerston, 'there is that child the Duchess of Lewes has taken up about to ruin herself by waltzing before she has leave. Go, quick, and bring her to me, that I may make it right for her. She is too entertaining a creature to be let destroy herself for a trifle.'

Palmerston bowed: 'Always considerate, divine Emily.' He led her to one of the seats reserved for the patronesses and hurried to intercept Jennifer and Mr Eltham. They were just taking the floor when he touched Jennifer's arm. She turned, haughtily, at the unwelcome interruption, then recognised him with a look of surprise.

'Miss Fairbank is it not? I had the honour of meeting you at Manchester House. Now, Lady Cowper desires the pleasure of your acquaintance.'

It was practically a royal command, and must be taken as such. Jennifer curtseyed apologetically to Mr Eltham and took Lord Palmerston's arm. Eltham followed as they approached the chair where Lady Cowper awaited them.

'Silly child,' was her greeting. 'Has no one told you you must not waltz till you have received permission from one of us?'

'No, indeed, ma'am,' Jennifer looked her surprise. 'I was quite unaware of it. I thank you a thousand times.' She turned a reproachful glance on Mr Eltham, who muttered something about not knowing this was Jennifer's first appearance at Almack's. It seemed unlikely. Jennifer was surprised, puzzled and suspicious, but thought it best to let it pass.

Lady Cowper dismissed her graciously. 'Go, then, and have your waltz. I can see that you are itching to be off and so, indeed, am I.' She took Lord Palmerston's arm again and the two couples were quickly lost in the exhilarating maze of the dance. Mr Eltham waltzed admirably and Jennifer had soon forgotten her uncomfortable suspicions in the excitement of the evening. She danced every dance, laughed with, and at, Mr Eltham, flirted with Lord Leatherhead, gathered in a *bon mot* of Lady Jersey's and another of Princess Lieven's for the delectation of the Duchess, and presented, altogether, a perfect picture of happiness. Only a very acute observer might have noticed how restlessly, from time to time, her eyes wandered about the room. She would be so much happier, she told herself, when Lord Mainwaring returned to town and the news of his engagement was final.

Lady Beresford returned home that night in a very ill humour which had not been improved by a half serious admonishment from Lady Cowper that she should take better care of her charge. Dismissing her maid, she summoned Pamela to her room. The thing was becoming serious; Lord Leatherhead had dangled after Jennifer all evening, and she was realist enough to be aware that Pamela's chances in the marriage market were strictly limited. If Jennifer could be removed from the running, Leatherhead would doubtless return to his first object – was he not known to have made the most encouragingly detailed enquiries about Pamela's fortune before Jennifer appeared on the scene and spoiled everything?

'But, come, my love,' said Lady Beresford to her daughter, 'this is no time for despondency. Dry your tears. I have a plan. The Duke of Devonshire, as you know, is giving a masquerade next Tuesday.'

Yes, indeed, Pamela knew. She and Jennifer had planned their costumes long since. She was to be Pamina in tulle, Jennifer the Queen of the Night in black satin. She was interrupted in an ecstatic description of these delicious costumes by her mother's impatient: 'Yes, yes, all very well, I am sure, but that is not my point. Luttrell was telling me only this evening that that same night there is to be another masquerade given at Watier's Club. Would you believe the effrontery of it? These same gentlemen, from the Duke downwards, who will entertain the *beau monde* at Devonshire House, are giving, the same night, a similar masquerade at Watier's for—' she paused, embarrassed.

'Yes, I know, mother,' chimed in her innocent daughter, 'for Harriette Wilson and her set. I heard Eltham tell Leatherhead it was a capital notion. The *beau monde* at one, he said, the *demi-monde* at the other, and the same dominoes giving admittance to both.'

Shocked at her daughter's knowledgeableness, or rather, at her admission of it, Lady Beresford reminded her that a young girl was expected to be ignorant of such things. 'But it comes most happily for us,' she went on, 'it is but to contrive that Miss Fairbank go to Watier's in mistake for Devonshire House, and the thing is done. Even if she escape unscathed, it will be more than anyone will believe.'

Pamela, who was not so much cruel as silly, protested a little at this scheme, but her mother soon distracted her by drawing her attention to the practical difficulties it entailed. They would have first to contrive that the Duchess did not attend the ball and then arrange that they should be unable to pick up Jennifer on their way as they usually did. Finally, the coachman would have to be bribed to deliver her to Watier's instead of to Devonshire House.

'Luckily,' said Lady Beresford, 'the Duke is but today returned from Chatsworth. It is impossible that Jennifer should have been to Devonshire House and as for Watier's, that is out of the question.'

Pamela still looked doubtful. 'But suppose her suspicions are aroused and she enquires before she is well inside?' she objected. 'Then we are blown and all for nothing.'

'Yes, it is indeed a puzzle,' said her mother. 'If we could but contrive some escort for her, who should hand her in before she had time for suspicion. But who could we trust? Not, certainly, Lord Leatherhead, and she might twig Mr Eltham after this night's work.' She tapped her teeth with her fan, deep in thought, then brightened. 'I have it. Is not Miles Mandeville one of her train?'

Pamela nodded. 'Yes, and she abuses him unmercifully for his strong language.'

'Excellent. He is deep in debt to Beresford – and an old admirer of mine as well. I'll send for him in the morning. Now, to bed, my love, and leave all to me.'

Miles Mandeville, a hard-drinking, hard-riding Leicestershire squire who liked hunting, shooting and women in that order, was more surprised than pleased to receive a scented note next morning summoning him to the presence of his old inamorata, Lady Beresford. He was still more surprised and, at first, still less pleased, when he found her in a strictly businesslike mood, with a bundle of his IOUs in her hand. But when she had put her proposition to him, he burst into a delighted guffaw of laughter that almost blew Pamela's listening ear from the keyhole.

'No need to bribe me with these, ma'am.' But he tore up the IOUs as he spoke. 'Damme, but I'd do it for love – or for hate – if you'd rather. If that chit of a girl has affronted me once, she's done it a thousand times. Turned her back on me at Almack's only last night and all to listen to Luttrell and his nonsense. Leave me alone to take care of her.'

Lady Beresford was glad that Pamela was not in the room to

see the expressive leer with which he finished his sentence. So accompanied, Jennifer's chances of escaping with virtue – let alone character – unscathed from the masquerade of the *demi-monde* were slight indeed.

The next point was to ensure that the Duchess did not attend the Duke of Devonshire's masquerade. This was more difficult, for the Duchess dearly loved a masked ball. Lady Beresford consulted Marsham who shook her head. 'No, my lady, to persuade her grace to stay at home from that is what I could never undertake to do. She is all in a pucker of excitement about Miss Jennifer's costume and is bound to go and see her triumph, as she claims it will be. And poor Miss Pamela to be totally eclipsed, I have no doubt, by this upstart Queen of the Night. But I'll tell you, my lady, what I could do, though for no one in the world but you and Miss Pamela would I consider such a thing, but knowing as how you are such a good friend of mine' (at this point she quietly pocketed the plump purse that Lady Beresford had as quietly handed to her) '. . . It is but to slip a few drops of laudanum into her grace's chocolate that she always takes when she is dressing and I warrant there will be no more talk of balls and masquerades. No, no,' she cut short a horrified protest from Lady Beresford, 'nothing to harm her dear grace, just a couple of drops that shall give her a better night's sleep than she has had this many a long day. For indeed I have tried and tried to persuade her she should take it now and then, when her sleeplessness is at its worst, the poor lamb, but she never would, and so it is the bell ringing all night long and "Marsham, another pillow," or "Marsham, some hot chocolate if you please," as if a body had no more need of sleep than she has.'

Lady Beresford, who had listened with concealed impatience to this tirade, now interrupted: 'Excellent, Marsham; I can see you are in the right of it. It will be doing my mother a true kindness. And indeed she is too old to be jauntering off to balls and routs. So,' she rose, 'I shall rely on you, Marsham.'

'And may, your ladyship.'

CHAPTER IX

Jennifer, who had designed her own costume as Queen of the Night, gave a sigh of pure pleasure when she was dressed at last and turned to survey herself in the glass. It had succeeded *à merveille*. If Pamela's white tulle confection, which she had designed with equally loving care, only made her as striking a figure, they should indeed be the belles of the ball. She re-read Pamela's note which had just been brought to her by a footman. It was disappointing that the Beresfords had to go first to Lady Cowper's and that she and Pamela cóuld not, therefore, make their complementary entrance together. But no matter for that. They would meet soon enough once there. She smiled her thanks to her adoring maid, Betty, picked up her mask and hurried along the wide corridor to the Duchess's boudoir.

Marsham met her at the door, finger on her lip. 'Hush, Miss Fairbank, the poor lamb is asleep. Look,' standing aside, she pointed to the still form of the Duchess, recumbent, deep breathing, on an unwonted sofa.

'She is not well?' Jennifer would have hurried into the room, but Marsham stopped her.

'No, no, it is nothing. She falls, sometimes, into this exhausted slumber. She has been wakeful, you must know, these many nights past, the poor lady. I doubt she is vexed at Lord Mainwaring's silence and such worrits always prevent her from sleeping. She is sound, now, till morning and it is best for you to go happily off to your masquerade with Lady Beresford who is doubtless calling for you.'

'No.' In her anxiety for the Duchess, Jennifer had not thought how her indisposition might affect her own plans. 'No. I had just now a note from Miss Beresford. They are to go first to Lady Cowper's and cannot therefore take me up. Nothing for it; I must go alone. I will hit upon them soon enough when once I am there.'

Well coached by Lady Beresford, Marsham was loud in protest against the impropriety of this plan. The argument was interrupted by a footman who announced that Mr Mandeville was below to attend upon her grace.

'Tell him her grace is indisposed,' began Marsham, then turned in well-simulated inspiration to Jennifer, 'but stay, he goes, no doubt, to the masquerade. Why not request his services as escort? For to let you go unattended is what I know her grace would never countenance.'

Jennifer made a *moue*. She did not like Miles Mandeville's looks, nor his license, nor his language, and would infinitely have preferred to go alone than in his company. But she could see that Marsham was set upon the point, and after all the drive to Devonshire House was a matter of but a few minutes. It would be refining too much to object to Mandeville's company for so short a distance.

'Very well,' she said to Marsham, 'I will go down to him.'

She found Miles Mandeville resplendent in a sky blue domino and was so absorbed in her own embarrassment at having to ask a favour of someone she disliked that she quite forgot to enquire what was his business with the Duchess. As he, for his part, had equally forgotten to invent any, this was just as well for the success of his plan.

When she put her difficulty to him and requested the favour of his escort to Devonshire House, he agreed at once with the greatest gallantry, but stipulated that they must go in his carriage rather than the Duchess's. 'Damme, Miss Fairbank, I'll not have it said that Mad Mandeville is dependent on any old dame for his transport. You shall come with me and ride behind such a pair of greys as you never had the good fortune to see. Never fear, I'll drive you home after, or' – he saw that this was going too far, 'I have no doubt that Lady Beresford will set you down.'

This was true enough, and so was his argument that he would need his own carriage to take him home when the masquerade finally ended in the small hours of the next morning. Jennifer yielded with the best grace she could muster.

After all, time was running on, the main thing was to get to the masquerade.

Mandeville handed her into his carriage with a flourish, gave an unintelligible order to the coachman and sat down himself rather too close beside her. He had his plan of campaign well worked out: 'Rattle the girl badly enough and she'll be so glad to arrive, she'll not notice if it were Old Bailey instead of Devonshire House.'

So he took her reluctant hand and began an impassioned speech. 'Charming Miss Fairbank, how I have longed for this opportunity . . .'

She pulled her hand away and interrupted: 'Indeed, sir, you much mistake the matter if you think my most unwilling request for your company licenses this familiarity.'

'Oh, so it was unwilling was it? There's a fine sweetener for a cavalier. You shall pay for that Miss Fairbank.' He again secured her hand and tried to pull her towards him, but she dealt him a resounding blow on the cheek with her free hand, and, as he let her go with an oath, retreated to the farthest corner of the carriage.

'Shame on you, sir. If I had a father or a brother to protect me you would not use me thus.' She looked in vain, as she spoke, for the check string. It was on his side of the carriage; quite out of her reach.

He was still swearing to himself. Her father's signet ring, which she always wore, had cut open his cheek and it was bleeding profusely. 'Damme, you have no need of protection, Miss Fairbank. I'd sooner have to do with a wildcat or an amazon. But here, at last, we are.'

And indeed Jennifer felt with relief that the carriage was stopping. A liveried footman flung open the door and she glimpsed a brilliantly lighted entrance hall, and, by the light of the flambeaux on either side of the door, a small crowd gathered to watch the arrivals. She was aware of a faint feeling of surprise. Did not Devonshire House stand in its own grounds? Was the Duke so liberal-minded that he allowed the mob inside his gates?

But Mandeville's unwelcome hand was under her arm urging her forward. As he guided her up the carpeted steps, she heard a cockney voice exclaim, 'There's another on 'em. Only see how innocent the drab looks.'

Blushing, she hurried inside. How could Lord Mainwaring maintain his radical opinions in the face of such mob crudity? But this was no time to be thinking of him. Mandeville was muttering an angry apology. He must attend to the cut on his cheek. She proceeded, alone, into the crowded rooms. For the first time, as she looked at the masked and dominoed crowd, she began to think it might be no easy matter to find Pamela and Lady Beresford. But surely Pamela's white tulle would be conspicuous enough, for the ladies of this assembly were clad in what seemed to her a garish motley of brilliantly coloured silk and satin. There was a something, too, about the noise of the crowd that she found disconcerting. She was used, by now, to the babble of society; here, surely, the note was higher, the voices shriller. But then, this was her first masquerade. No doubt the knowledge of anonymity brought with it a relaxation of decorum. Just the same, she would be glad when she found Pamela and her mother.

Eagerly searching for them, she made her way through several crowded rooms where dancing and cards were in lively progress and was surprised, as she went, by the freedom of the remarks addressed to her by many of the dominoed figures she passed. A gaudily costumed pirate seized her hand as she brushed by him.

'It is,' he said, 'it must be, by this tiny hand I swear it. You are the divine Harriette herself.' And he printed a damply burning kiss on her hand and would have continued up her arm if she had not snatched it away with such obvious indignation that he drew back in surprise.

'Damme, such airs and graces here?' He would have caught her hand again but to her relief he was suddenly surrounded by a bevy of young women costumed as gipsies who claimed him as their lord and master – being a pirate – in language that amazed Jennifer by its freedom. Hurrying away, she was relieved to find herself in a rather quieter room where hangings of pale green satin set off a profusion of hothouse flowers. She sat down on an ottoman, determined to wait there until she should be so fortunate as to recognise someone she knew and could ask their safe conduct to Lady Beresford. If she had had any idea what a masquerade was like, she would certainly not have ventured here with no more reliable companion than Miles Mandeville. She saw him now in the next room, in animated conversation with a nun and a country girl in an Indian glazed gown. Anxious to avoid him, she got up and hurried into a further room which she was surprised to find quite empty. But she had been followed.

The pirate who had previously molested her came up behind her and seized her in his arms. 'Divine Harriette, so you have led me here at last. I should have known that your coyness was but feigned.'

And to her speechless and enraged astonishment, he took her in his arms, forced her mask over her chin and kissed her fiercely through his own mask of black crape.

This was too much. 'Is all the world gone mad?' She tore herself away from him and hurried back into the next room, only to be seized upon by Miles Mandeville's two companions.

'Here she is at last,' said the nun. 'Where have you been hiding yourself all this time, Harriette, my love?'

'Here is some strange mistake,' she tried to free herself. 'My name is not Harriette, I assure you.'

'Excellently feigned,' said the country girl. 'Even the voice is missish. But we have smoked you, Harriette, through all your airs. Now come, take a turn of the room with us and tell me who you will have home with you tonight.' And, forcing her along between them, they began a discussion of the good and bad points of the men they passed which made her blush hotly behind her mask.

'But here,' said the nun, as Miles Mandeville approached them again, 'here if I mistake not, is a gallant of yours. We'll not spoil sport.' And she detached her arm from Jennifer's, gave a bold laugh, and moved away, arm in arm with the country girl.

'Sir,' Jennifer turned to Mandeville with appeal in her voice.

89

'I cannot find Lady Beresford anywhere and truly I cannot stay here alone. I must beg you to take me home.'

'Home?' He had taken her arm and was leading her through the crowd. 'Do you jest? The evening is but beginning. And, moreover,' here he whisked her through a doorway concealed behind some draperies, 'you and I have a score to settle.'

She found herself alone with him in a small withdrawing-room whose most conspicuous article of furniture was a sumptuous ottoman covered with green satin and fringed with silver. He led her, resisting, towards it. What should she do? The noise of the party, and the music playing in the next room would drown her cries. And, even if she did manage to summon assistance, what an appallingly compromising position in which to let herself be found.

'Mr Mandeville,' she began to appeal to him when a voice behind her made her turn.

'Miss Fairbank? Can it be?'

'Lord Mainwaring!' She snatched her hand away from Mandeville and hurried towards the tall figure in a black domino who had entered the room behind them. 'Oh, I am so thankful. I beg you will take me home. I cannot find Lady Beresford anywhere and indeed I was mistaken to come alone.'

'Mistaken?' His voice was cold as ice. 'So it would seem if you expect to find Lady Beresford. I am at a loss to understand what folly brings Miss Fairbank here.'

The doubt that had been gnawing away at the back of her mind came to the surface at last. 'Is not this Devonshire House then?'

'My poor child,' his voice softened, 'it most certainly is not. Who has beguiled you here?'

'Why, Mr Mandeville brought me.' She turned to where he still stood, rigid, in the middle of the room.

Now he came forwards with an uncomfortable assumption of ease. 'Miss Fairbank is pleased to be forgetful, my lord. She begged me to give her a sight of the Cyprians' Ball and – I own I am to blame – I thought I might harmlessly indulge her, since, you see, she is well masked.'

Jennifer gasped. 'The Cyprians' Ball?' Her surprise and

shock were so evident that Lord Mainwaring, taking her arm, softened still further towards her. 'Come, Miss Fairbank, you have been here too long already. My carriage is without. We will not wait, now, to clear up this strange misunderstanding.' He turned, without a word of farewell to Mandeville, and led her from the room.

Her confusion was such that she remained speechless as he led her back through the crowded rooms towards the entrance hall. Once there, she began to speak, to try and explain, but he silenced her by a warning pressure on her arm. 'Wait,' he said.

So she waited, in silent agony, while his carriage was summoned. Fortunately, it was now late enough so that the crowd of arriving carriages had dwindled, while still so early that they were the first to leave. To her infinite relief, Lord Mainwaring's carriage was soon announced and he handed her silently in.

'What must you think of me, my lord?' She sank back into the corner of the carriage.

'I think you very foolish, Miss Fairbank. Even your slight knowledge of the world must have taught you that Miles Mandeville is not a suitable cavalier for so very young a lady as yourself.'

The slight to her good sense was almost harder to bear than one to her character. She began a protest: 'But Marsham urged it . . .'

'Marsham?' His voice was cold again. 'An abigail's advice? But where, pray, was my grandmother? I cannot believe that she had any part in this escapade.'

'Oh, no,' Jennifer hurried to explain. 'If *she* had been able to come, none of this would have happened. But she fell fast asleep and Marsham said she must not be roused. And Lady Beresford could not come for me, so it seemed the only thing to go with Mr Mandeville. But I see now that I was wrong.'

'You see it a little late in the day. We must earnestly hope that I was the only person who recognised your voice, which is indeed likely since it was your mention of Lady Beresford that raised my suspicions. Mr Mandeville, I apprehend, will be silent for his own sake, and thus all may yet be well. But it has been a most mismanaged business. I thought I might trust you with my grandmother, but I fear I overestimated both her vigilance and your prudence.'

It was too much. As if she had gone to the wrong masquerade on purpose! She blinked back angry tears and was about to protest when she observed that the carriage had turned in at a pair of ornamental gates. 'Oh,' a new and unwelcome thought struck her. 'Are you not taking me home?'

'Home?' His voice queried her right to use the word, 'I most certainly am not. We cannot be sure you were not recognised at Watier's. You must, of course, appear at the Duke's masquerade and you will be well advised to affect a calm enjoyment even if you cannot feel it. This night's work might damage your reputation irredeemably.'

'Watier's?' she asked, puzzled, as the carriage came to a standstill in the long line of conveyances that was still setting down at the entrance of Devonshire House.

'Yes, yes,' he said impatiently, 'you are just come from Watier's Club. You must, I apprehend, be the first lady of any pretensions to respectability who ever set foot there.'

She was silent, enraged by that word 'pretensions'. So that was what he thought her, a hoydenish country girl, always in scrapes, pretending to a respectability she could not compass.

If he was aware of her fury, he ignored it. 'We must think of a story,' he said, 'to explain your late arrival. Trust no one with the truth. Not even Lady Beresford, nor Pamela, nor Marsham, though she is such a confidante of yours, nor your own maid. No one, I tell you. This is no subject for girlish confidences.' She seethed, but he went on, ignoring her increasingly furious silence. 'First, we must make some change in your costume. For many of the men at Watier's will doubtless come on to Devonshire House before the night is out. If there was time, we should find you a new one altogether. But time is of the essence. What's to be done?'

Jennifer thought rapidly. 'My cloak,' she said, 'it is black, as you see, but lined with silver. It is but to turn it and I will present quite a different appearance.'

'Excellent,' he said, as she did so. 'And if you will be ruled by me, you will discard that highly becoming headdress. There could be no mistake about that. No, give it to me.' He took the coronet with a crescent moon on it which she had designed with so much pride, twisted off the moon, and returned it to her. 'There, now wear it the other way round. And, remember, no word of the change to anyone.'

'But Pamela will notice. We planned our costumes together.'

'Pamela?' He paused for a minute, thinking. 'Pamela?' he said again, a question in his voice, then went on. 'No matter. Tell her you changed your mind before you left home. That will help to explain your tardiness. But not enough. No young lady would be wilfully so late as this for the greatest ball of the season.' He paused, thinking, then, 'I have it. We will say that I arrived unexpectedly at my grandmother's . . . offered to escort you to the ball . . . had to procure a domino . . . and kept you, most ungallantly, waiting. You may be as angry with me about that as you please. It will, no doubt, be a relief to your feelings. But,' the carriage was moving forward again, 'here we are.'

'But the servants?' she asked as the carriage again paused for a moment. 'Marsham?'

'I will take care of them. And I trust, for her own sake, that Marsham is not so deeply involved in this night's business as I find myself suspecting. Remember, not a word of Miles Mandeville. I have done myself the honour of bringing you here.'

'I am vastly obliged to you.' Fury trembled in her voice, and she could not prevent herself from adding, 'I am sorry it is so distasteful to you. I apprehend you find the company at Watier's more to your liking, since you went there first.'

He was about to make some reply, whether of explanation or, more likely, of rebuke when he was interrupted by the carriage's stopping at last at the entrance of Devonshire House. He helped her to alight.

'Remember,' he said again. 'You have been waiting this half-hour or more for me to bring you. You can be as much out of patience with me as you please.'

'I do not think,' she withdrew her hand from his arm, 'that that will overtax my powers as an actress.'

'Excellent.' He took her arm more firmly and led her into the splendid entrance hall. 'You do it to a nicety. And here, if I mistake not, is the Duke himself and with him,' his arm tightened warningly on hers, 'is, I fear, an acquaintance of yours.'

With horror, Jennifer recognised the pirate from Watier's. Would he recognise her? Had she made a sufficiently drastic alteration to her costume? Too late now, if she had not. She went forward boldly on Mainwaring's arm. Only he was aware how cold her hand was, and could feel it tremble.

The entrance hall was so thronged with people that it took them some time to make their way to where the Duke and his companion stood. Watching them anxiously from behind her mask, Jennifer saw the pirate start at sight of her, turn and say something to the Duke, who was unmasked as were many of the other costumed figures. He turned at once to survey her as she approached.

'Come,' Mainwaring said, 'no trembling now. Your only hope is to brave it out.'

The crowd parted. The Duke came forward and greeted them courteously.

'But,' he added, 'you are come so late, I think I must ask you to unmask and make your apologies in person.'

This suited Mainwaring admirably. 'With pleasure,' he said, removing his mask. 'I have but had it on these few minutes and I find it plaguily inconvenient. How does your grace?'

'Mainwaring!' said the Duke. 'This is an unexpected pleasure. I thought you still in the country a-wooing.'

'I am but just now returned and would hardly have ventured here so soon, but I paid a visit to my grandmother and found her charge, Miss Fairbank, languishing for lack of an escort to your house. You must blame all our lateness on me, I promise you it was no wish of Miss Fairbank's, but I had to procure myself a domino. I fear she is quite out of charity with me.'

'Miss Fairbank?' The Duke darted a questioning glance at the pirate, who had stood just behind him, an interested auditor of all that passed.

'Yes. Your mask, Miss Fairbank.'

Jennifer, who had waited with unwonted docility for her cue, now unmasked and saw the Duke's start of surprise.

'Let me present my grandmother's ward, Miss Fairbank,' said Mainwaring, and Jennifer made her deepest curtsy in acknowledgement of the Duke's low bow.

'Remarkable,' exclaimed the pirate behind him and the Duke turned.

'It seems that you owe Lord Mainwaring and Miss Fairbank an apology, Lovell.'

He came forward. 'I confess it freely. I am the victim of the most damnable coincidence – I beg your pardon Miss Fairbank. You must forgive me, Mainwaring,' he turned a little away from Jennifer who was exchanging compliments with the Duke. 'I am but now come from Watier's where Harriette Wilson is peacocking it in a costume most remarkably like Miss Fairbank's. Only, now I consider, the cloak was of a different colour and the crown another style.'

'No small difference, surely,' said Mainwaring dryly.

'No, I apprehend it is not. And now I come to reflect, I see how I was mistaken. Harriette's costume had not the – what shall I say – none of the distinction and elegance of Miss Fairbank's. But you must forgive my mistake, Mainwaring. I truly believed you were some good friend of Harriette's, passing her off here for a wager.'

'You did me too much honour,' said Mainwaring sardonically. 'Harriette, I collect, is most particular in her affections. The Beau himself has sighed away many a night under her window, if she is to be trusted, and how should I be so honoured?'

'Aye, but you see I did not know it was you, Mainwaring. To tell truth, I thought it some freak of Ponsonby's.'

'You are now the wiser. But, tell me, by what secret token did you recognise Harriette at Watier's since, I apprehend, she must have been masked like the rest?'

'So she was indeed, and putting up a devilish good imitation of a prude, I assure you. But Mad Mandeville had smoked her and spoiled her game by whispering about the room who she was. After that, her protestations, of course, were useless.'

'I see,' said Mainwaring, and indeed he did, much more than

Lovell could understand. He now realised the full extent of the conspiracy against Jennifer. Someone had seen to it that his grandmother was asleep when Jennifer was ready to go to the Ball. Someone, too, had arranged that Lady Beresford could not fetch her and had sent, instead, Miles Mandeville, who had not only lured her to the Cyprians' Ball but had ensured that she would be molested as much as possible by putting it about that she was the notorious Harriette Wilson. He smiled grimly to himself. There would be a score to settle with Mr Mandeville. In the meantime, he found himself perturbed about his grandmother. By what means had she been put to sleep? Had she been drugged? He must lose no time in ascertaining. The Duke and Jennifer, he was pleased to see, were getting on famously. Jennifer, her first hurdle safely past, had recovered colour and composure and was blossoming under the Duke's compliments. Lovell, too, seemed even more taken with her in her own character than he had been when he thought her London's most famous courtesan. Under the balm of their admiration, she was visibly relaxing, soon she would be enjoying herself. He could safely leave her and take care of the loose ends of the conspiracy that still threatened her. Anyway, she was so visibly out of patience with him, so clearly preferring the Duke's company to his, that there was little purpose to be served by staying here to dangle after her in hopes of a dance. And why should he wish to do so? Having gone so far as to ask himself the question, he wisely did not stay to answer it.

Hearing Jennifer accept the Duke's hand for a forthcoming quadrille, he broke into the conversation to suggest that they should first find Lady Beresford.

'Yes indeed,' said Jennifer, 'and Pamela. I long to see her costume, for I designed it as well as my own.'

This admission brought on a fresh spate of compliments from Lovell and the Duke, but Mainwaring took her arm and led her into the card rooms, in one of which he knew he should find Lady Beresford losing money as usual.

Seeing Jennifer on Mainwaring's arm, Lady Beresford paled, played the wrong card and burst into a flood of apologies to cover her confusion. But Mainwaring had noticed it all. Still, he thought, she had a right to be surprised, since everyone thought him still in the country and he knew well that if he had not told her he considered himself pre-engaged to Miss Purchas she would have hoped for his hand for his cousin Pamela. It must be more surprise than pleasure to see him with the unknown heiress. Her high colour and ill humour, too, might well be attributed to her invariable ill luck at cards. But was that all that discomposed her, he wondered. He had never loved his scheming aunt since he had caught her in a self-interested falsehood when he was a knowledgeable boy at Eton, and he was all too ready to believe that she was the mainspring of the plot against Jennifer's good name. If so, let her beware. Of course, he assured himself, his concern for Jennifer was purely protective, for was he not in honour bound to that insipid white mouse of a girl in the country? But since he had taken Jennifer up, and had, indeed, put her in the position to be an object of Lady Beresford's jealousy, he was bound to take care of her.

He greeted his aunt with his usual courtesy, explained to her that he had been the cause of Jennifer's lateness, and added, for good measure, that he was anxious about his grandmother, who had been strangely fast asleep when he arrived at her house, and proposed, therefore, to leave Jennifer with her and go back to Grosvenor Square to make sure that all was well with the Duchess.

Lady Beresford, who had been alternately crimson and pallid around her rouge as he spoke, now exerted herself to greet Jennifer and wonder where Pamela was. 'We have so longed and worried for you, my love, you can have no idea. Pamela was bound she would not dance till you were come, but then, of course, she was overpersuaded. The Duke, you know . . .'

Poor Lady Beresford. She had never been able to help lying, even when it was not strictly necessary. It was a pity for her story that the Duke himself appeared at this moment to claim Jennifer's promised hand for the quadrille. Jennifer, who had been a silent audience to Mainwaring's interchange with his aunt swept a haughty curtsy to them both and went away on the Duke's arm, determined to enjoy herself if it killed her, furious that Mainwaring should insult her by leaving at once, without even doing her the common courtesy of asking her hand for one dance. Of course, if she could possibly have justified it, she would have taken great pleasure in refusing him, but that was nothing to do with the matter.

She was particularly charming to the Duke as he led her to the room where the quadrille was about to begin and he found himself seriously considering her as a possible duchess. What matter that his heart had been broken by Caroline Lamb, his ambition thwarted by Princess Charlotte? Must he always remember them?

As they approached the set, Jennifer saw Pamela, on the other side of the room, drop her fan. It was picked up for her, with assiduous gallantry, by her partner – Miles Mandeville. Passionately Jennifer now wished that her own partner was Mainwaring instead of the Duke. He would know what to do, how to protect her from Mandeville. But, to her relief, she saw that the Duke was taking her to the very top of the set. Her normal bashfulness and uncertainty of her own capacity to support such an honour were quite lost in relief at seeing Pamela and Mandeville find a modest place at the bottom.

And, surely, she consoled herself, as she made her opening curtsy to the Duke, Mandeville would never try to shame her here. The risk to himself would be as great as that to her. And – she was dancing with the Duke. That, in itself, was considerable protection. She would do very well without Mainwaring. She flashed the Duke a particularly brilliant smile as they passed each other in the intricacy of the dance and for a moment Lady Caroline was forgotten, Princess Charlotte unimportant. When the dance was over, he did not offer to take her back to her aunt. The great doors of the supper room downstairs had been thrown open. She must be his partner, too, for this. So, over cold chicken and champagne, she forgot her terrors of Miles Mandeville. He could hardly touch her here.

And indeed Mandeville had only summoned up courage to come to Devonshire House because he felt it imperative to explain his failure at once to Lady Beresford. But, arriving, he had found her immobilised at the card table; to approach her there would have made their meeting dangerously conspicuous.

He had been obliged instead to find Pamela and lead her out to dance, telling her, as the opportunity offered, as little as he dared about the evening's fiasco, urging her to forget the whole affair and accept whatever story Jennifer should choose to tell in explanation of her late arrival. The sight of Jennifer at the top of the set with the Duke at once enflamed his rage at her escape and increased his terror of the possible consequences to himself. He had not expected her to be so powerfully befriended.

CHAPTER X

Arriving in Grosvenor Square, Mainwaring demanded imperiously to be taken to the Duchess at once. The footman looked embarrassed and muttered something about the lateness of the hour and her grace's indisposition. Mainwaring's frown had once subdued a French outpost. The man wilted and fetched Marsham. She, in her turn, told him with suitable regret, that his grandmother was seriously unwell and could not see him. She, too, rashly, ventured something about the lateness of the hour. His explosive reception of this was interrupted by the clamorous ringing of the Duchess's own bell. Marsham's look of surprise and alarm told him much that he needed to know. She had not expected her mistress to wake again tonight. Ignoring her renewed protestations, he followed her upstairs and was close behind her when she entered his grandmother's boudoir.

The old lady was sitting up on the sofa, her cheeks flushed, her scarlet wig awry, her eyes flashing fury. 'I have been asleep,' she said to Marsham. 'Me! Asleep after dinner like an old dotard in a country vicarage. Why did you not wake me, Marsham? What excuse have you to offer? And where is Miss Fairbank? It is long past time for us to leave for Devonshire House.'

Marsham had hardly begun her flustered apologies when the old lady saw Mainwaring behind her. 'George,' she said with pleasure, 'the very person. It is not often you come so exactly when needed. Marsham, summon the carriage and tell Miss Fairbank and Betty to attend me. It is but to repair my toilette and you shall escort us to Devonshire House, George.'

'But Miss Fairbank is there already,' began Marsham.

Mainwaring interrupted her: 'Yes, ma'am,' he darted a formidable look at Marsham. 'This is not the first time I am come to your house tonight. I came some hour or so ago and found Miss Fairbank all impatience to be gone and – I hope with your approval – I took her there myself.'

Marsham went scarlet. The old lady beamed. 'Excellent, George. You were always one for action. And how does the child take?'

'Beyond anything, ma'am. When I left she was leading the quadrille with the Duke himself.'

The old eyes sparkled. 'Just what I hoped. George, I owe you much for this night's work. But still I wish I could be there.' Her hand went up to her lop-sided wig. 'It is but to prink a little . . .'

But Mainwaring had noticed her distended pupils which confirmed his suspicion that she had been drugged. 'No, ma'am,' he said firmly. 'You cannot be altogether well. You know yourself you never sleep in the daytime. This drowsiness of yours can be no good omen. Stay here, I beg, with me. Miss Fairbank is well enough. Pamela is in the set with her, Lady Beresford in the card room near by and the Duke her devoted slave. You and I will await her here, like Darby and Joan over your fireside.'

The Duchess smiled and sank back among her scarlet cushions. 'Very well, George, if you can play Darby while Miss Fairbank conquers the world, I'll be your Joan. And you shall entertain me with the tale of your country wooing about which, I may tell you, you have been most unconscionably slow. Marsham, you need not wait. Tell Betty she shall put me to bed when Miss Fairbank returns.'

'Indeed, ma'am,' protested Mainwaring, when Marsham had flounced from the room, furious at this preference of Jennifer's raw country maid over herself, 'I do not recommend your waiting up for Miss Fairbank. I doubt the ball at Devonshire House will end before morning and I am sure her partners will not let her leave before then, even if Lady Beresford should consider going before she had lost the greatest possible sum at loo.'

'Ah, George, you never loved your poor Aunt Beresford, and indeed she is but a frippery creature, but then consider that ramshackle husband of hers.'

'You are right, ma'am. He is enough to try the patience of a saint. And Aunt Beresford is no saint. But – he is of her own choosing; you know you had no hand in the match.' He was tempted to go on and tell his grandmother just how far from saintly he suspected Lady Beresford of being, and of the night's plot against Jennifer. But the old lady looked far from well. The effect of the drug he was sure Marsham had administered had not entirely worn off. This was no time to agitate her. And, clearly, she had struck on suspicion of Marsham for herself. He need do no more. So, to distract her, he launched forth upon the story of his adventures in Sussex.

'You see before you, ma'am, a most unlucky lover.'

'Unlucky! You, George? It cannot be that they look askance on your suit. You, who are now to be a duke, wooing a little country miss no one has ever heard of? Fiddlestick!'

Mainwaring laughed. 'Fiddlestick it is, ma'am. Of course you are right. That is not at all where my trouble lies. Miss Purchas's family – or, to be precise, her banker uncle and her vulgar aunt, greeted me with the greatest *empressement* and indeed I was like to run away for very disgust at their enthusiasm, which seemed to me somewhat strange when you remember how they put me off when first I wrote to offer for their niece's hand.'

'Indeed I do recollect something of the sort. They wrote, did they not, to say she was but young yet, and had not fully recovered from the shock of her father's and brothers' death – and they must beg you to give her time. Some such nonsense as that, was it not?'

'Just so. A strange letter, I thought it, almost insolent, but urgent in its plea that I put off my proposed visit. And so I did, of course, since my father and brother were killed, the very day I received it, in that damnable accident – I beg your pardon.'

'No need. It was damnable. And all the more reason, as I've told you before, why you must marry. No need to beat about the bush with you, I know. If that father and brother of yours left you anything but debts, I'm wide of the mark. And you know what an expense your grandfather is. I'm a selfish old woman, George. And Miss Purchas has £80,000, if she has a penny.' It was very far from being a *non sequitur*. 'But to your story, George. You've been down to Sussex and seen the girl?'

'I have indeed. That uncle of hers kept putting me off with this excuse and that so in the end I simply wrote announcing my arrival next day – and arrived.'

'And?'

'Was greeted with unction by the uncle, with titters of pure fright by the aunt.'

'But the girl herself, George,' interrupted his grandmother, 'what of her?'

'Patience, ma'am, I am coming to her. She was still mighty indisposed, they told me, over her father and brothers – I tell you, ma'am, though they were my friends I was tired of their very names by now. But I should see her tomorrow . . . For tonight I must make shift with such poor company as they and their ward could offer. For there is a ward, a poor booby of a country boy with a scarlet face and a stammer, who looked at me all evening with such unconcealed loathing that I was soon aware of a part of my trouble.'

'He loves the girl himself?' said the Duchess.

'Indubitably. He looked daggers and hinted at insults till I was glad to get myself to my room without giving him the thrashing he deserved. And then, tossing all night on as hard a bed as ever I encountered in Spain, I determined to show them all a clean pair of heels in the morning and be damned to my promise to Purchas.'

'But you did not?'

'No, I wish I had. But in the morning I was summoned with such fanfare to Miss Purchas's presence as if she had been the Princess Charlotte herself. And, I must confess it, curiosity got the better of me. Having come so far, I would see my enchanted princess, if I died in the attempt.'

'I am glad to see that you have not done so.'

'No; but I am not sure that is any cause for congratulation. I am not dead, but I am engaged to be married, which may be worse.'

'Oh, my poor George, is it as bad as that? I feared these romantic notions of yours might lead to no good. But take heart, remember the £80,000 and forget the girl who brings it to you. Besides, she cannot be so bad as all that; her brothers were your friends . . . But tell me quick, what is she like?'

'What like? A poor little white mouse of a thing, red eyes and all, for it was all too evident she had cried all night and was no better pleased to see me than I her. She caught her breath, swallowed a sob and made me a country mouse's curtsy, and I tell you ma'am, if I had not been so amazed, I should have been sorry for the child. For indeed, short of witchcraft, how Richard and Francis Purchas should come to have so insignificant a chit of a sister is what I cannot bring myself to understand. I never heard but good of their mother, either.'

'Oh, poor George,' said his grandmother again. 'Is she indeed such a cipher? And I remember I cried her up to you as the very wife for a politician.'

'For a politician? She is no wife for a country curate. She could not say good-morning to a parishioner at the church door without blushing and begging his pardon. I tell you, ma'am, I am in despair.'

'Best cut your losses, George. Cry off and be done with it. It will but be a nine days' wonder.'

'Indeed, ma'am, I tried. Oh how I tried. I took her by her little limp paw and told her I feared I had discomposed her by proposing for her so soon – God help me – after her father's and brothers' deaths . . . I begged her pardon, said I would not trouble her peace for the world . . . we would forget it all for a while . . . and a plenty more mealy-mouthed stuff of that kind by which I hoped to talk myself out of my scrape and indeed flattered myself I had well nigh done so when, hey presto, in comes my friend the uncle, for all the world as if he had been listening at the door, as, I have no doubt, he had, congratulates me on our good understanding, takes her hand from mine (it had got left there, I cannot think how) gives it to me all over again: "Take her, my boy, she is yours," for all the world like the last act of a tragedy.'

The old lady could not help laughing. 'Capoted,' she said. 'I had not thought it could happen to you, George. So what did you do?'

'Bore it with the best grace I might. One look told me I should get no help from my betrothed. I could have pitied her terror of that uncle of hers if I had not pitied myself so much more.'

'It is an engagement then?'

'Yes; signed, sealed and delivered, but not to be gazetted for a few months: "Till you are out of black gloves and we all know each other better," says my new uncle, wrings me by the hand and begs me to consider his house (or, to be precise, his niece's) my own. But that was too much: another day there and I'd not have answered for the consequences. I pled urgent business, my father's death, anything, nothing . . . And, the business settled, he was as glad to be rid of me as I to be gone. As for my white mouse, she never said another word, but snuffled a little in her corner and let me kiss her hand. It will be a lesson to me, ma'am, against knight errantry.'

'And yet you have but proved yourself right. The uncle is wicked; the maiden does need rescuing.'

'Yes, but I am the wrong rescuer. I can well imagine that the bumpkin of a ward – what was his name, Edward, Edmund something-or-other – might well be more to miss's taste than I. But it is too late now; I have made my bed . . .'

'And Miss Purchas must lie in it?' said the old lady with her wicked twinkle. 'Well, I feel for you, George, but £80,000 is a powerful consolation.' She yawned and rang her bell. 'Now I am going to dismiss you. You are quite right; it would be an absurdity for me to stay up for Miss Fairbank who will no doubt end by taking breakfast with the Duke.'

He took his leave of her. Now to find Miles Mandeville and ensure that he breathe no word of Jennifer's adventures. Not for the first time, he found himself thus thinking of her by her first name and took himself to task for it. But, he explained to himself, it was merely that he was convinced that while Fairbank was not her name, Jennifer certainly was.

How strange it was, he thought, as he alighted from his carriage in Piccadilly, that he should be concerned with two so dissimilar Jennifers. For the Sussex white mouse to whom he found himself, albeit reluctantly, betrothed, bore the same name as his London heroine. It was the only similarity between them. Miss Fairbank might get into scrapes but at least she was no white mouse.

He turned into St James's Street and proceeded to make the rounds of the various clubs and gaming houses he knew Mandeville to frequent. Drawing a blank, he came, at last, as the first light broke down Piccadilly, to Watier's, where he found the masquerade still continuing, though few of the participants pretended any longer to either sobriety or anonymity.

Here, he found Mandeville surrounded by Harriette Wilson and her sisters. Harriette, who had once written Mainwaring one of her famous letters of invitation, beckoned to him to join them. This suited him admirably. He did so and observed with satisfaction that Mandeville was considerably drunker than his companions. Cold sober himself, he should find it easy enough to provoke Mandeville by a series of pinpricks into a state of fury. And indeed Mandeville, who had been drinking hard to drown his anxiety over the possible consequences of his night's work, was soon whipped up into simmering, heedless fury. Mainwaring judged that the time was ripe.

'Come,' he held out his hand to Harriette, who was sitting on Mandeville's lap, 'a turn of the room with me, Miss Wilson?' Taking her hand, he contrived 'accidentally' to upset Mandeville's champagne into his lap. Mandeville sprang up with an oath, accusing him, quite rightly, of doing it on purpose.

'No,' said Mainwaring blandly, 'but I will, if you wish.'

The matter was soon settled. They would fight that very morning. Mandeville insisted on it and, after protesting in vain, the friend who had agreed to act as his second hurried him away in search of black coffee. The crowd around them merely thought it was one more quarrel provoked by Harriette Wilson and her sisters – the dangerous Three Graces. Having made sure that this was the case, Mainwaring went calmly home to change his clothes and collect his pistols, then set forth without delay to Wimbledon Common where the meeting was to take place. So far, so good. The question now was whether Jennifer's position demanded that he kill Mandeville. He could do it, he knew, easily enough, but the idea was repugnant to him. The man was drunk ... Besides, he did not particularly wish to have to leave the country. He would have to content himself with giving Mandeville a salutary fright.

Mandeville, meanwhile, had been sobering up much too rapidly for his own peace of mind. A coward as well as a bully, he had always before seen to it that he fought only men like himself who could be relied on to lose their nerve or their aim. Mainwaring, he began unhappily to remember, was a very different character. He had heard enough about his army career to know it was idle to hope his aim might be false. If only he could apologise ... But Mainwaring was technically the offending party and it was for him to do so. Mandeville arrived at the windmill where they were to meet a thoroughly chastened man.

Mainwaring and his friend were there already with the surgeon. The preliminaries were soon accomplished. The time was near ... The seconds drew apart for a moment to examine the pistols. Mainwaring spoke: 'Would you prefer,' he asked, 'to be killed outright or merely winged?'

Mandeville blanched: 'You are pleased to jest.'

'On the contrary, I assure you, I was never more serious in my life. I can do the one as easily as the other. And as readily. Promise me your absolute silence over this night's work and it shall be but the right arm.'

'The right?' Mandeville's nerve had completely given by now, his chances of saving himself by shooting first were gone. 'I'll promise anything.'

'Good. Then we will make it the left. It would be a pity to interfere with your elegant taking of snuff. But remember,' the seconds were returning, 'one word of what happened tonight and I meet you again – fatally.'

They took their places, Mandeville half conscious with fright.

The signal was given, he fired, simultaneously felt Mainwaring's bullet enter his left arm and saw, with amazement, that by pure chance his own bullet had grazed Mainwaring's cheek.

Mainwaring came forward, dabbing the wound with his handkerchief, and shook hands. 'Remember your promise,' he said to his half-fainting adversary, then, handing him over to the care of the surgeon, said good-bye to the seconds, jumped into his curricle and drove rapidly away. The streets were waking up as he drove back into London, but it was still early. Yielding to a sudden, irresistible temptation, he swathed himself once more in his domino, donned his mask which effectively covered the bullet graze and turned his horse towards Devonshire House. It was suddenly important to ascertain whether Jennifer had indeed finished the evening in the company of the Duke of Devonshire as his grandmother had prophesied. Besides, he told himself, he was in honour bound to give her early information of Mandeville's silencing.

But he was doomed to disappointment. Jennifer had been carried home at what seemed to her a deplorably early hour by Lady Beresford. Pamela had seized the first opportunity to take her mother aside and tell her Mandeville's bad news. Lady Beresford was at once on thorns. The return of Mainwaring, and his interference in the affair, boded ill for her. She must get to her mother's as fast as possible and concert a strategic retreat with Marsham.

When they set Jennifer down in Grosvenor Square she trumped up an excuse of anxiety for her mother to come in with her, only to find that both the Duchess and Marsham had retired. She heard, however, with alarm that Mainwaring had spent some time with his grandmother first, and went home in a great state of fright and fury, which she took out upon her daughter, whose fault it all inevitably became. Pamela retired to bed in tears and Lady Beresford sat down to undo her face and fabricate a new plan.

CHAPTER XI

Waking late next day, Jennifer learned that the Duchess was already gone out leaving a note for her in which, after explaining her absence, she went on: 'George tells me you were quite the belle of the ball. Best have a quiet day to recover from your late night, for we are promised to join Lady Sefton's party at Almack's tonight.' And then, casually, 'George has good news: his engagement is a settled thing at last.'

Tearing up the note, Jennifer walked to the window with an angry swish of her silk négligé. Why had the Duchess thought it necessary to write to her? The reminder about Lady Sefton was too obviously a mere pretext. Did she think it necessary to warn her of Lord Mainwaring's engagement? Intolerable thought!

But so much was intolerable. She paced up and down the room, going drearily over the events of the night before. Why had Mandeville lured her to Watier's? In pursuit of some private vengeance of his own or in concert with Marsham and perhaps even Lady Beresford? Of the seriousness of the threat she had no doubt, nor of her debt of gratitude to Mainwaring for his intervention. But this was the worst of all. She could not forgive him for having found her in such compromising circumstances, still less for having deserted her so callously after their arrival at Devonshire House. He might at least have given himself the pain of one dance with her ... But then he had obviously been prepared to think the worst of her from the beginning. He had jumped at once to the conclusion that it was her own folly that had brought her to Watier's. It was unpardonable. So, too, were his strictures on her acceptance of Mandeville's escort. How was she supposed to know he was unreliable? She had seen him often enough in Mainwaring's own company. And as for the last taunt, about her accepting advice from an abigail – it was beyond forgiveness.

Her angry cornering of the room had brought her back to the window and she stopped for a moment to look out. A barrel-organ was playing *Cherry Ripe* in the square. The trees were in their first leaf, the grass was green; it was spring. On an impulse, she rang and ordered Starlight to be brought round. Changing hurriedly into her habit, she refused to let herself remember that it was Mainwaring who had arranged for Starlight to be housed in the Duchess's stable and for a groom to be available to ride with her. She was much too angry with him to be fair.

Out of doors, she found the fresh air soothing and set forward more cheerfully for the park. If only, when she got there, she could let Starlight out in a good gallop instead of being compelled to the decorous paces of society. Almost, for a moment, she was tempted to return home and face her uncle. Life in London had become intolerable, her whole position a false pretence, her path bedevilled by unknown enemies. And, as a last straw, she had learned by accident only the day before that Lucy Faversham, on whom she had perhaps absurdly relied to extricate her from her difficulties, was to stay several months more in the north, where her father was busy settling his brother's estate. For the first time, she began to realise what it was to face London alone.

More and more, as she became aware of the complexities and pitfalls of society, she understood how rash she had been to leave her uncle's protection. If protection, she told herself angrily, it could be called. But the fact remained that her chances of getting out of the scrape in which she found herself without irrevocable damage to her good name were slight indeed. She had been mad to run away, madder still to let Mainwaring plant her, so casually, upon his grandmother. The stormy day of discovery lay inevitably before her. She could see neither how to avoid, nor how to ride it out. Or rather, suddenly brutal, she made herself face it: when she had let Mainwaring impose her upon his grandmother she had thought . . . She had imagined . . . She had dreamed . . . Enough of that. She had been mistaken. He was engaged to someone else, some puling Sussex heiress who would, no doubt, bore him to extinction and bear him ten children.

The thought was unbearable. She was glad to be distracted by the problem of crossing Park Lane and entering the park. Successfully dodging between Lord Petersham's brown carriage and Mrs King's yellow one, she turned Starlight's head resolutely away from the fashionable end of the park. It was early still for the *beau-monde*'s promenade, but she wished to take no chances; she was in no mood for flirtation and gossip today. She wanted to ride among trees, not people; to be miserable at leisure, to think.

But her luck was out. She had hardly got Starlight beyond the entrance of the park when the Duke of Devonshire rode up to join her. Almost, in her misery, she would have enjoyed snubbing him – as a Duke – but, as a man, it was impossible. He was too gentle, too kind. And besides, it was not his fault that she had not enjoyed his ball. She complimented him on it properly and he in return congratulated her on her fresh appearance and bewailed her early departure the night before. 'I had hoped to have had the pleasure of leading you in to breakfast.'

She murmured something, she knew not exactly what, about her own disappointment, and Lady Beresford, and then regretted it, when he took her up exactly as she least wished.

'Yes,' he said, 'you are, I apprehend, in Lady Beresford's charge for the season?'

It was the question of all others she most longed to avoid, but now it must be hedged somehow. 'I am living,' she hated herself for the evasion, 'with Lady Beresford's mother.' How long could the pretence last? She had been insane not to foresee all this. Suppose the Duke actually intended to propose for her hand. What could she tell him? That the Miss Fairbank he wooed was in reality Miss Purchas, a fugitive from her home? The only thing, she thought gloomily, that was genuine about her was her fortune which was doubtless why the Duke and such dandies as Leatherhead who, now, to her great relief, joined them, were apt, instinctively, to hang about her. Well, if her uncle had not managed to play ducks and drakes with it before she came of age, her fortune bade fair to be her only consolation. She would retire with it to Paris, refuge of tarnished names, or set up for a lady bountiful, dispensing soup and unwelcome advice, in some remote country district. For all the flirtation that she was automatically carrying on with Leatherhead and the Duke, it was plain that she would never, never marry.

But she had missed some remark of Leatherhead's. She looked at him in polite enquiry.

'I knew it,' he reined his grey in more closely beside Starlight. 'Miss Fairbank is in the dreams today. I was telling the Duke of the latest *on dit*: they say there was a duel fought at Wimbledon Mill this morning, and two of his guests the protagonists.'

'Not guests of mine when they quarrelled,' said the Duke. 'That I apprehend, was at Watier's. I had thought Mainwaring a cooler head than to fight over so trifling a cause.'

'Mainwaring?' She started.

'I had quite forgot. He is your Duchess's grandson, is he not? Well, you can set her heart at rest when you go home. See, here he comes. And in Harriette Wilson's carriage, too,' he added in an undertone to Leatherhead.

'You see, I am right,' answered Leatherhead, obviously pursuing some earlier argument. 'She was undoubtedly the cause and now fêtes the victor. But, Miss Fairbank, we neglect you shamefully. Tell me you will be at Almack's tonight to justify the fatigue of knee buckles. Did you hear, Duke, that Willis turned away the Beau himself the other night for having the temerity to appear in trousers?'

'Turned away Wellington? Willis is a brave man.'

'No braver than the dowager who turned the Beau out of her pew in Deal. But, Miss Fairbank, I await your answer. Am I to mortify myself in court dress and be rewarded by your hand for the quadrille or are you, alas, promised elsewhere?'

Jennifer, who had overheard the entire interchange between Leatherhead and the Duke, and whose eyes had been involuntarily following the *vis-à-vis* in which Mainwaring was flirting so obviously with the notorious Harriette, now collected her wits: 'Indeed, sir, I believe we are to attend Almack's with Lady Sefton's party,' she said. 'I shall be most happy to dance the quadrille with you.'

'And the waltz with me,' said the Duke.

Accepting, her cup of happiness should have been full. Was he not the most eligible bachelor in town? But her eyes were still following the carriage where Harriette Wilson's white velvet bonnet, with its flaunting plumes, nodded so close to Mainwaring's head. Had he really fought a duel this morning? And about Harriette Wilson? But Leatherhead was claiming her attention.

'I observed, ma'am, that the town is filling up. I have seen Petersham's brown carriage this morning, and here, if I mistake not, comes Lady Laverstoke, fresh up from the country and languishing as ever.'

The name made Jennifer start and turn. And there, indeed, approaching at a distance, was Lady Laverstoke's well-known barouche, yellow liveries and all. Madness not to have expected such an encounter. She put an anguished hand to her head, pleaded a headache which her previous absentness did much to justify to her concerned companions, turned Starlight quickly about and made for the park gates. The Duke and Leatherhead rode beside her till she reached them, full of concern and condolence, urgent that she return home and recover herself, pressing that she should not fail them at Almack's. It was all very flattering and yet curiously tedious. She left them with relief to ride home in the pleasantly silent company of James, the groom. By now, the headache she had feigned had become a disagreeable reality. It was in throbbing misery that she reached Grosvenor Square.

But her hopes of rest and solitude were thwarted. She found Lady Beresford sitting with the Duchess.

'There you are at last, my dear,' said Lady Beresford, giving her one of her highly perfumed kisses. 'I have been waiting for you this age to tell you again how sorry I was we could not take you up last night.'

Hard, bright little eyes probed at Jennifer's composure, but she was ready for the attack. 'Indeed, it was nothing, ma'am.

Lord Mainwaring was so good as to escort me.'

'Mainwaring?' said her ladyship on a rising note. 'And that reminds me, the most amazing story is going round the town. Have you heard it, ma'am?' she asked her mother.

'A story about George? There are so many,' said his grandmother. 'Not, I collect, the old one about his wager with Alvanley?'

'No, no, nothing so paltry. This, I fear, will shock you a little. That is why I thought it best to tell you myself.'

'You have taken your time about it,' said her shrewd mother. 'You have sat here this half-hour and talked of nothing more significant than India muslin and the Princess Charlotte. Perhaps you wished Miss Fairbank too to have the benefit of your *on dit*?'

This shot went too near the bone for either Jennifer's comfort or Lady Beresford's. Reddening, she muttered something about having clean forgot the matter till Jennifer's mention of Mainwaring reminded her. 'But the short of the matter is, ma'am, that he has fought a duel.'

The Duchess laughed. 'Another? Is that such a piece of news? I collect he is not injured?'

'A grazed cheek, no more. But you have not asked for his opponent.'

'No,' said the old lady, 'why should I? George is not such a fool as to have killed him. But I apprehend you wish me to ask why they fought.'

Lady Beresford reddened still more around her rouge. She was never a match for her mother. 'Nothing of the kind, ma'am; I only wish it could be kept from you. But I would rather you heard the unpalatable truth from me than from another. His opponent was Mad Mandeville' (again the sharp eyes darted to Jennifer) 'and they fought' (she paused in seeming embarrassment) 'they fought over Harriette Wilson.'

'Did they so?' The Duchess sounded amused. 'I knew she had sent George one of her letters, but hardly thought the matter had gone further. But, since I see you must tell me, how is poor Mr Mandeville?'

'Wounded in the left arm, ma'am. It seems he resented some

familiarity of Mainwaring's with Miss Wilson at Watier's this morning.'

But her mother stopped her. 'That will do, Jane. It is hardly a subject for Miss Fairbank's ears.'

Defeated, Lady Beresford flounced angrily out of the room, only to be waylaid in the hall by Marsham.

'Oh, my lady, what shall I do? Her grace has given me my notice.'

'Her grace? You?' Lady Beresford did not need to simulate astonishment and concern.

'Yes. This very morning and I am to go at once, my lady, as if I had never served her so faithfully all these years. In truth, my heart is breaking; I have hardly the strength to pack my box, and as for where to go, I have no more idea than a baby.' She paused and waited sharply for Lady Beresford's reaction.

It was not what she had hoped for. Lady Beresford had no intention of taking this now useless tool into her own house. But, on the other hand, she was well aware of the danger she would run if she affronted Marsham. She thought for a moment. Then, 'Come, Marsham,' she said, 'do not put yourself into such a pucker. I have thought of the very thing for you. My friend Lady Laverstoke is but yesterday come to town and is new forming her establishment. I will give you a line for her which will, I am sure, make all smooth for you.'

If Marsham was disappointed, she was too clever to show it. An hour later she was admitted to the house Lady Laverstoke had taken in Bruton Street and received with open arms by her new mistress, whose own maid had formed an attachment for the bailiff on the Sussex estate and had given in her notice rather than be separated from him by this visit to London. Lady Laverstoke, who had never dressed herself in her life and who had been dependent, the night before, on the bungling ministrations of a housemaid, was more than delighted to engage Marsham and was soon chattering away to her as if she had known her all her life, while Marsham went straight to work to prepare her for her first appearance of the season at Almack's.

'Though really,' sighed Lady Laverstoke, 'it is such a fret to prevail upon dear Charles to accompany one, I sometimes wonder whether it is worth the pains. He would much liefer be losing his money with his low friends at Limmer's – if he would only do it elegantly at Brooks' it would not be so bad. Or better still if he would fix his attentions on some suitable girl: but sometimes I am in despair of him; he cares no more for girls than his little brothers. Yes,' she broke off to admire her reflection in the glass, 'that is excellent. I have always wished to try my hair *à la giraffe* but poor silly Edwards could never compass it. I begin to think I shall do very well without her.'

'Indeed,' Marsham sniffed, 'I believe your ladyship is well rid of her. The condition of your gowns ... But I will say no more.'

'Nor need you, Marsham. I can see we shall suit excellently. And truly I have been so dogged with ill luck it has quite distracted me. First there was poor Milward – the governess, you know, who ran off with the curate and not a penny to bless themselves with so that I am sure they will end by coming on the parish, and no more than she deserves for leaving me so in the lurch. And then when I thought I had got Miss Fairbank to replace her and she seemed such a treasure – why, she proved nothing but a fribble after all. What is it?'

For Marsham had paused, a bunch of artificial poppies suspended over Lady Laverstoke's high-piled curls: 'Miss Fairbank?' she asked.

'Yes, my late governess. *Most* strongly recommended to me by my cousin, Miss Faversham, and to all appearances a treasure. Why, the children actually minded her. I never saw the like of it. And if she did play some hoydenish tricks, well, she was but a young thing after all, as I told Lord Mainwaring. I confess I was a thought anxious when it seemed Charles was *épris* in that direction; but Mainwaring soon took care of that, and though I was sad to have them leave, yet it seemed all for the best. I think the poppies a little further this way, do not you?'

Marsham, who had been listening with fixed attention as she put the finishing touches to her new mistress's coiffure, hastily complied, paid the expected compliment to Lady Laverstoke's taste and then steered her back to the matter in hand: 'And Miss Fairbank proved unsatisfactory after all?'

'Unsatisfactory? Worse; a thousand times worse. Why, you never heard the like of it. Milward and her curate was bad enough, but at least she had the common courtesy to leave me a note, explaining she was off to Gretna Green, or wherever that kind of person goes to be married out of hand. But as for Miss Fairbank! She just disappeared, scarce a sennight after Mainwaring took Charles away, and the children at their most restless, poor little lambs, because of their brother's being gone so suddenly. I declare, I did not know which way to turn. And indeed Mainwaring might have saved himself the pains and stayed – for they always mind him – if we had but known she was going to do anything so inconsiderate. But it is always the way, no one has the least consideration for my feelings, just because I am a widow, and have no husband to protect me.'

'You had not considered,' Marsham paused for a moment to resettle a recalcitrant curl and make sure of her ground. 'You had not thought that the two departures might be in any way connected?'

'Connected? You are pleased to be insolent, Marsham. You suggest that my son, that Lord Laverstoke . . .' She paused, speechless for once.

'No, no,' Marsham pacifically held a hand mirror so that her new mistress might see the elegant back of her head. 'I am sure Lord Laverstoke is far too much the gentleman for such carryings on, but from what I have heard of Lord Mainwaring . . .' She waited anxiously for Lady Laverstoke's reaction.

'Oh, Mainwaring.' She paused for a moment, ogling her reflection in the glass. 'Yes, I had not thought of that. He has, it is true, something of a reputation. But I have never credited much that I have heard. He is, I must tell you, the guardian of my children and most punctilious in their care. And now he is to be a duke . . .'

'I have never understood,' said Marsham, greatly daring, 'that such elevation necessarily had a sobering effect on a gentleman. But, my lady, I am loth to tell you what I think it well you should know . . .' She paused, assuming an air of diffidence while she considered rapidly how best to tell her story.

'Well? You kill me with curiosity. Proceed, Marsham. What is it that I should know?'

'My lady,' said Marsham with an air of frankness, 'it makes it exceeding awkward that he should be the guardian of your children, but I think it still more my duty to tell you that my former mistress, the Duchess of Lewes, has for many weeks past had under her protection a Miss Fairbank who was, unless I am much mistaken, committed to her charge by Lord Mainwaring himself.'

'Lord Mainwaring? Miss Fairbank? Impossible! You are trifling with me, Marsham.'

'Indeed, my lady, I wish I were. For, from what you have told me, it would seem that my poor lady has been most grievously imposed upon. We always thought Miss Fairbank an impostor, ma'am, a snake in the nest, but we had no idea of such treachery, such duplicity . . .'

'We, Marsham? This has been a matter then for the servants' hall?'

'No, no, ma'am, I would not so demean myself. I should, in truth, have said Lady Beresford and I, for, you must know, I have known her ladyship ever since she was the most winning baby that ever cut tooth or wore curlers, and feel for her quite as if she was my own child. And indeed, ma'am – my lady, I should say – this predilection of her mother's for an unknown upstart like Miss Fairbank is not at all what she could like.'

'No,' said Lady Laverstoke shrewdly. 'I dare swear it is not. The Duchess still holds the purse-strings, I collect, since the Duke is no better than in Bedlam, poor man. But tell me, does Miss Fairbank go into society?'

'Into society! I should just about think she does. You will meet her tonight at Almack's, my lady, and had best decide what you propose to say to her. She is quite the talk of the town, I can tell you, with the Duke of Devonshire and I don't know who else dangling after her. There is a story afloat that she has a fortune. I know not who put it about, but the results are easily enough to be seen. I do not know when I have seen the Duchess's house so gay as since she has been living there. Morning callers, bouquets, *billets doux* ... It has quite made her grace young again. And all for a fraud, my lady, a one-time governess, if, I hope, no worse.' Marsham's ominous pause made it clear how very much worse she in fact hoped the case to be.

'And Mainwaring introduced her to the Duchess?' Lady Laverstoke returned to this point. 'I can hardly credit it. I knew his *morals* have never been of the most immaculate, but surely his *manners* must preclude such an imposition. Quick, Marsham, the hare's-foot and the rouge. I must make time to visit Lady Beresford before I go to Almack's. She, I apprehend, knows nothing of all this. We must put our heads together as to what is best to be done.'

'Excellent, my lady, the very thing of all others I should have recommended. Lady Beresford will be only too happy to take Miss Fairbank down a peg, I can tell you, for indeed her success has been excessively hard on my poor Miss Pamela. But how will you contrive, my lady, for her grace has so prevailed upon poor Lady Beresford that there is nothing for her but to take up Miss Fairbank and give her the undeserved benefit of her protection at Almack's or wherever else she goes. Unless, of course, her grace goes tonight herself, as, now I recollect, she well may, for I believe she was promised to join Lady Sefton's party.'

'Good,' said Lady Laverstoke picking up gloves and fan. 'And if not, let me alone to contrive something.' Pausing for one last, satisfied glance at her new coiffure in the glass, she hurried away to tease her son into spoiling half a dozen more cravats than usual in her efforts to hasten his dressing. At last, he begged her to go on to Lady Beresford's without him, promising to meet her at Almack's.

This suited her well enough, and she was still more pleased to find Lady Beresford alone, attending, with the help of her maid, to the last refinements of her costume. Pamela, she explained, had gone to Lady Sefton's with the Duchess and Miss Fairbank.

'Ah,' said Lady Laverstoke, with deep meaning, 'the very subject. My dearest life, hasten your toilette, I beg of you. I must speak to you *alone*.'

Puzzled and intrigued, Lady Beresford hurried to dismiss her maid, and her friend then lost no time in pouring out the tale of Marsham's discoveries. This time she told the story of Miss Fairbank's governess-ship in full, making the most of such scandalous exploits as her borrowing of Lord Mainwaring's horse and her excursion in Laverstoke's carriage.

Having punctuated the story with proper exclamations of amazement and horror, Lady Beresford summed it up at last: 'A hoyden indeed, and an impostor to boot. But what purpose, think you – if indeed he is behind it – can Mainwaring hope to serve by this imposture? And, truly, my dearest creature, from what you tell me of his behaviour to her at your house, it is hard to believe him enamoured of her.'

'No, I confess, I had no idea of such a thing. Had you but seen his fury when she came cantering up, all blowsy with exercise, on his Lightning, you would have thought him safe enough. But how else to account for his foisting her upon his grandmother?'

'It is indeed a puzzle,' said her friend. 'Or, – I believe I have it! Could it be for a wager? My dearest life, that is it for a certainty. And, if so, Mainwaring will not thank us for spoiling his game. There must be a fortune at stake or, so wild as he is, he would never have involved his grandmother.'

Lady Laverstoke looked doubt and then, slowly, conviction. 'You must be right. But how then shall we proceed? What shall I do when, as I apprehend I will, I meet my former governess at Almack's?'

'Why, that is easy. Behave as if you have never seen her before in your life and tell Laverstoke he must do the same. Only think of the anguish the silly creature will suffer wondering when you will choose to expose her. It is almost better than to do it at once. For she will be in a sad puzzle to account for your not recognising her.'

'But are we then to let her get off scot free?' asked Lady Laverstoke.

Here was a difficulty. Neither lady had the slightest inclination to show mercy to Jennifer, but both were extremely anxious not to offend Mainwaring, Lady Beresford because she began to think his engagement would come to nothing and had hopes of his hand for her daughter, Lady Laverstoke because she had similar ambitions on her own account.

'And besides,' said Lady Laverstoke, summing up much that had been unspoken between them. 'It would be the greatest pity in the world to do anything precipitate and so alienate his grandmother from him.'

'Yes, indeed,' agreed her friend. 'I do not like to think what she would do if she were to learn what kind of a ladybird Mainwaring has foisted upon her. We must proceed, my dearest creature, with the greatest circumspection.'

So agreed, they admired each other's toilettes and left for Almack's. To Lady Laverstoke's relief, she found her son positively there before her and took him aside to prepare him for a meeting with Miss Fairbank. He looked amazed.

'Miss Fairbank? Here? You are roasting me, ma'am. I always thought Miss Fairbank a prime article, but to get herself here is a trifle above her touch.'

'You might well think so, Charles, but you will find yourself mistaken. Only, I must beg you to do nothing to disclose her true identity!'

'What? Let her get away with it? Mother, that is the outside of enough. Only consider what those starchy lady patronesses would say if they knew.'

'That is exactly what I am thinking of. Imagine the scandal. And she is living, I must tell you, in Grosvenor Square with the Duchess of Lewes.'

'With Mainwaring's grandmother!' He let out a low whistle. 'Sits the wind in that corner. Very well, ma'am, I am dumb. But may I not tease her a little with our previous acquaintance? No need to say where or when, after all?'

This seemed entirely reasonable to his mother, who had never objected to his teasing his horse or dogs – or even his younger brothers and sister – when he was a boy. He left her almost at once and made his way through the crowded rooms, eager to find Miss Fairbank and commence operations.

But when he found her, she was in animated conversation with Pamela and the Duke of Devonshire, of whom he was in considerable awe. It did not, somehow, seem the moment to begin his campaign. And, besides, he had not seen Pamela for several years and now found her most remarkably improved from the shy miss he remembered. He begged her hand for the waltz that was then commencing, was accepted, and forgot all about Jennifer.

She meanwhile, having steeled herself for this moment ever since the morning's near encounter with Lady Laverstoke, was amazed and relieved to receive nothing more than a conventional bow and greeting. Could it be that he and his mother would not expose her after all? As the agonising evening wore slowly away, she began to think that this must indeed be the case. It was impossible, but it must be true. She could not understand it. She saw Lady Laverstoke in deep confabulation with Lady Beresford and soon afterwards received haughty but impeccable notice from both. The disaster that had loomed so large before her all day was incomprehensibly postponed. Could it be that they feared the scandal of a scene at Almack's? Or did they hesitate to expose her for fear of the shock to the Duchess? Whatever the reason, for tonight it seemed that she was safe.

For the hundredth time she looked eagerly round the room for Lord Mainwaring. If only he would come and she could ask his advice in her new predicament. But he was doubtless celebrating his morning's victory in the arms of Harriette Wilson. Furious with him, and with herself for her fury, she took the floor to waltz so vigorously with the Duke that Mrs Drummond Burrell raised her eyebrows and Lady Laverstoke and Lady Beresford exchanged one silent, speaking look.

CHAPTER XII

As for Mainwaring, he had spent a maddening day in pursuit of Jennifer, who must be told of Mandeville's silencing. Calling in Grosvenor Square at what he considered the earliest possible moment, he had found her just ridden out; returning, later, he had learned from his friend the butler that Lady Beresford was in possession of the field, and had retired without leaving his name. He was in no mood for his aunt. The butler, however, had told him that the Duchess and Jennifer were engaged to Lady Sefton and he had gone there, hoping for a quiet moment with Jennifer, but had encountered Charles Laverstoke on the way. This was a fresh shock. Jennifer must be warned of the Laverstokes' presence in town. But Charles, who was genuinely fond of his formidable guardian, proved hard to shake off and Mainwaring arrived at Lady Sefton's only to learn that his grandmother and Jennifer had just left for Almack's. His luck was out indeed, for Lord Sefton then pounced on him with a long account of a recently contested by-election in one of his boroughs. It was impossible not to listen politely to his host and essential to pretend an interest in a subject supposed to be so near to his heart. When he finally managed to disengage himself, it was only to realise with something like despair that it was half past ten and he was wearing trousers. There was no hope of getting home, changing into the knee breeches essential for Almack's and reaching there before the doors' inexorable closing at eleven o'clock.

He spent a bad-tempered, restless evening wandering between various clubs and gaming houses in St James's, choosing them more for their nearness to King Street and therefore to Almack's than from any preference of his own. He did not admit to himself that he hoped, by 'accident' to encounter his grandmother and Jennifer on their way home, but the fact remained that he spent a remarkable amount of time in and about King Street. Inevitably, as he went from place to place, meeting a friend here, joining in a game of cards there, he drank rather more than he would have if he had fixed himself in one spot. This did nothing to improve his temper. It had been a long, hard day; in fact, he reminded himself, saying an irritable goodnight to the doorman at Brooks', it had been two hard days; he had not been to bed at all the night before. It was not surprising that he was feeling a considerable effect from the wine he had drunk.

But at last his patience, such as it was, was rewarded. Loitering in the doorway of Frank's Parlour in King Street, he heard, from across the road, the stentorian cry for the Duchess of Lewes's carriage. He said a brisk farewell to the friends to whom he had been saying a slow one for ten minutes and walked casually across the road, arriving at the entrance of Almack's as the Duchess and Jennifer came out to the carriage. But, to his fury, he saw that they were accompanied by Pamela and, of all people, Charles Laverstoke. Impossible to speak freely in front of them. He ground his teeth – a habit for which his nurse had often rebuked him as a child – and watched, from the shadows, as Laverstoke handed the ladies into the carriage. Then he came forward, greeted, and firmly dismissed him. Charles Laverstoke was far from pleased; he had counted on seeing Pamela home and thus cementing their new friendship; but he was too thoroughly in awe of his guardian, who looked more than usually formidable this evening, to protest. He turned reluctantly towards Bruton Street and dreams of Pamela.

Mainwaring, meanwhile, had given the coachman his orders and taken his seat in the carriage beside Jennifer. He was at once aware of a stiff withdrawal on her part and understood it when his grandmother began to twit him unmercifully about his duel with Mandeville.

'I apprehend you think yourself heroic, George,' she began the attack, 'having wounded a poltroon in a duel about a piece of Covent Garden trash. Miss Fairbank and I were vastly entertained when we heard the story, were we not, Miss Fairbank?'

'Oh, excessively.' Jennifer seemed to shrink still further into her corner of the carriage.

'And you are wounded yourself, I see.' The old lady pointed her fan accusingly at the piece of court plaster with which he had covered the graze on his cheek. 'Love's scars indeed: I hope Miss Wilson has proved sufficiently grateful for the honour you have done her. But in truth, George, I am angry with you. Your grandfather killed his man, of course, but his opponent was worthy of his notice and it was politics, not petticoats they fought over. You have done yourself harm, I fear, among thinking people, by this day's work, and if you will be ruled by me, you will find yourself some urgent business to take you out of town. Join your fat friend Prinney in Brighton, or find yourself a political pretext elsewhere, but at all costs get away and let the tittle-tattle die down. We can well spare your escort, now young Laverstoke is come to town, can we not, Miss Fairbank.'

'Oh, admirably,' said Jennifer. 'We have managed excellently well tonight under his care.'

'And the Duke's,' said the Duchess, 'it would be ungrateful in you, child, to forget the Duke of Devonshire who did much, I apprehend, to make your evening pleasant.'

'I would not forget him for the world,' said Jennifer, delighted with this opportunity of making clear to Mainwaring how little she had missed his company.

He ground his teeth silently, realising, too late, that in his anxiety to protect Jennifer's good name he had done his work too well. To Jennifer herself he might, he thought, have explained the true reasons for his duel with Mandeville, but not now, not since he had felt her scorn and seen how easily she believed the story against him. Surely *she* should have realised that he had used Harriette merely to spare her? Having failed to observe Jennifer's quick retreat in the park that morning, he was not aware that she had been a witness to the flaunted flirtation with Harriette Wilson by which he had hoped to lend credence to that explanation of the duel. It seemed, therefore, to him that Jennifer had decided against him on the very slightest of grounds. He was in doubt whether to be angrier at her stupidity, or at her readiness, after all he had done for her, to believe ill of him. But if that was what she thought of him, very well, he was glad to have discovered it. He proceeded to take the best revenge he could by paying his entire attention to Pamela and talking to her extensively about his friends, the Laverstokes, sure that with every reference to them he must be increasing Jennifer's anxieties. When they reached the Beresfords' house in Bruton Street, he took his leave of his grandmother.

'You have Miss Fairbank's admirable company; you can have no need of mine.' His tone made it an insult to Jennifer, to whom he contrived to pay no further attention while taking an elaborate farewell of the Duchess.

'Think well of my advice,' she reminded him. 'You had much best leave London for a while.'

'Ma'am, you have already persuaded me. I shall go down to Sussex tomorrow. I recollect that my esteemed uncle-to-be spoke of a forthcoming meeting of the Hampden Club at which he anticipated some trouble with the more radical elements in the district.' (His tongue blurred a little on the words and he pulled himself more upright as he leaned in at the carriage door.) 'I shall be happier, I am sure, talking sense to his Sussex bumpkins than exchanging nonsenses with Harriette and her kind.' He closed the carriage door with a bang and none too steadily, helped Pamela up the steps to her front door.

His grandmother, meanwhile, had settled comfortably back against the squabs. 'Remarkable,' she said conversationally. 'In all his thirty-five years, I do not recollect ever to have seen George disguised before. Miss Wilson must be attractive indeed.' She waited for Jennifer's answer.

But Jennifer was too angry to speak.

As for Mainwaring, waking next morning with a rending headache, he convinced himself that he was delighted Miss Fairbank would never know he had fought his duel on her account. His grandmother was right, although, of course, for the wrong reasons. The sooner he left town the better. But could he honourably do so leaving Jennifer in what had become a highly explosive situation? Apparently, from Laverstoke's amicable presence with them last night, he and his mother had made no sign of recognition on encountering their vanished governess at Almack's. But that might well have been out of respect for the portentous lady patronesses. No doubt Lady Laverstoke's first action, this morning, would be to hurry round with the whole amazing story to his grandmother, or, worse still, to Lady Beresford who, he remembered, was a strong friend of hers. He groaned, drank a little more soda water and looked at his watch. As he had feared, it was very late indeed. Whatever Lady Laverstoke's first action might be, it was far too late to prevent it. Cursing himself for a bungler, he began angrily to shuffle through his post letters. Bills, bills, invitations, bills, a political manifesto – and then a delicately scented lavender-coloured note in Lady Laverstoke's unmistakably illegible hand. Her first action, it seemed, had been to write to him, and in the most affectionate terms too. Not for the first time, as he deciphered the much-crossed, spidery hand-writing, he cursed his friend Laverstoke who had died leaving him his children's guardian and therefore subject to his widow's unwelcome advances. The letter seemed to be about nothing whatever, or rather a concatenation of nothings. He threw it down angrily and drank some more soda water, thinking about his friends and the trouble they had brought on him. Laverstoke's wife, the Purchases' sister ... Odd, he thought again, that she, too, should be a Jennifer. A Cornish name. Was Miss Fairbank perhaps a fugitive from some fierce moronic Cornishman? Well, the sooner she went back home to him, the better for everyone. Thinking of her, he caught sight of her name on the second, still unread page of Lady Laverstoke's letter and, thus aroused, applied himself once again to deciphering it. At last he made it out. With much would-be kittenish teasing and much hinted self-praise for her silence, Lady Laverstoke accused him of foisting her ex-governess on his grandmother for a bet. If she suspected more, and worse, she was far too much the lady even to hint at it. All she wanted, it seemed, was proper credit for her amazing discretion and that of Lady Beresford, whom, she boasted, she had contrived to silence.

So his aunt knew the story too. He crumpled the fragrant paper angrily in his hand. A bet. It was a lucky thought. Perhaps all might yet be well. But he must think it out . . . he must have time.

His head ached worse than ever. He rang for his man and demanded champagne. Getting it, and a reproachful look from Hudson, who had served him through the Peninsular war and thought him above such things, he applied himself to composing a letter to Lady Laverstoke which should at once satisfy and silence her – and tell her nothing. It was not easy and he was not altogether pleased with the result. Vying with her in the elegant saying of nothing, he seemed to have caught some of her coyness. But no doubt that would please her. And it would give him time to think of some stratagem for bringing his grandmother out of the imbroglio unscathed. Jennifer was unimportant; he no longer cared, he told himself, what became of her, but his grandmother must at all costs be protected from scene and scandal. Thinking thus, he conveniently forgot how she loved them both, reminding himself instead that the political meeting he had mentioned the night before was not for another week. He would take her first advice and pay a last bachelor visit to his friend the Prince Regent in Brighton before he gave himself up to meek Miss Purchas and marriage.

Receiving his note, Lady Laverstoke was delighted. If not, alas, a proposal of marriage, it seemed to her the next best thing, strong encouragement. Rereading it, she was less pleased. There was disappointingly little in it that one could get hold of. Though full of admiration at her perspicacity in deducing the bet that had placed Miss Fairbank in the Duchess's house, he gave her oddly little information about it. But then, he had always been silent and secretive. Her problem now was to see that Lady Beresford maintained the silence he asked for without giving her any inkling of her own hopes.

This proved easier than she expected, for Lady Beresford had her own hopes about Mainwaring. Had he not brought Pamela home last night, ignoring the rival attractions of Miss Fairbank? And was not Pamela, today, in that wide-eyed dreamy state that to so experienced an eye as her mother's betrayed the pangs of dawning love? It was disappointing, of course, to hear from Lady Laverstoke that Mainwaring had had to leave town suddenly on urgent business, but then, they reassured each other, there was the small matter of yesterday's duel to be taken into account. He was doubtless well-advised to go away and let the resulting gossip die down. For each of them had her own reasons to be concerned for his political career. Lady Laverstoke fancied herself as the great Whig hostess, Lady Beresford thought how admirably she would control Pamela in a similar situation. Visions of salons bright in their heads, they answered each other somewhat at cross-purposes, but were too preoccupied with future bliss to notice it. The first point upon which they easily reached agreement was a compact of silence as to the odious Miss Fairbank. If Lord Mainwaring wished it, of course it should be so.

Thus their resolution, faithfully adhered to by Lady Laverstoke, who had, after all, the more personal stake in the matter. With the incentive of so prosperous a marriage before her, she contrived, for once in her life, to be totally discreet. Lady Beresford on the other hand, had a less powerful motive for secrecy – and her temptations proved greater. A few days after they had reached their agreement, she was visited by Miles Mandeville, pale, interesting, his arm in a sling, his temper in shreds. She greeted him with all the enthusiasm due to a hero. Pamela was out riding in the park with young Laverstoke, her childhood friend, whose escort her mother thought unexceptionable. She and Mandeville were alone, free to talk, to hint, to be silent; in short, to mystify each other to their hearts' content.

Both had, as a matter of fact, intended to keep their secrets, Mandeville from dread, Lady Beresford from hope of Lord Mainwaring. But the availability of so admirable a listener proved too much, in each case, for discretion. Lady Beresford broke down first and gratified Mandeville with the full history of Jennifer's career as a governess. He could hardly do less than reciprocate with the true story of his duel with Mainwaring. Both, naturally, promised secrecy all over again. Lady Beresford intended no less. The explanation of the duel was only what she had long suspected. It was merely added to the general sum of her knowledge, to await the long deferred day of vengeance on Miss Fairbank. If only Mainwaring would return to town ... But in her heart she hoped that he was occupied in Sussex in disentangling himself from the deplorable engagement of which her mother had told her. This was more important than anything. When he returned there would be time enough to learn the full story of the bet that had placed Miss Fairbank in Grosvenor Square, to compass her disgrace and to fix his attentions, so promisingly begun, on Pamela.

Mandeville, on the other hand, while promising secrecy as a matter of course, was already considering what use to make of this amazing piece of information. Miss Fairbank, on whom with Mainwaring he had vowed revenge, was in his hands. It was but to decide how best to use his knowledge. He brooded over it happily for a few days, making a point, the while, of seeing Jennifer in society and paying her extravagant attention. Watching her nervous reception of his gallantries he inwardly considered and dismissed various courses. It was such pleasure merely to consider what he would do to her, that he purposely delayed acting. Besides, would it not be better to wait for the climax until Mainwaring, against whom he felt still more bitterly, should have returned to town? He must share to the full in the moment of disgrace. So he watched, and waited, and waltzed with Jennifer at Almack's.

CHAPTER XIII

Jennifer was distracted. Mainwaring had left town with no more word to her. Lady Laverstoke's strange silence continued and became every day more mysterious and somehow more menacing. The Duke of Devonshire had gone down to Chatsworth for a few days and she was left to the unremitting pursuit of Mandeville whom she increasingly detested. Lord Laverstoke tormented her by teasing innuendo in the intervals of his more and more assiduous courting of Pamela. Lady Beresford, fortunately for him as well as for Jennifer, had caught a feverish cold and stayed in her room solacing herself with laudanum drops, *The Black Dwarf* and the latest issue of *La Belle Assemblée*. The Duchess had a cold too and a new maid who reduced her to frequent explosions of bad temper by her ignorance.

Jennifer was only too grateful for the excuse this offered her to stay at home and entertain her benefactress. She read *Tom Jones* aloud by the yard – for the Duchess thought nothing of the anonymous author of *Waverley* and immensely enjoyed Jennifer's blushes over the more scandalous passages in Fielding. When Jennifer's voice failed, they played piquet and Jennifer lost imaginary thousands to her astute opponent. As a last resource, the Duchess demanded to be entertained with gossip. What folly was the Princess of Wales committing now? And Lady Caroline Lamb? Was she really shut up in an asylum? Failing to answer these, and many other similar questions, Jennifer was more and more tempted to take her kind-hearted, bad-tempered patroness into her entire confidence and ask her advice. Only the difficulty of explaining Mainwaring's part in the affair held her back. She hesitated, somehow, at the thought of describing the ups and downs of their relationship to this all too acute listener. For she was only too well aware of the Duchess's intentions for her grandson. They had been made almost brutally plain. He was to marry his Sussex heiress and lead the Whig party. Nor, she told herself, did she wish him any other fate, though she reserved the right to feel a little sorry for the unknown heiress. If it occurred to her, sometimes, that she was an heiress herself, and quite capable of handling a constituent or organising a political dinner, she suppressed the thought. It was perfectly clear to her that she would never marry: good causes and a companion were her fate.

Just the same, it would be an immense relief to have the Duchess's advice as to how to extricate herself from her immediate predicament. In fact, one rainy morning when the hours had dragged by particularly slowly, when *Tom Jones* was finished and the Duchess's cough was worse, she decided to yield to temptation. After all, the story of the masquerade at Watier's was calculated to delight the wicked old Duchess: it would be true kindness to tell her about it.

But they were interrupted. A footman came in with the post. None, of course, for Jennifer, whose total lack of out of town correspondence was, unknown to her, a source of much speculation in the servants' hall.

The Duchess riffled through hers. 'Ah,' she said with satisfaction. 'Mainwaring at last. Let us hope that milk-and-water miss of his has been prevailed upon to name the day.' She read; she beamed upon Jennifer. It was settled. The wedding would be a quiet country affair in deference to the recent mourning of both parties. Telling Jennifer all this, the Duchess thought it best not to mention a certain lack of enthusiasm in Mainwaring's tone. He was to be married; that was enough. Enthusiasm might – or might not – come later.

It was indeed enough for Jennifer. The room was stifling hot. Her head ached. She jumped at the excuse offered by a dwindling supply of tincture of lavender. No, no need to send a footman, who would certainly return with the wrong kind. She knew exactly what the Duchess liked. She would get it herself.

If the Duchess saw through the pretext, she was, for once, too kind to say so. Instead, she urged Jennifer to take advantage of the rain's having ceased and go for a turn in the Park. 'Take that horse of yours with the absurd name. The air and exercise will do you good. I have been a selfish old monster to keep you here tied to a sick bed so long. And mind you talk to everyone you meet and bring me back a prime collection of the *on dits* of the town.'

It was dismissal and Jennifer took it, thankfully, as such. But she took her troubles with her. James, the groom, who had become something of a privileged companion, took one look at her ravaged face and left her undisturbed by his usual conversational openings. She rode on ahead of him, silent, preoccupied and wretched.

She was roused from her depressing thoughts by a shout from the other side of Park Lane. 'Jenny! Hey, Jenny!'

She looked up in astonishment at the nickname, then paled at sight of her uncle's ward, Edmund Butts. What was he doing in London? Was he helping in the search for her? For a moment she was tempted to put Starlight to an indecorous gallop and escape into the park, but wiser councils prevailed. There was no need to tell Edmund where she was staying, and no reason to suppose he was really looking for her. It had been all too clear at their last interview that there were few things he desired less than marriage with her. Away from his uncle, he might even prove an ally. She reined in Starlight and waited patiently while Edmund dodged between a smart barouche and a shabby travelling carriage and came over to join her.

'Jenny, by all that's wonderful. Where have you been hiding yourself all this time?'

She looked down at him gravely. 'I do not know that I will tell you, Edmund.'

'Not tell? But, Jenny, you quite mistake the matter. I am run away from Uncle Gurning too. That is why I am so glad to see you, for, to deal plainly with you, I have not a feather left to fly with. I had no notion life in London was so dear. And poor Elizabeth is in no better case.'

'Elizabeth? Is she here too? What madness is this? But, come, we cannot stay talking here. Walk with me into the park and you shall tell me your whole history.' She turned to the groom who had been an all too interested audience to their interchange, sent him off to fetch the Duchess's tincture of lavender and told him to come back for her in half an hour. 'My cousin will stay with me till you return.'

The man was too well trained to show his surprise at Miss Fairbank's finding a strange cousin in Park Lane and went obediently off to do her bidding. Once in the park, Edmund looked up at Jennifer pleadingly. 'Jenny, we are in the greatest straits, Elizabeth and I . . . And it is all your fault, too.'

She looked at him in amazement: 'My fault? What absurdity is this?'

'It is nothing of the kind. If you had not run off like that none of this would have happened to us. Indeed, you are in honour bound to help us.'

'I will certainly do everything possible, if you will tell me what's the matter. But lose no time about it, I beg. We may momently meet one of my acquaintance and I must know how to explain you to them. I am passing as Miss Fairbank, by the way.'

'Miss Fairbank? I cannot think it right for you to be masquerading under an assumed name, Jenny. I am much afraid your whole proceedings are very far from being the thing. What Elizabeth's feelings will be is more than I like to consider, and indeed I wonder whether I should ask you to visit her. The poor angel's position is so delicate already I feel that I cannot be too careful.'

She lost patience with him as she so often had before. 'For pity's sake, Edmund, this is no time to be reading me a lecture. Tell me instead what you are doing in London and whether Elizabeth is truly here too. I only hope you have not ruined her, between you.'

'Nothing of the kind, Jenny, and besides, I collect you are in no case to accuse me of impropriety. It is true that Elizabeth has left her father's protection but I assure you she could do no other. And since she was bound she would come I could not but offer her my escort for the journey. But I assure you she is very respectably settled with her mother's sister, Mrs Foster, in Holborn.'

'Holborn?' Jennifer was enough in the social swim by now to recognise this as a deplorable address. 'And no doubt you are in Cheapside?'

'No, no,' he said seriously. 'Mrs Foster found me a very eligible lodging in the Strand, but,' he hesitated for a moment, 'but to deal plainly with you, Jenny, I am sadly pressed for money. It was like a miracle when I saw you.'

'I hardly think you will find it one,' said Jennifer dryly. 'My pockets are far from well lined either, but I will do my best to help, if you will but tell me what folly has brought you and Elizabeth jauntering to London without, I apprehend, my uncle's permission.'

'I should think so indeed,' said Edmund proudly. 'You think you are the only person with enough spirit to run away, Jenny, but believe me the case is quite other. You should have seen poor Elizabeth's tears and her despair in the stage-coach.'

If Jennifer thought tears and despair an odd manifestation of spirit, she wisely forbore to say so, pressing instead for an explanation of their elopement.

'Elopement?' He reddened at the word. 'It is no such thing, Jenny. I will not have Elizabeth so slandered. She has done me the great honour of entrusting herself to my protection and of course I cannot but hope – but indeed, Jenny, no word of love has crossed my lips. The poor angel has been browbeaten enough as it is.'

'Browbeaten? Elizabeth? But she was ever the apple of my uncle's eye. I beg of you, Edmund, quit your prosing and *explain*.'

He looked affronted. 'I am doing my poor best to do so, Jenny, only you will keep interrupting.'

'I do no such thing,' she began angrily, then caught his eye, laughed and apologised. 'Proceed with your story. I am all ears.'

'Well you must know that after you fled the house in that hoydenish way – for indeed climbing out of a window in the dark is what no right-minded young female would think of doing . . .' He caught her furious eye and closed his parenthesis in a hurry. 'Well, the long and the short of it is that Uncle Gurning went off after you in a rage, and returned without you in – as you can imagine – no better temper. Even Aunt was afraid when she saw his face, and you know she does not usually notice his passions. As for me, I kept out of his way, for fear he should blame me for not wooing you harder, but how could I when my heart was another's?'

'Elizabeth's?'

'Always. How could one live in the same house with that angel without . . . But I digress. Uncle said nothing about you, but it was evident he had not found you. A few days passed. He went about the house like a thunder-cloud. Even his bitch Flora kept out of his way. Then, one day, all was changed. Uncle Gurning came to dinner all smiles – but Elizabeth's eyes were red with weeping.'

'Again?' asked Jennifer, but luckily he did not hear her.

'She made an opportunity to be alone with me after tea and told me all. Would you believe such villainy, Jenny? Uncle Gurning insisted that she allow him to pass her off to Ferris – or whatever his name is now – as you.'

'As me?'

'Yes. He said Ferris had never met either of you and it could make no difference to him which he married. All he wants, it seems, is a girl who can act as hostess for his political parties – and, a fortune, of course, but uncle said that with his prospects it could not signify whether he got your £80,000 or what he can give Elizabeth.'

'Infamous,' said Jennifer. 'And what did Elizabeth do? Wept I apprehend.'

'You do not understand her sensibility, Jenny. Her own father, too! How could she hold out against him? Particularly – well, you know Uncle Gurning. He is not of the gentlest when his temper is up.'

'No,' agreed Jennifer. 'He most certainly is not. So my cousin Elizabeth was prepared to masquerade as me. What, I wonder, caused her to change her mind?'

'Why, the man himself. He came next day to make his proposal in form. A great black-browed brute of a Corinthian, Jenny, old enough to be my poor angel's father. A bow-window dandy if ever I saw one, polished and prinked as if he was in St James's instead of Sussex, and proud as the devil with it all.

Treats me as if I were a country lobby, scarce grants a polite word to my uncle and aunt – not that I cared a fig for that – and reduces my poor little Lizzy to strong hysterics.'

'To his face? What a droll betrothal!'

'No, no. After he had left. You must understand that he merely stayed one night; had not even the courtesy to stay to dinner next day after he had seen poor Lizzy, but called for his curricle and was off, back no doubt to his boon companions at Watier's. And leaves us in a fine pucker, with Lizzy in the vapours, my uncle swearing at her for not encouraging my lord's suit – as if that brute needed encouraging. Why, he'd make a mouthful of Lizzy. Someone like you would be more up to his weight, Jenny. You were never troubled with my poor darling's sensibility.'

'No, I collect you think me a complete amazon. But tell me how this fragile Elizabeth of yours nerved herself to so desperate an expedient as flight.'

'What else could she do? With her father talking settlements and her mother talking bride-gowns!'

'She did not think to tell her wooer of the deceit that was being practised on him? That I apprehend would have settled his business fast enough.'

'Tell him? Why the poor child was too terrified even to look at him. And besides, my uncle was listening outside the door the whole time.'

'Oh,' said Jennifer. 'That, I grant you, is another story. So the poor child took her courage in both hands and ran away with you.'

'Yes, was it not famous? We planned it that very day, but of course we waited until her situation became desperate before we put it into execution. If only there had been more time . . . But hardly two weeks passed before my lord wrote another of his bullying letters: he is urgent to have the knot tied as soon as possible. He will do himself the honour of visiting us the next day (no more notice than that, Jenny) in the hope that Miss Purchas (of course he calls poor Lizzy that) may be persuaded to name the day. And all this, I may tell you, without one word of kindness for my poor little Lizzy, but as curt and matter of fact as if he had been taking delivery of a bale of goods. It was too much for Lizzy: I feared she might be too affected to put our plan into execution.'

'Strong hysterics again?' asked Jennifer.

'No, the vapours. But she mastered herself heroically next morning and told my aunt she needed a ride in the park to cool her head. Of course Aunt sent me along as her escort and we showed them a clean pair of heels. Only I could wish that when Lizzy went to my uncle's desk she had found more than ten pounds in it.'

'She robbed her father's desk, did she? Most exquisitely sensitive.'

He reddened angrily. 'Jenny, you are not kind. What else could we do? You know what a short stint my uncle keeps us on. I could not even have paid our shot on the stage-coach to London. And, besides, it is hardly robbery when it is her own father. But the devil of it is, it was not more. For though her Aunt Foster received her kindly enough, it is all too plain she is terrified of her brother and dares not shelter her for more than a day or so at the most. By a fortunate chance, my uncle is promised to speak at a meeting of the Hampden Club tonight and will not, I apprehend, miss it even to seek for Lizzy who, besides, left him a most confusing missive which will, I trust, keep him for some time in a puzzle as to what she intends.'

Jennifer laughed. 'Every moment, my cousin and my uncle reveal new depths. She is a mistress of duplicity and he cares more for his political career than for his daughter. But I have no doubt you are right. Only, what advantage do you propose to take of these few days' start?'

'Why, marry Lizzy, of course. Then we are safe.'

'Edmund, you amaze me. I thought you had not spoken one word of love to her.'

'And no more have I, for how could I take such advantage of the poor innocent? But I must be able to protect her. Have you forgot, Jenny, that when I marry I obtain control of my fortune and can snap my fingers at my uncle? It is but to obtain a special licence and we can marry tomorrow. I have no fears of Lizzy . . .'

'A special licence? But are they not vastly expensive?'

'Yes, and that is why I am so glad to see you, Jenny. If you could lend me £50, purely as a loan, of course, until I am in control of my own estate, I will be indebted to you for ever.'

'£50!' She looked at him in amazement. 'But, Edmund, I have not £5.'

'What! Jenny, you are roasting me. That hat you have on cost more.'

Jennifer coloured. It was as impossible as it was distasteful to explain her real circumstances to Edmund. 'Yes,' she said, 'I suppose I do give an appearance of affluence, but truly Edmund it is deception, I am as much to pieces as you are.'

'I must, of course, believe you.' He clearly did nothing of the kind. 'Then we are undone. My uncle will certainly reach town tomorrow and if we are not married by then my poor little Lizzy will never be able to stand up to him.'

'No,' said Jenny, 'I do not suppose that she will. But wait a minute. I have an idea. I have my pearls with me. If I can but sell them. But how?'

'Sell your mother's pearls! Jenny, you must not. But you could borrow on them.'

'No, I thank you Edmund. I am not such a gudgeon as that. If I sell them, it's done; if I borrow on them, there's no end to it. I remember too well the lecture my father read Richard when he went to Howard and Gibbs for money to pay his college debts: I never saw him so angry. No, I have quite made up my mind. I will take the pearls to Gray's the jewellers. I have some acquaintance with Mr Gray and he will do the business for me. And I will visit you and Lizzy tomorrow and bring the money with me.'

He was too pleased at the idea of the loan to quibble over how it was to be procured. 'I knew you would stand our friend, Jenny. I will never forget this. How overjoyed Lizzy will be when she hears my good news.' He wrung her hand warmly and was turning to leave her when she called him back.

'Stay a minute, Edmund.' She had been thinking rapidly. 'I believe it would be best if you accompanied me to Gray's to-morrow. I could not easily explain such an errand, but if you

will meet me here at this time it will be easy for me to find some
pretext to send the groom home with Starlight and accompany
you to Holborn. Then you will be able to take the money and
obtain your special licence at once. And indeed I think that
would be wise. I cannot believe that even politics will keep my
uncle in the country beyond tomorrow.'

'I very much fear you are right. Till tomorrow then. For
here, if I mistake not, is your groom. You are mighty well
attended, Jenny.'

'Am I not?' she smiled, said no more, and left him.

CHAPTER XIV

Back in Grosvenor Square, Jennifer found the Duchess visibly
better. Mainwaring's letter had acted as a tonic. The old lady
was simultaneously teasing her maid, trying on wigs and considering whether to go to the opera, the play, or Lady Bessborough's drum. Appealed to, Jennifer strongly recommended
the opera. The crush at a drum, she said, would be the worst
possible thing for anyone in the Duchess's precarious state of
health. This was true enough, but privately Jennifer was thinking that Mandeville was no devotee of opera and that even if he
should, by ill luck, be there, it would be easier to avoid him
there than at Lady Bessborough's.

She found she had been mistaken. Mandeville's quizzing
glass was soon focused on the Duchess's box and he joined
them in the first interval. The Duchess was delighted. She had
observed his attentions to Jennifer and thought that a proposal
from him would be a most eligible way of rectifying what she
felt to be Jennifer's precarious position. With Mainwaring's
marriage a settled thing, it seemed to her more important than
ever that his equivocal, if all too attractive protégée should be
suitably disposed of. So, on Mandeville's appearance, she said
she felt faint and asked for her vinaigrette. Jennifer had already
played into her hands by showing an unguarded enthusiasm for
the opera. The Duchess wilted still more. She had been foolish
to come; she should have had more sense; her cold was growing
worse every minute; her head ached; in short, she must go
home to bed. Only – she did not want to spoil Miss Fairbank's
evening. Mandeville was at once all eagerness to oblige. He
would be delighted to see the Duchess safe home – still more
delighted, he made it clear, to stay and keep Miss Fairbank
company. And as to a chaperon – was not Lady Beresford in
the very next box?

In vain did Jennifer beg to be allowed to accompany the

Duchess home. It was most unsuitable that she should go alone; she would catch more cold . . . The Duchess laughed at her; her company, though delightful, was hardly a specific against the cold. Besides, she had been joined by an old friend, a General Sir Somebody-or-Other Something (Jennifer never did catch his name) who had known the Duchess all her life, and her husband in happier times. He would see her home and they would talk about the good old days and that never-to-be-forgotten one when the Duchess smuggled herself into the House of Commons with his help. It was all most satisfactory – except to Jennifer.

Left alone with Mandeville, she rose at once to go and join Lady Beresford in her adjoining box. But Mandeville felt the opportunity too good to be wasted. He took her hand to detain her.

'Charming Miss Fairbank, one word. You think me, I fear, your enemy; you must allow me this chance to tell you how truly I long for your forgiveness; how earnestly I wish to be considered your friend.'

She withdrew her hand. 'You will best show your friendship, Mr Mandeville, by conducting me at once to Lady Beresford's box. It is most improper for me to remain here alone with you.'

'Divine Miss Fairbank,' he had her hand again. 'What courage! What spirit! I confess it is impossible not to admire you. To think that you, of all people, dare speak of impropriety.'

'I do not understand you, sir.'

'My dearest creature, I would not pain you for the world, but I must tell you that I know all.'

'Indeed? You are pleased to be mysterious, sir. What, pray, does this formidable "all" of yours consist of?'

'Why, of your inevitable disgrace, my dear, if I was not kindly disposed towards you. It is one thing to disport yourself with Harriette Wilson and her kind at Watier's. That, though bad enough, might perhaps be glossed over as a girlish frolic. But to have let Lord Mainwaring pass you off – you, an ex-governess, a nobody, if not worse – upon his grandmother: that, I collect, my dear, could never be lived down.'

She made a gallant effort to rally: 'I do not know what you are talking of, sir.'

'I think you do. But I wonder if you have considered all the implications of your frolic – if it is no worse. Supposing that I was to whisper to a few of my friends that Mainwaring had passed his ladybird off on his grandmother as sterling ware. Imagine the talk of the town tomorrow. And imagine the effect on the Duchess! Scandal, I grant you, is the air she breathes, but to find herself the centre of so unsavoury a one as that! It would kill her, my dear creature; most indubitably it would kill her. And as for Mainwaring: it might not exactly kill him, but it would most effectively put paid to the political future he sets such store by. You are silent, my dearest life. I fear I have discomposed you. But do not fret, and pout, and stamp your little foot at me. You think me a monster, I can see, but I will prove to you that I am no such thing. I have no desire to kill the Duchess, nor yet to ruin Mainwaring, though, God knows, he has given me cause enough. Your secret is safe with me. But on condition . . .'

'Oh, conditions?' Jennifer, whose hopes had incorrigibly leapt up, despaired again.

'Well, yes, I am a man of the world, my dear, and I do not give something for nothing.'

'Not even silence?' asked Jennifer bitterly.

'Particularly not silence. Only think what a nine days' wonder it would be. What a story to have the starting of. What a revenge for this,' his good hand touched the sling that still supported his wounded arm. 'No, no, I must be bribed, my love, bribed and cajoled into silence.'

Jennifer's hopes dwindled and died. 'How?'

'Why, in the oldest way, the pleasantest way in the world. Your situation, I apprehend, is not of the easiest. If I do not discover you today, someone else will tomorrow. There is nothing before you but disgrace and disaster. Avoid them by leaving the Duchess and accepting my protection now – this very night if you will. I promise you every comfort, every luxury, and my unqualified adoration.'

She looked at him very straight out of deep blue eyes. 'You

are not, I apprehend, proposing marriage.'

'Well, no,' he laughed, a trifle awkwardly, 'be reasonable, my dear creature. It is hardly a case for that, is it?'

Jennifer was silent, fighting a mixture of rage and terror. It was all true. He had it in his power to ruin not only her but Mainwaring and, perhaps, his grandmother. This was not the moment to show the fury she felt; she must temporise, think, play for time. Her silence had lasted too long already.

'Well, Miss Fairbank,' he asked. 'I await your answer. Come, my dearest creature, be reasonable. We will deal admirably together, you and I. Shall we go to Paris? You would, perhaps, be happiest out of London for a space, and, to be plain with you,' again the sensitive hand touched his sling, 'so will I. An apartment in the Rue St Honoré now; I can just see you there, and myself, the happiest of men, at your side.'

'Can you?' she looked up at him, thinking, thinking . . .

'And moreover,' he played what he considered to be a trump card, 'I have it on good authority that your friend Mainwaring is to marry forthwith. You can hardly wish to remain in London and see some country nobody my ladying it at his side. You have played your cards ill, my dear, but trust me to make your losses good.'

There was, horribly, something in what he said. She let him see her waver. 'I do not know; I had not considered . . . It is true that my position is not an easy one. Sir,' she seemed to make up her mind. 'You must give me time. Let me sleep on your . . .' she hesitated for a word . . . 'on your proposition. Paris, it is true . . . Paris, they say, in the spring time . . . Send to me tomorrow for my answer. I must consider, you understand, how most honourably to remove myself from her grace's protection.'

'Oh, never trouble your pretty head about that.' He was sure, now, that he had her. 'You will care little enough for her, and such as her, when you are safe with me.'

That would, she was sure, be all too true, nor, of course, would they care for her. If she had needed it, these thoughts strengthened her resolve to escape him at all costs. But how to ensure that he should not, in his fury at being rejected, publish his slanderous story and destroy Lord Mainwaring? No time to think of that now: she must get away from him and, for the moment, continue to play his game. She smiled up at him: 'And now,' she said, 'indulge, I beg you, my missish notions for tonight, and take me to Lady Beresford.'

He laughed and obeyed. The hand that guided her lay hotter and heavier on her arm than usual, but she pretended not to notice. For the rest of the evening, she sat in a daze, doing her best to return his gallantries, and all the time thinking, planning, rejecting one project after another, hardly aware of what went on around her. At last she was safely home in Grosvenor Square, grateful, for once, for Lady Beresford's safe conduct home. Odd, she thought, dismissing her maid, that she had indeed come to think of the Duchess's house as home.

The word, with its inevitable thoughts of her real home, gave her her cue. That was where she must go. She must give herself up to her uncle's mercy and accept the match he had planned for her. Only thus could she at once escape Mandeville's advances and tie his hands. Miss Purchas's engagement had been given out; the marriage would follow immediately; Miss Fairbank would disappear as if she had never been. And at least, she consoled herself, it should be easier, now, to deal with her uncle, whose embarrassment must at least equal her own. Perhaps, by good management, they might be made to cancel each other out. Since Elizabeth had run away, Uncle Gurning must be in despair as to what to tell her betrothed. Well, he might tell him the truth: that a substitution had been planned but had failed. Here, he could say, and prove it, was the true heiress, the real Miss Purchas, fortune and all, ready, nay eager, to marry him. For it had come to this, thought Jennifer, pulling the comb savagely through her hair, after all her gallant attempts (for she still respected herself for them) she must be grateful if the wooer she had run away from would consent to marry her. For in marriage, it was clear, lay her only salvation, and, more important, that of Mainwaring and the Duchess. Only as a married woman, as – what was the man's name? – as Mrs Ferris could she afford to snap her fingers at Mandeville's threats. And, after all, why should Ferris complain? He had never pretended to want anything but a hostess and a fortune. He would get both. And, from what Edmund had said, she had not got the impression that he had been particularly pleased with Elizabeth's timid charms.

Black-browed and a bully, Edmund had said . . . Resolutely, she put away the thought of someone else who was black-browed and, often, bullying. Mainwaring's marriage was a settled thing. She might just as well have this Ferris. But she must lose no time . . . It was of the first importance that she reach her uncle before he discover Elizabeth and Edmund. What was best to do?

Then she thought again. Her uncle had no terrors for her now. He was still more deeply embroiled than she. Why not go to Elizabeth in Holborn, explain the situation to her, and wait there for Uncle Gurning to arrive, as doubtless he would, breathing fire and fury, in the course of tomorrow. Her unexpected presence would quite take the wind out of his sails. He would, no doubt, be only too relieved to hear that she was prepared to ignore his double-dealing and marry Ferris at last, and would, she thought, in all probability give his consent to Elizabeth's marrying Edmund. On this thought, she fell asleep.

Rising early next morning, she wrote two notes. The first, to the Duchess, was comparatively easy. It expressed her heartfelt thanks for all the kindness she had received, then went on to say that she had recognised, she feared rather late in the day, how odd her presence in Grosvenor Square must seem to the world. 'I do not blame people for thinking ill of me,' she went on. 'My dear madam, I should never have so trespassed on your great kindness. I am doing now, what I should have done at first, going back where I belong.' With further protestations of gratitude, she signed and sealed the letter, refusing to let herself add any message to Mainwaring, then turned to the more difficult of the two – that to Mandeville.

This one called for much diplomacy and some pen-chewing. He must not be enraged into precipitate action. She drafted and redrafted, finally achieved a version that almost satisfied her. 'Sir,' she wrote, 'I must do myself the honour of declining your proposals. But at the same time, let me thank you with all my heart for the plain speaking that has brought home to me the true danger of my position. I tell you solemnly that I am innocent of all but folly, and my lord and his grandmother of all but ill-placed kindness. I am returning to those whose duty it is to protect me and I warn you that I hope soon to have a husband who will take any action necessary to defend my good name. If you carry out your last night's threats, you will regret it most bitterly.' She stopped and reread it. It would do, she thought, remembering his cowardly behaviour over his duel with Lord Mainwaring. It would frighten him ... Anyway (she signed and sealed it, then addressed it in her neat small hand) it would have to do.

For time was passing. The Duchess would soon awaken and send for her. She wished, at all costs, to avoid the pain of a final interview. Ringing, she gave the two notes to a puzzled footman, and ordered the groom and Starlight to be summoned. She would be early for her rendezvous with Edmund, but that did not matter. It was, to be sure, slightly inconvenient that she would have to face the world equipped with nothing but her favourite green riding habit, but Elizabeth or her aunt would doubtless lend her whatever she immediately needed, and as soon as she had had her *éclaircissement* with her uncle she could go home to Sussex.

It was a happy thought. In the park, birds were singing, trees in leaf. In Sussex, summer would be in full splendour, with sunshine heavy on the hills. It was time she went home. She put Starlight to a canter, partly to banish less happy thoughts, partly to avoid any of her acquaintance who might have been lured by June sunshine to come out so much before the fashionable hour. This was no day for the rubbed coin of society small talk. She wanted to be alone to face alike her past and her future.

Lucky for once, she saw no one. Edmund appeared, meticulously prompt upon his hour, his plain, conscientious face red with hurry. Seeing him, she felt her first qualm. Would it all be so easy as she had thought? But the die was cast now. The Duchess was no doubt sitting up in bed, sipping chocolate and reading her note. Mandeville might well have received his.

There was no going back. Instead, she must go forward as rapidly as possible. This was no place to be loitering.

She turned to the groom: 'I have recollected an errand which I must do on foot, James. My cousin will accompany me. Do you take Starlight home.'

He looked at her doubtfully. All his training indicated implicit obedience, but it seemed to him that there was something very smokey indeed about this behaviour of Miss Fairbank's. And he had grown to like her. He ventured a protest. 'But, Miss Fairbank, I doubt her grace will be displeased.'

'I have explained everything to her grace,' Jennifer interrupted him. 'Do as you are bid, James, and do not come the old family retainer with me.'

He grinned ruefully and obeyed her without further protest.

Alone with Jennifer, Edmund looked at her with awe. 'Her grace?' he asked. 'You have been flying high, Jenny.'

'Yes,' she said. 'But it is a long story and one that I do not think I will burden you with at present. There is much else, more urgent, to be talked of. I have changed all my plans and do not intend selling my pearls after all. I am sure that you will be relieved to hear it.'

'Not sell them? But, Jenny, the money? The special licence?'

'Never trouble yourself about them. You will need neither. You may woo your Elizabeth in the most respectable leisure and wed her in Hanover Square. I am sure you will both infinitely prefer it.'

'Why, of course we should. My poor Lizzy was in tears only this morning because she would have no bride-clothes, and I confess to you that this hugger-mugger way of proceeding is not at all to my liking. But how is it to be contrived? I cannot believe that my uncle will not find us today, and my poor darling is but wax in his hands.'

'Never fear for that,' said Jennifer cheerfully. 'I am going to talk to Uncle Gurning myself and, if I mistake not, by the time I have finished with him he will be on his knees to you to marry Lizzy.'

'Shame on you, Jenny,' he flared up at once. 'You are not to slander the poor angel. I will not permit it.'

'Why should I? There is no need. The facts speak for themselves. Married she must be, and forthwith. What, ride to London with you in the common stage-coach? Oh, fie!'

She never could resist teasing Edmund and now he reacted exactly as she had expected. 'It is not half so bad as climbing out of the window in boy's clothes, or riding to town on horseback,' he said angrily.

'No, nor nearly so entertaining. But I am going to do penance, too. I am going to marry Ferris.'

'What?' he exclaimed. 'After all your heroics and gallivantings about the country to escape him! Jenny, I do not believe it.'

'You may well be surprised, Edmund, but it is true for all that. To deal plainly with you, I see no alternative. And you must see that it will make things vastly easier for you and Elizabeth. Once I reappear and claim my own name (which I can tell you I shall be glad to do, for I am heartily sick of being Miss Fairbank) my uncle will find himself in a sad quandary.'

Edmund's eyes sparkled. 'He will indeed. Jenny, this is famous. Let us hurry home and tell Elizabeth the good news.' He summoned a hackney carriage and helped her in. Neither of them noticed Miles Mandeville, who had been watching them fixedly for some minutes past from the vantage-point of his high perch phaeton. When Edmund called the hackney carriage, he muttered an oath to himself, turned his phaeton out of the park, and followed them to Holborn. Having seen Jennifer alight and enter a prosperous-looking house in this unfashionable district, he turned homeward, excessively puzzled. He had intended to call at the Duchess's house as early as he decently could and receive Jennifer's answer – which he was sure would be favourable – in person. Now, he changed his mind. Something odd was afoot; he would send for her answer instead.

By so doing, he missed a notable scene. The Duchess, a strong-minded woman, had not gone into hysterics when she read Jennifer's note, but she had lost her temper more completely than the servants could remember her doing since the day the Duke finally proved his madness by breaking every bottle and every looking-glass in the house. She was still scarifying the unfortunate groom, James, who had returned alone just as she was getting her second wind, when she was interrupted by the arrival of Lord Mainwaring in a temper even more savage than her own. They talked, or rather shouted, for a while at furious cross purposes, then, inevitably, the Duchess got the floor.

'They have let her run away, the dolts,' she said. 'The numskulls, the ninnyhammers; a parcel of idiot servants with not an eggsworth of wits between them. Took her farewell note with a "thank you, miss" and a "yes, miss" and did not even have the sense to wake me before my usual hour. And why she should be writing to Mad Mandeville at the same time is more than I can rightly understand. I have half a mind to open her letter and find out; for if this is not some plot of his and your Aunt Beresford's, I am very wide of the mark.'

Mainwaring, who had been trying in vain to make head or tail of this tirade, now intervened: 'My aunt? What has she to say to the matter? And who, pray has run away? Not Pamela, I trust.'

'Pamela indeed! What a slow-wit you are, George! No, it is your precious Miss Fairbank, of course. "Gone back where she belongs," she tells me, as calm as you please, with a parcel of "deepest gratitude" and "eternally indebted" and other rubbish of the kind. "Eternally indebted", she says, and goes off and leaves me just when I have taught her to wind my wool as I like and play a game of piquet that's worth the answering. "Deepest gratitude" and does not even tell me who she is, after all, or where she is going, or who has frighted her into this folly. I tell you, George, I am out of all patience.' Her angry old hands broke the fan she was holding and tossed the pieces aside. 'You will laugh at me, George, I have no doubt, but I had grown fond of the girl, and to have her run away like this: why, it has made me quite angry.'

Mainwaring, who had been struck speechless by her revelations, could not restrain an angry laugh of his own at this understatement. 'I see that it has, ma'am. But it cannot be so serious. She has gone off for the day – perhaps to some friend we do not know of.'

'Yes, a friend indeed. A red-faced bumpkin fresh up from the country: that fool James saw her meet him yesterday and arrange all this – and had not even the wits to mention the matter, so today off she goes with this "cousin" as cool as you please, sending James about his business when he tries to protest. I had thought at first it was Mandeville she was gone to, for I tell you George I had expected daily to have him propose for her hand, but it seems I was mistaken, for how else would she have left this note for him which I am now determined to open. Here, read you hers to me, while I see what she has to say to him.'

Mainwaring protested in vain against this high-handed behaviour and applied himself to reading Jennifer's letter to his grandmother, while she exclaimed over that to Mandeville. Then, with a near oath, he exchanged letters with her. 'So,' he said at last, 'Mandeville is a villain, as I always thought, and must be dealt with. Leave me alone for that, ma'am. But as for your Miss Fairbank, she seems well enough able to take care of herself. She is gone back where she belongs, she tells you, and does not think to mention – as she does here (an angry hand crumpled the note to Mandeville) that she has a husband in view. No doubt the country bumpkin James saw her keep assignation with. We have been mightily deceived in her. What does all this fine talk amount to? A few elegant phrases of thanks for those who have turned their lives topsy-turvy on her behalf. Excellent: "her undying gratitude" forsooth! "Nothing she can do to repay." She has certainly seen to it that there shall be nothing she can do.' He took a turn about the room, then returned to the sofa from which his grandmother was keeping an anxious eye out for explosions. 'She leaves you in the lurch, ma'am, in the very midst of the season, to run off God knows where and marry God knows whom. And she leaves,' (here, thought his grandmother, comes the heart of the matter) 'she leaves, for all her gratitude, without so much as a "thank you" for me, who brought her here in the first place. I tell you, ma'am, I thought I had had, already, enough to drive me to distraction, but this is the outside of enough. Well, why do you look at me like that? I collect you find me vastly entertaining.'

She smiled up at him, her own poise entirely restored by the collapse of his. 'Yes, George, I fear I do a little. If I understood your first fury aright, you arrived here in a state of distraction because your Sussex match is off again. Can you really be in such a rage about two young women at once? You are a regular bluebeard, George. I begin to think that Miss Fairbank's disappearance is not such a bad thing after all.'

'Not bad! You are pleased to jest, ma'am.'

'Not at all. To deal plainly with you, your Aunt Beresford has been pulling long faces at me these several weeks past about Miss Fairbank and her dubious position in this house and in society, and dropping such portentous hints about disgrace and disaster that I cannot but think it vastly considerate of the girl to have taken her own means to end a difficult situation. She is gone back, I have no doubt, like the sensible young woman I always took her for, to say "yes" to the match her family arranged for her. If it is indeed the country bumpkin, I am sorry for it, but trust Miss Fairbank to make something of him if she puts her mind to it. And at least she is taken care of. Mandeville has his answer (though you are right, I think a word from you in addition will do no harm); the voice of slander is stifled and you, George, are saved from a mighty awkward position. Had you considered how your country-mouse bride might feel about your knight-erranting it round London rescuing unknown damsels in Parliament Square? How are we to know some whiff of scandal has not reached them in the country and accounts for their blowing hot and cold on you? No, trust me, George, you should be grateful to Miss Fairbank for showing some sense at the last, and I am sorry I let myself get into such a passion about it. I can see there is nothing for it but to take Jane Beresford's youngest (what is her deplorable name – Clorinda!) and teach *her* piquet and my bad habits. Lord knows her mother has been angling for it long enough, and the child is certainly so plain that I should have her for some time on my hands. I have no doubt that that is exactly what Jane intended. She was ever a great schemer, was Jane.'

She spoke with a near approval that infuriated Mainwaring. 'So, I apprehend you believe my Aunt Beresford and Mandeville between them to have frightened Miss Fairbank with I know not what bug-a-boo of scandal so that she has quitted your protection and returned – at the best of it – to a match we know is abhorrent to her. And all this we are to look on as a matter for rejoicing. Ma'am, I have never found myself so out of patience with you. And as for my Aunt Beresford, let me but encounter her . . .'

He paused expressively, only to be taken up gaily by his grandmother: 'And so you shall, George, for if that is not the rattle of her ill-hung carriage in the square I am very much out of my reckoning. She will be with us as soon as she has given Tullett her day's catechism about my affairs. So hurry, George, and tell me what difficulty they are making in Sussex this time. Is the match truly postponed again?'

'Postponed, ma'am? If it were only that! No, I have never been so insulted in my life. The child is run off, gone, bolted – and all for fear of me, of her brothers' friend, who only offered for her out of kindness. I – ma'am – words fail me . . . They tried to keep it from me. That mealy mouthed vulgar aunt of hers waylaid me, on my arrival, with talk of the poor child's nerves – a bride's timidity – confined to her room – her uncle away, so sorry to disappoint me and much more rubbish of the kind. I had almost let her gull me, but they are not even good conspirators: in comes a servant all in a pother to say Miss and Master Edmund's horses have been found at the Swan in Petworth. Then it is all out: she is bolted, ma'am, and with that lubberly cousin I told you of, and her uncle gone after to bring them back. I shall be the laughing-stock of the town.' He paused, words really failing him at last.

She flashed him a humorous and not unsympathetic glance. 'Indeed, George, you do not seem over lucky with the ladies. Have you, do you think, been taking them a trifle for granted? And might you not be well advised to consider which of these runaways you really want, and concentrate on pursuing her?

153

But I hear Jane on the stairs. Do not call her out, George, I beg of you.'

He picked up Jennifer's note to Mandeville. 'I cannot trust my temper, ma'am, if I meet her now. With your permission I will retire and compose a covering note for this missive that shall send Mad Mandeville on his travels forthwith.'

She nodded approvingly. 'Do that, George. I will not have a guest in my house insulted. And besides,' she twinkled up at him mischievously, 'a little action may improve your temper.'

So Lady Beresford was half disappointed, half relieved, to find her mother alone.

'All alone, ma'am? I had hoped to find Mainwaring with you.'

'He has but this minute left me,' said her mother, and offered no further explanation. 'How are you, child?' She held up an unenthusiastic cheek to receive her daughter's dry kiss.

'Indifferent, mama. You know my wretched health.' For once she did not dwell upon it further. 'But what is this I hear of Miss Fairbank's being run off? I always thought you would find yourself much mistaken in that girl. Has she truly left you without a word? I never heard of such base ingratitude.'

The Duchess sat up straighter on her sofa. 'Now that is exactly what she has not done, Jane, and if I hear that you are spreading any of your malicious rumours to that effect, I shall change my mind about taking Clorinda in her place.'

'Taking Clorinda? Are you serious, ma'am?'

'Never more so. I have learned to like having a young creature about the place to bully, and Clorinda will do as well as another chit. She has her father's meek disposition and your long nose, so that I do not expect to be overmuch troubled with wooers. In short, she should suit me admirably. You will send her to me tomorrow, if you please.'

Lady Beresford, who had six daughters to bring out, thought it best to swallow the insults that accompanied this most welcome offer and after expressing effusive gratitude and prophesying Clorinda's transports at such an invitation, she returned, her sharp nose acquiver with curiosity, to the fascinating subject of Miss Fairbank. She had left a note had she? What did it say? Where was she gone? Might one . . . trembling at her own daring, she hinted a desire to see the note.

Her mother was short with her. 'No, Jane, it was addressed to me, and to me only. But I will tell you that Miss Fairbank is very properly gone home to her family and intends (here the old lady thought fit to draw on the letter to Mandeville) to make a very suitable match in the near future, so I would advise you to be excessively careful in what you say about her. I have my suspicions, Jane, as to what has led Miss Fairbank to take this step, and if you will be advised by me, you will not rouse me to look into the matter any more closely. As things have turned out, I am not altogether displeased that she has chosen to go home, but interference in my domestic arrangements is what I never have and never will tolerate. If you know what is good for you, Jane, you will be more careful in future . . . But what is this, another caller? I would seem to be keeping open house this morning.'

Lady Beresford, who had found her mother's last remarks come uncomfortably near the bone, was considerably relieved when Lady Laverstoke was announced, and appeared all agush with excitement.

'Oh, my dear Lady Beresford,' she exclaimed, 'have I found you at last. I beg your pardon, ma'am,' she turned to the Duchess, 'for this intrusion, but I declare I have been running after dear Lady Beresford all over the town, and with such a piece of news: I know it will delight you as much as it does her.'

The Duchess raised her eyebrows. 'You amaze me. It must be wonderful indeed so to move us both.'

'Oh it is, the very best in the world. I vow it quite threw me into one of my spasms when I first heard it: "Charles," I said, "not another word till you have fetched me my vinaigrette. I have never been so delighted in my life," I said: "you must fetch me my vinaigrette this instant." And there was the poor dear boy all in the midst of his passion and his adoration and a great deal more that was most excessively poetic; but he is a good boy, Jane – I am sure I may call you that now. Oh, I am so happy I do not know how to bear it. Anyway, the long and the short of it is, that he fetched me the vinaigrette like the good son he has always been to me and I am glad to be able to tell you the spasm is quite passed away and here I am able to come out and rejoice with you, my dearest Jane.'

'So we see,' said the Duchess dryly, 'but what, pray, is the reason for all this rejoicing?'

'Lord bless me, have I not told you? Really, my wits are all to pieces today; I am in such a seventh heaven, but I made sure I had explained. Why, not to make a Canterbury story of it, my dear Charles is going to propose for your sweet Pamela, Jane. Is it not famous news? I was never more astonished in my life than when he broke it to me over breakfast this morning: "Charles," I said, "I am so delighted my head is all in a whirl: you must fetch me my vinaigrette at once, or I will not be answerable for the consequences." And so he stops, right in the midst of "love" and "beloved", and goes like the good boy he is and fetches it for me – indeed, dear dear Pamela is an excessively lucky girl, though I do say so. Such a dear boy, who would never do anything without consulting his mother: and such an old lady as it makes me feel: only fancy having a son old enough to be married.' She waited in vain to be flattered and contradicted, realised she had mistaken her audience, and went on: 'But that is nothing to the question, and perhaps I shall surprise you all yet. Matrimony, they say, is catching . . . But how I do run on, I tell you I was never more overjoyed in my life. Dear Charles and sweet, sweet Pamela. It has been going on, Charles tells me, ever since we came to London, and I with no more idea than the man in the moon; but such meetings in the park, such waltzings, such languishings . . . Why, it positively makes me a girl again to hear of it.'

She stopped at last for breath, glancing eagerly from one lady to the other, waiting for their enthusiasm to match hers.

The Duchess spoke first: 'A very proper match,' she said. 'I felicitate you both. They are both young and both silly; they should deal admirably together. Charles's fortune is not large, I apprehend, but he is a viscount already and at least, thanks to Mainwaring's guardianship, the estate is unencumbered. And you, I collect, will not be able to do a great deal for Pamela,' she spoke, with a warning note in her voice, to Lady Beresford, whose face had throughout been a perfect study in chagrin.

'That is nothing to the purpose, ma'am,' she said now. 'For I am persuaded that Lady Laverstoke in her most understandable mother's enthusiasm has quite mistaken the matter. Charles may be in love with Pamela – it is natural enough – he is at the age for such infatuations; boyish fancies that will soon be forgotten. But as for Pamela, she, if I mistake not (and I seldom do) is looking in quite another direction. Have you not noticed, ma'am,' caution thrown to the winds, she turned to her mother, 'how her eyes follow dear Mainwaring about the room, and how he has begun to address himself to her? His bringing her home the other night was such a signal attention: why, it put her into quite a flutter. And what could be more suitable? With her beauty and his brains . . .'

But the Duchess had gone off into a paroxysm of silent laughter, while Lady Laverstoke who had been fidgeting agitatedly with her vinaigrette throughout this unguarded speech, now burst out: 'Pamela marry Mainwaring? Fiddlestick! Why, he is old enough to be her father and wise enough to fly after higher game. I had not intended to mention the matter; for indeed it is a most delicate subject; but in fairness to everyone; since such false hopes seem to have been raised; I think it only right to tell you that I am confident Mainwaring only waits till Charles is settled in life before he pays his addresses to me, and I . . . I . . .' She let a delicate blush finish the sentence for her.

'You are a couple of idiots,' said the Duchess roundly. 'I never heard such a parcel of nonsense in my life. Are you not aware that George is betrothed to a young lady in Sussex?'

'Oh yes,' said Lady Laverstoke sweetly, 'his sense of duty, you know, but his *heart* is not in it. You will see: he will cry off.'

'Yes, indeed,' chimed in Lady Beresford, 'it has been clear enough from the start that *that* affair would come to nothing. But as for these delusions of yours, Lavinia, I tell you you are out of your mind.'

Lady Laverstoke's coy blush had deepened into one of anger.

'You are pleased to laugh at me, Lady Beresford. I tell you; you will regret this.'

But it was the Duchess who was laughing. 'My poor dear creatures,' she said, controlling herself with difficulty. 'I do not know when I have been so entertained. I find myself vastly indebted to you both, for indeed I was in the dumps and, to deal plainly with you, this loss of Miss Fairbank has left me thoroughly blue-devilled.'

'Loss of Miss Fairbank?' Lady Laverstoke looked her surprise.

'Ah, you have not heard yet? You do not, I collect, acquire information quite so fast as my dear Jane here. Yes, Miss Fairbank has left me. She is gone back to her family to make, she tells me, the highly suitable match she disliked so much in the first place. But that is not, I should warn you both, at all what I expect to have happened. Since you have both been so mightily indiscreet, I think I will blab a little too, to keep you in countenance. George is back in town. You knew, (to Lady Beresford) 'you did not' (to Lady Laverstoke). 'But neither of you knows why he is come. You were right on one point: that country miss of his has given him the slip at last: I am persuaded she will have none of him in the end and that he will be vastly relieved (if either of you breathes a word of this outside this room you will have me to reckon with). So far, indeed you have understood aright: that match will come to nothing. But do you seriously think he will throw away his freedom on your ripe charms' (to Lady Laverstoke) 'or Pamela's raw ones' (to Lady Beresford). Surely if you have eyes in your heads, you must have seen that *he* has eyes for no one but Miss Fairbank? If he finds her before she marries, he'll have her. If not – I pity her husband. There: now you know where you stand. If you will be ruled by me, you will forget all that has passed in this room today and clap hands on a bargain over Charles and Pamela. An excellent, dull match. Now, I am tired. Will you ring, Jane?'

The two ladies took the hint (if such it could be called) and withdrew in mutual and silent fury, to their carriages. At home, Lady Beresford sent for Pamela, gave her the worst half-hour of her life and finally bowed to the inevitable. She was fool enough to throw away all her chances and love Charles Laverstoke: very well, she was doubtless fit for nothing better: she might as well have him. As for Lady Laverstoke, her recovery was still quicker. In her carriage she remembered Mainwaring's bad temper; half-way down Brook Street it occurred to her that he would very likely be mean about pin-money, and in the park she caught sight of an old gallant of hers whose existence she had forgotten. By the time she got home, she had a new love and a new hope.

CHAPTER XV

Arriving in Holborn, Jennifer was surprised at the size and appearance of Aunt Foster's house, and delighted with Aunt Foster herself who hurried downstairs to greet her with such unaffected warmth and kindness that she felt she, too, might be her niece.

'My dear Miss Purchas,' said Aunt Foster, taking her warmly by the hand, 'this is an unexpected pleasure. My poor Lizzy will be overjoyed to see you, for there is no concealing that she has been sadly down in the dumps since she came to me. She's as good a girl as ever drew breath, and this defying of her father sits very ill with her. I cannot conceive of what her mother was about to let the poor child be forced into so disagreeable a position: but then poor Maria was ever shatter-brained and too terrified of my brother to cross him in anything. But come you up, my dear Miss Purchas, for I know my poor lamb is all agog to see you. And to tell truth, the sooner matters are settled between you all, the better I shall be pleased, for one of my brother Gurning's tantrums is what I have no desire in the world to encounter. And as for you, Edmund, I thought you were to be off at once and procure that special licence you spoke of, for though I cannot at all approve of so desperate a proceeding, yet I do not see how else you are to contrive, for have my poor Lizzy here beyond today I dare not.' This sentence brought her to the head of the second pair of stairs, and, with a parenthetical apology for bringing Jennifer up so high, she flung open a door and continued: 'But I doubt my poor Lizzy will be pleased enough to see you, Edmund, just the same, and it will be a regular tonic for her to see Miss Purchas, for cast off by her family is what she has been expecting to be, and in tears about it the whole morning long, the poor innocent. But what am I thinking for to be keeping you tittle-tattling here, Miss Purchas? Come you in and give the poor child a good kiss and tell her all is forgiven, for I tell you she has been in such a pother at the thought of having lent herself to anything so wicked as impersonating you, that I can tell you there has been no doing anything with her. There, Lizzy, see who has come to kiss and be friends!'

Elizabeth, who had been drooped upon a sofa, jumped up and ran to Jennifer. 'Oh, Jenny, is it really you and do you truly forgive me? Indeed, indeed, I never meant to harm you, and have felt so wicked ever since, I cannot bear even to think of it. I thought I would go distracted for very joy when Edmund came last night and said he had met you and told you All and you were not angry, for, indeed, Jenny, I would not blame you if you never spoke to me again, only I tell you I could not bear it and would very likely die of grief.'

Jennifer gave her a kiss and a bracing pat on the back, very much as if she had been a child with hiccups. 'No, no, Lizzy, I beg of you do not start to cry again: I can forgive anything in the world but that, and your eyes are quite red enough already. Besides, there is nothing to be forgiven, for, to deal plainly with you, I find myself much beholden to you. Do you not see that by falling in with his plan to marry you in my stead, you have delivered my uncle into my hands? It is but to threaten exposure, and he cannot help but do what I demand. I shall be my own mistress at last, and you shall marry Edmund (if that is in truth your wish) at leisure in all the gauze and illusion your heart can desire.'

Elizabeth's tear-drowned eyes began to shine. 'Oh, Jenny, what a wonderful girl you are! I knew all our troubles were over once Edmund had found you. Oh, how happy I am! Can I really have bride-clothes, and favours, and a honeymoon just like everybody else? Of course I do love Edmund dearly, dearly, but, Jenny, a girl only gets married once, and to do it in such a hustle-bustle, with no proper announcement, or wedding gifts or anything, and all in some hole and corner of a city church, when I had always meant to be married in Denton Chapel with bridesmaids, and primroses on the window-sills and mother in tears ... Oh, Jenny, can I really have it all just as I planned it?'

Jennifer patted her hand soothingly and darted a quick glance at Edmund to see how he was taking his prospective bride's childish raptures. But he was gazing at her with fond enthusiasm: they would make an admirable pair. 'Yes,' she said, 'if you will just dry your eyes and compose yourself, Lizzy, and do exactly as I bid you, you shall have it all exactly so, if I have to give you away myself. But I have no doubt your father will be prepared to hear reason, by the time I have finished with him. But listen! Can this be he already?'

For a violent knocking had sounded on the street door below and now sounds of altercation rose up the stairwell and in at the open door of the room. Mrs Foster, who had been a sympathetic observer of all that passed, stood as if turned to stone, Edmund went red and Elizabeth white. Jennifer eyed them all with wry amusement. They were not, she thought, a very promising set of allies. But – how odd it was – she herself had lost all her fear of her uncle's blusterings. It seemed absurd now that she had ever let him impose upon her. At any rate, those days were done, as he would soon discover.

An agitated maidservant appeared at the door. 'Excuse me, ma'am, Mr Gurning is below and wishes to speak with you.'

'Oh, my dears, what shall I do?' wailed Aunt Foster. 'I cannot, I positively cannot face him. I shall faint with fright, I know I shall.'

'No need for that, ma'am,' said Jennifer. 'I will see Mr Gurning. He and I have much to discuss. Do you all wait here until I send for you. I promise you, by then, he will be in a more reasonable mood.'

Elizabeth clasped her hands. 'Oh, Jenny,' she said, 'you are superb. But would you not like Edmund to support you? He is a *man*, after all.'

Edmund looked anything but grateful for this suggestion of his beloved's and muttered something unconvincing about being always willing to oblige a lady, but, to his great relief, Jennifer cut him short.

'No, no, I will go to him alone,' she said. 'Take me to him, pray.'

The servant girl dropped a curtsy in tacit acknowledgement

of her tone of command and led her to a small downstairs parlour where she found her Uncle Gurning angrily pacing up and down. He turned: 'What, ma'am, is the meaning—' He stopped. 'Jennifer!'

'Yes, Uncle. That will do, my dear.'

The maid, who had paused in the doorway, unable to tear herself away from a scene the whole household had been betting on, curtsied reluctantly and withdrew. Jennifer advanced into the room and held out her hand to her uncle.

'How do you do?' she asked politely.

It set him off, as she had expected it would. She waited patiently, eyebrows slightly raised, while his wrath erupted. At last, when she thought he had blown off the worst of it, having accused her, among other things, of debauching his daughter and deluding his ward, and having passed, in his description of her, from the language of the stables to that of the stews, she decided she had born enough.

'That will do, Uncle.' He paused and stared at her, momentarily deflated by her calm, and she went on: 'I have let you say your say and curse your fill, now I trust you are rational enough to listen to me for a change. You are entirely right in supposing that your daughter is in this house. No, you will hear me out before you go to her. Join her in your present mood and you will have her in hysterics, or worse. And, besides, I have something to say to you that cannot wait.'

He looked at her in amazement. This was not the girl he had been used to bully into submission, down in Sussex. 'Something to say to me indeed,' he tried to bluster it out, 'and so have I something to say to you, miss. Running away in the night, forsooth, like a hussy, like a trollop, like a . . .'

'Yes, yes,' she said, 'you have said all that once already. But now we are come to my case against you, Uncle, which is quite another story. Because I was a child, I did not, as I should have, resist your high-handed taking over of my household and my affairs. Because I was a fool, I let you frighten me into running away, which, I grant you, was a mistake, though I still do not see,' she added reflectively, 'what else I could have done. But now, Uncle,' she saw that he was again rising towards explosion point and thought it best to come quickly to the heart of the matter, 'now, the case is altered. You have thought fit to compel your daughter to masquerade as me and accept a suitor in my stead. What do you think the world will say if that becomes known? Where then are your hopes of Parliament? A petty tyrant, a common trickster . . . And,' she paused, 'I wonder if you can face an accounting of my estate?' His silence gave her her answer and she went on: 'No, I do not believe you will wish your activities of these past few months to become known.'

He burst once more into angry speech. 'The jade! I might have known she would betray all. Let me but get my hands on her.'

He started for the door of the room, but Jennifer was before him.

'No,' she said, 'I have told you, Uncle, you do not see Elizabeth until you are in a fit state to meet her. There has been enough of this bullying. I collect that you have not fully comprehended your position. I can ruin you if I wish.'

He looked at her sharply. 'Yes, but not without ruining yourself at the same time. By my contriving, the world thinks that Miss Purchas has never left her home: accuse me and you shame yourself. I have not asked you, miss, where you have been all this time, but I apprehend that you would not relish the question.'

'I certainly should not answer it,' she replied coolly, 'but that is in the main because I do not wish my friends troubled with your ill manners. But, I will be plain with you, there is something in what you say. And besides, dearly though I would love to bring you to book, I do not wish to embarrass my poor aunt any more than she already is by the mere fact of marriage with you. And, by the same token, I have a great fondness for my cousin Elizabeth. So, Uncle, I think you and I will have to make the best of the matter and be friends despite ourselves.'

'Friends?' he snorted angrily. 'I'd as soon be friends with the pig-faced lady.'

'Very well then.' She shrugged her shoulders. 'I do not insist on friendship, for indeed it would go sadly against the grain with me too. But allies, I think, we shall have to be. Let us consider our position. You have, I collect, made free with a part of my fortune (let us hope not too large a one) and have attempted to marry off your daughter in my place. To add to your difficulties, Elizabeth is now run away from you, doing you know not what damage to her good name. Your case is not a happy one, but I think it admits of improvement, if you will be ruled by me. Elizabeth, to begin with, is deep in love with Edmund. Her marriage with him will take care of her good name and – again if they are not too great – I am prepared to write off your depredations on my fortune against her marriage portion. You cannot, I apprehend, have touched the principle of my money, nor sold any of my land. If you agree to Elizabeth's marriage we will not look too closely at your inroads into my income. There remains then the matter of the engagement with Mr Ferris – no, do not interrupt me – which you have entered into apparently on my behalf and from which I collect you will find it sufficiently embarrassing to withdraw. Well; you need not. I have decided, for reasons with which I do not propose to trouble you, that I will go through with the match.'

Now he did interrupt her. 'You, Jennifer? But he has already been presented to Elizabeth and has wooed her in your stead.'

'Yes, but not, I apprehend, altogether happily. It shall be your part in the business, and your penance, to see my wooer and explain to him, I care not by what glossing of the truth, that a substitution was made. I can rely on you, I think, in the circumstances, to take the utmost care of my good name . . . Apart from that, tell him what you like, so long as you tell him that the true heiress – and the fortune – are now at his disposal.'

He looked at her in amazement. 'But what a *volte-face* is this! You, who have gone to such lengths to escape him! Are you out of your senses?'

'I think perhaps I have come to them at last. I begin to see that marriage is a more practical matter than I had thought. And Edmund tells me Ferris and I will deal admirably together: he is a bully, it seems, and I am a shrew. I shall suit him much better than poor Lizzy.'

He looked at her with reluctant respect. 'You have the right of it, Jenny, I do believe. I only wish you were my daughter:

we should manage the world famously together, you and I. But as it is, I can see there is nothing for it. I will do my best to retrieve this wooer of yours, though it passes my imagination what story I am to tell.'

'If you will be ruled by me, Uncle, you will tell as much of the truth as you can get your tongue round. It is not as if there had ever been any question of love in the matter: it is nothing more than a business arrangement; so long as the fortune is there, why should it matter whether Lizzy or I is the happy bride? Surely you have talked your way out of worse corners than this in your time? But you must hurry; Lizzy's marriage must not be long delayed, and mine, I think, should precede it. So, if you will take my advice, you will go at once to find this suitor of mine. Does he know, by the way, of Lizzy's running off? That might make matters more difficult for you.'

His face darkened with anger. 'Yes, your fool of an aunt let a servant blurt the whole business out in his presence and he is returned to London in a rage. It will not be easy to school him, Jenny.' He was talking to her now, she noticed with amusement, almost as if she were a fellow conspirator.

'Of course, it will not be easy, but I have the greatest confidence in your powers of persuasion. Best lose no time, however. It would sadly mar matters if he were to cry off publicly.'

'You are right again. I will seek him out at once; do you be ready to receive him if I can bring him to see reason. Have you nothing more becoming than that shabby green habit? It is hardly the costume to be receiving a wooer in.'

'No, I fear this is the best I can do for him. But after all, he is marrying my fortune, not my clothes. They can be remedied easily enough afterwards. This will do well enough for so unromantic a bargain. But will you not see Lizzy before you go?'

He gave her a wry smile. 'No, I thank you. If I am not to thrash her as she deserves, I had best not see her at all. Next time I try my hand at a plot, you shall be my accomplice, Jenny. Tell her from me that if I can settle your affairs to my satisfaction I may be prepared to listen to Edmund's suit. If not – but time enough for that. Expect to hear from me directly.'

He bowed, and left her at once amused and delighted at the ease of her victory.

Hearing the front door slam behind him, Elizabeth peered anxiously over the banisters. 'Jenny, is he truly gone without even seeing me?'

Mindful of the listening servants, Jennifer ran lightly up to join her. 'Yes, he said if he saw you he would certainly beat you, so he is gone, instead, to see if he can restore my suitor to me. For it seems the poor man learned of your being run away, Lizzy, and is come back to London in a sad passion.'

Elizabeth paled with fright. 'Oh, Jenny, how can you face him? Are you sure you are acting for the best? I cannot bear to think of your throwing yourself away on such a tyrant as I am sure he will prove. You should but see his eyebrows, Jenny, and the way he looks right through one with those piercing eyes of his. I was never more frightened of anyone in my life.'

'Except, I apprehend, your father. But you see, Lizzy, I have destroyed one giant today already: now I am ready for anything. No, seriously, never fret for me. My romantic days are over. Now I am ready to settle down and be a good, dull wife with naughty children and a box at the opera in recompense for a husband. And I am persuaded he and I will rub along well enough together. He will give me much that I have always wanted: a London life and a place in the world. Do you not see me, Lizzy, as a First Minister's wife, scribbling little notes to this minister and that placeman, famous for my diary and my intimate suppers? I shall do well enough, I promise you. We cannot all find romance like you and Edmund. Oh, by the by, I had quite forgot to tell you that my uncle says if he can settle my affairs – which I am persuaded he will, since he has such a stake in them himself – he will be prepared to listen to Edmund's suit.'

Elizabeth's eyes filled with tears as she embraced her cousin. 'Oh, Jenny, you are so good to me. I cannot bear to think that you are not going to be as happy as us.'

'I intend to be much happier,' said Jennifer briskly. 'I shall have the most elegant equipage, and the newest liveries and the most splendid jewels in town. I shall make bishops and unmake generals (I must, of course, first make my husband First Minister!) . . . I shall become a patroness of Almack's and dandies shall tremble at my frown. And now, Lizzy, my love, I would give all my future wealth for half an hour alone. Do you think your good Aunt Foster could be prevailed upon to allow me to stay here? I see that it is getting late, and, to deal plainly with you, I am as much of a runaway as you are. I had hoped it might prove possible to start for home today, but as it is . . .' She paused, suddenly exhausted.

Elizabeth took her hand. 'Oh, Jenny, how could I be so shatterbrained? Aunt Foster will be most happy to have you stay, I know. She is so grateful to you, Jenny, for facing my father that there is nothing she will not do for you. But come to my room and rest a while, I beg of you, while I seek her out.'

She insisted on seeing Jennifer laid down upon her bed and after supplying her with her aunt's spirits of lavender and her own vinaigrette, left her, at last, alone. Jennifer turned her head into the pillow and burst into a passion of tears.

Gradually recovering her composure, she lay quietly for a while, grateful for the solitude, letting herself, at last, wonder what kind of a man this unknown husband of hers would prove to be. She had often thought it strange that she had neither encountered him in society, nor heard his name mentioned, but had hesitated to make any enquiry about him, for fear of drawing unwelcome attention upon herself. She cared nothing for Elizabeth and Edmund's opinion of him. Their fright and resentment might, after all, be his best recommendation. Anyway, the die was cast now. If her uncle could prevail upon him to renew his suit, she was determined to have him, were he ten times a bully. As she had told Elizabeth, her days of romance were over. Now it was time to dwindle into a wife.

CHAPTER XVI

Mainwaring, meanwhile, had composed a fulminating note to Mandeville, enclosed Jennifer's in it and sent it round to his lodgings. That done, he resisted a strong temptation to cross-examine his grandmother's servants in what he knew would be a vain attempt to discover Jennifer's whereabouts. She was gone of her own free-will, he told his grandmother, and – incidentally – himself. If that was how she wished it, her wish should be respected. *He* would not attempt to pursue her.

'No, indeed, George. Why should you?' asked his grandmother blandly.

This apparently innocent answer so enraged him that he slammed out of the house and took his fury to Brooks', where the porter confided to a footman that he had not seen his lordship in such a tearer since Boney escaped from Elba. Mainwaring did not stay there long. The news in the papers was insipid, the faces of his friends infuriated him, and he was disappointed in an unadmitted hope that he might encounter Mandeville and have a chance of giving him the thrashing he deserved. Instead, he met young Laverstoke, who had been searching for him to get his approval for his match with Pamela and, incidentally, to babble what seemed to Mainwaring a great deal of nonsense about his extraordinary good fortune and unprecedented happiness. Mainwaring cut him off in the middle of his transports with an abrupt farewell. It had suddenly occurred to him that Lady Laverstoke might just possibly know something of Jennifer's whereabouts. Of course, he had no personal reason for pursuing her, but he told himself that he owed it to his grandmother to make quite sure that she had, in fact, returned safely to her family.

Thus convincing himself, he hurried to Bruton Street, only to be told that Lady Laverstoke was driving in the park. He was setting off, on a forlorn hope, to pursue her there, when he heard himself hailed from across the street. The sight of the odious Mr Gurning hurrying towards him did nothing to improve his temper. He would dearly have loved to cut him dead, but his inherent good manners were too much for him, and he waited furiously while Gurning hurried up to him.

He was out of breath. 'Thank God, I have caught you at last, sir . . . Been looking for you all over town . . . Never was more embarrassed in my life . . . Owe you the humblest of apologies . . . Must crave the honour of a few minutes' private conversation with you.'

The black brows rose. 'I can think of nothing in the world, sir, that you and I can have to say to each other. Unless, of course, you are come to discuss the means by which we may least disagreeably release each other from an engagement into which I, for one, heartily wish I had never been fool enough to enter.'

'No, no, sir,' Gurning had got his breath back. 'You are quite wide of the mark, I assure you. You must, you positively must, give me an opportunity to explain.'

'Explain, Mr Gurning? I cannot conceive how you propose to explain away the fact that your niece has chosen to run away from home rather than entertain my suit. No, sir, I repeat, we have nothing further to say to each other. Choose your own means of breaking off the match. I owe Miss Purchas that much consideration for her brothers' sake, but farther than that I will not go.'

He turned and resumed his impatient progress towards the park, only to find Mr Gurning bobbing along irrepressibly at his elbow.

'My lord, you do not understand. You *must* let me explain.'

'I understand well enough that I have been made a laughing-stock among you. That is enough for me. Now I must wish you a very good day. Give my respects to your niece and tell her that she need fear no resumption of the attentions that were so unpleasant to her.'

'But that is the whole point,' Gurning got it out at last. 'You have never met my niece.'

'Never met your niece? What madness is this? I have spent

two endless hours trying to fix her attention. And now, if you please, sir . . .' again he turned away, but Gurning laid a restraining hand on his arm.

'My lord, I am trying to tell you. That was not my niece, but my daughter.'

Mainwaring swung round to face him. 'Your daughter?'

'Yes. It is a most painful subject to me, my lord, and, I apprehend, a highly delicate one for us both. Let me beg you to do me the honour of accompanying me to Holborn where I am at present residing, and I will explain the whole.'

'Accompany you to Holborn? Why, in the name of all that's ridiculous should I do that?'

'My lord, because my niece awaits you there.'

'Ah. So you have a niece. I am relieved to hear it. I was beginning to think you must have made away with her.'

'I? My lord, you are pleased to jest. No, no, it is, I admit, a painful story, but not so bad as that. I have indeed a niece, the most self-willed ungrateful hussy that ever drew breath. I mean,' he remembered his brief, and hurriedly corrected himself, 'I intend to say that she is an excessively high spirited young lady and took some notion into her head that – as her brothers' friend – you should have come to her sooner.'

'Oh, she did, did she?' But Mainwaring was listening now, and allowed Gurning to walk on beside him. 'And what is that to the purpose?'

'Why, to be short with you, my lord, she took such an unreasonable prejudice against your lordship that – I am sorry to have to say it to you – rather than meet you she thought fit to leave home.'

A sharp burst of laughter acknowledged this confession. 'Ha! Ran away too, did she? You do not seem to be happy in your family, Mr Gurning.'

'My lord, I am the most unfortunate man in the world, so plagued with females . . . But, to deal plainly with you, my wife has not the sense of a pea-hen and I fear her conduct of the girls has been sadly at fault. Not that I would say a word against Miss Purchas: a high spirited filly, that is all, a trifle heavy-at-hand, but nothing that a husband will not remedy.'

'I am delighted to hear it,' said Mainwaring dryly. 'But let me understand you aright. First Miss Purchas ran away from you. Then, for reasons of your own, you substituted your own daughter for her and let me pay my addresses to her (I see now why she was in such a pother, the poor child; it positively does her credit). And now, to complete your confusion, she, too, is run off. It is not an edifying story, Mr Gurning.'

'No, my lord, I blush to recall it.' He did nothing of the kind. 'But if you will only be patient, I think all may yet work out for the best. For, I will have you know, I have found them both. Jennifer – I mean Miss Purchas – is but this morning returned to her senses and to my protection. She is a changed girl, my lord. She has got over her childish follies and entirely acknowledges the honour you have done her by proposing for her hand. If you will but forgive and forget and resume your suit, all will yet be well.'

A great light had dawned on Mainwaring in the course of this speech. 'Jennifer Purchas,' he exclaimed, 'by all that's holy! But this morning returned, you say, and handsomely prepared to marry me at last. It is mighty good of her, sir. I am not, I collect, to ask where she has been spending her time, or what she has been doing.'

Mr Gurning had prepared himself for this question. 'Why, as to that, my lord, I can only tell you that some considerable part of the time has been spent with Lady Laverstoke and her family at Laverstoke House. But no doubt Miss Purchas will be glad to give you the fullest satisfaction on this point herself.'

Mainwaring walked on for a while in silence. It all fitted together now. Miss Purchas was Miss Fairbank. He had been purblind not to have realised it before. She had taken some miff or other at the manner of his suit (he resolutely refused to let himself remember that his grandmother, too, had thought him dilatory) and as a result had run off like the hoyden she was and contrived to meet him without his having any idea of her true identity. How she must have laughed in her sleeve at him, how triumphed at his deception when he went off to pay his court to her cousin. For, of course, though her uncle would naturally not admit it, she must have been a party to the whole plot.

Mr Gurning was looking at him anxiously. He made up his mind. 'It is a strange story, sir, and hardly an elevating one. I collect I am to marry Miss Purchas in haste to protect her from the consequences of her folly. Well, I promised her brother I would look after her, and I am a man of my word. I will do it. But we'll have no more hole-and-corner work, no more pigs in pokes. Take me to her directly.'

Mr Gurning was only too happy to comply, though he shot many an anxious glance at his saturnine companion as they made their way to Holborn. His respect for Jennifer was by now considerable. She had worsted him, but would she be a match for this furious nobleman?

Jennifer was listening patiently to Elizabeth's plans for her wedding when a maid told her that Mr Gurning and another gentleman were awaiting her company in the small downstairs drawing-room.

Elizabeth clasped her hands: 'Oh, Jenny, they are come. Do you really dare face him?'

It was what Jennifer was rather wondering herself, but she put a good face on the matter: 'Of course I do,' she said briskly, 'it will be over soon enough, and he cannot eat me. After all it was not I that tricked him.'

'I wish he may be aware of that,' said Lizzy presciently. 'And, Jenny, you did run away from him.'

'Too late to worry about that now. Is my hair tidy, Lizzy?'

'Yes, you look very becomingly, my love, though I could wish . . .'

'Yes, I know,' interrupted Jennifer impatiently, 'you wish I had a different gown. Well, to deal plainly with you, so do I. One does not feel at one's bravest looking a dowd.' But in her heart she consoled herself with the knowledge that the dark green became her. As for its shabbiness, she was, oddly, quite pleased about that. She would not flaunt the fortune for which this unknown suitor was prepared to marry her. It seemed, as she slowly descended the stairs, a mad venture. But what else could she do? She summoned up her courage and entered the

173

drawing-room. Her Uncle Gurning was standing facing the door, talking, it seemed with some embarrassment, to a tall man whose back was towards her. But that back – could she be mistaken? He turned. Mainwaring.

She very nearly turned herself, and fled, as it all fell into place in her mind. How could she not have guessed? His brother's death, of course, accounted for the change of name that had misled her. It had been he, all the time, from whom she had fled, and to him that she had turned to save her from disgrace. It was impossible, intolerable. But there was no time to think. He was coming towards her, she saw the colour in his cheek, the little flame in his eye, and knew that he was in one of his cold rages.

'Miss Purchas,' Mainwaring bowed over her hand, 'this is a pleasure to which I have long looked forward.' His eyes gave her a more savage message. For the first time, she was frightened.

But her uncle was elaborately taking his leave of them. They would have much to discuss, he hinted. He was happy to see them so well in agreement at last ... With this final unfortunate phrase he got himself out of the room.

Mainwaring looked down at her. 'Well, Miss Fairbank,' he said, 'or rather, I beg your pardon, Miss *Purchas*. How do we play this scene of your comedy? Or have you finished your game with me at last?'

'My game? I do not understand you, sir.'

'Why, this pretty game of hide-and-seek by which you have made a laughing-stock of me. How you and your cousin must have laughed, comparing notes over my follies. To "rescue" you one day and go a-wooing of her the next. Good God, I can hardly forebear laughing myself to think what a figure of fun I have proved.' He looked very far from laughter.

Jennifer was appalled. This was worse than anything she had imagined. 'But, my lord, it was not like that at all! There was no plan, no stratagem of the kind you hint at. If I had but known – but believe me I did not ... You must have seen, when I came into the room, that I was as astonished as yourself.'

174

He looked at her grimly. 'On the contrary, Miss Purchas, I saw you as little astonished as myself. I had already collected all too much of the truth from your uncle's speeches. And you, I apprehend, are far too accomplished an actress to let a little thing like "surprise" defeat you. Do but consider the performances I have been favoured with: the errant heroine, the faithful friend, innocence affronted . . . And I, all the time, the deluded fool. Pah! It makes me sick to think of it.'

She was white now, holding on to the back of a chair for support. 'My lord, you must let me explain. I did, I confess, take your first proposal amiss . . .'

He interrupted her. 'My dear ma'am, that is ancient history. We have no time to lose over it now. It seems you are come at last to a stand. Your play-acting is over; your fingers are burned; you find your good name endangered and turn to me for the protection of mine. Well; you shall have it, as I have already told your uncle. I promised your brothers I would look after you, and by God, I will. We marry tomorrow, by special licence. We must, I think, to make the thing complete, set up house together, however much it may go against the grain. I suggest that we dispense with the mockery of a honeymoon and proceed at once to Shaws, my house in Derbyshire, which will, I trust, be large enough to hold us both without too great inconvenience to either. As soon as I may do so without arousing gossip, I will rejoin the army and you shall be rid of me.'

She was crying now, she was not sure whether from anger or despair. But she must be angry, only so could she save any shred of self-respect. She lifted her white face to his. 'My lord, that is enough. When you recollect yourself – and understand the matter more clearly – you will be sorry to have insulted me so. For the present, there is nothing for me to do but to thank you for your generous offer, however worded, and to decline it. My brothers loved me too well to wish me married to a man who loathes me. You are absolved from your promise to them. As for my name: let the world chatter. I am beyond caring for reputation. Good-bye, my lord. I am sorry you should think I ever mocked you.' The last words were forced out with difficulty over the rising tide of tears. She turned and quickly left the room.

He started after her: 'Jennifer, stop!' But she was gone, running up the stairs, her handkerchief over her face. And in the hall, inevitably, lurked her uncle, all aswim with felicitations.

It was too much. Mainwaring muttered an oath and slammed out of the house. He went, instinctively, straight to his grandmother, who took one look at his face and rang for restoratives. 'I shall need them, George, even if you do not. Now, pour me some ratafia and help yourself to what you will and tell me what is amiss.'

'What's amiss? Everything, ma'am. I am a fool, a brute, a bully . . . I have lost her, ma'am.'

'What, so soon? I did not even know that you had found her.'

'Yes, found and lost all in a moment, and all through my own vile temper. But, ma'am, you amaze me. Did you *know*?'

'Know that you loved Miss Fairbank? George, I am an old woman, but not a fool. Of course I knew.'

'But did you also know who she was?'

The wise old eyes looked at him speculatively. 'Shall we say I guessed, George? You see, I had the advantage of not being in love, which, we all know, is not the most clear-sighted of passions. Yes, I confess, I have been enjoying your little comedy of mistaken identities; though I must own to some curiosity as to who the white mouse down in the country might be.'

'Oh, her cousin, daughter of the wicked uncle. So you had guessed it all, ma'am, and let me go off to ruin myself without a word.'

'I am sorry for it if you have indeed done so, George, but I find it hard to believe. I thought all was in train for a perfect climax of discovery and delight. Pray, what has marred it?'

'Why, my vile temper, ma'am. That uncle of hers came to me – you must understand I still had not guessed who she was and, to tell truth, was on my way to Lady Laverstoke's in hopes that she might have some news of her – when up comes my friend the uncle with a long story of apology, and deception, and substitution, and more apology ... and suddenly, from something he said, I saw it all, or rather, saw too much, as I now understand. For, ma'am, I was convinced Jennifer (Miss Purchas, I should say) had been a party to it all; had been mocking me from the start, looking me over as a prospective husband very much as one might consider a possible carriage horse. I thought – God help me, ma'am – I thought it was all a plot; the meeting at Lady Laverstoke's, even the encounter that night, in Parliament Square. I was a fool, ten times a fool. I see it all now, but the uncle – God rot him – left me no time for thought, but hurried me off to Holborn, where, it seems, his niece had taken refuge, and presented me to her all in my first rage.'

'Ah,' said the old lady thoughtfully. 'It was all his fault, I apprehend.'

'Oh, ma'am, do not mock me. Of course it was my fault. You have told me many times that my temper would be my ruin. You were right; it has been. I have lost her, ma'am. I'll never marry now.'

'What did you do, George?'

'Why, insulted her as deep as I could. Oh, I offered for her hand, ma'am, but in such terms ... I told her I had promised her brothers I would look after her and would be as good as my word. And all with such an accompaniment of insults that I wonder she stayed to hear me finish.'

'And what did she say?'

'Cut me short in my raging. Oh, ma'am, there's the woman for me. *She* could control me! Declined my "generous" offer. Absolved me from all contract with her brothers. Shamed me by her quietness, broke my heart with her tears – and left the room before I could stop her.'

'But surely you went after her?'

'Yes, and found that uncle of hers lying in wait for me in the hall. It was more than I could bear. I left the house. No, it is all over, ma'am. It is not possible that she should forgive me. I shall rejoin the army and go to the devil as best I may.'

'Leaving Miss Purchas to suffer for your sins?'

It pulled him up short. 'You think I might have another

chance? That she might forgive me? But it's impossible. I have not told you how I insulted her.'

'You need not. I know you, George. I can guess. But I still say you have a chance. She loves you, George. Why do you think she was prepared to go back and yield to her uncle's wishes? I have something to show you. Betty found this letter from Mandeville in her room and brought it to me. She must have forgotten to destroy it in the hurry of her flight. Read and see by what means he was blackmailing her: it was disgrace to you and me that she feared, not to herself. She was prepared to marry you (the unknown you) to save you (the known) from disgrace. But read for yourself.'

He read and then threw the letter angrily from him. 'Yes, I understand it all now. What a villain that Mandeville is. And what a wretch I am to have used her so. I cannot forgive myself. How then can I expect her to forgive me?'

'But that is quite another matter. Self-love has never been your vice, and what I am trying to prove to you is that she loves you, George, and love will forgive much. Go to her again, beg her pardon, on your knees if you will, tell her how you mistook the matter. Trust me, all will yet be well. Love does not die overnight, and she is a girl of too much spirit to let her life ruin itself over a misunderstanding, whatever you may do. Stay, I have a better idea still. You were never much good at pleading. I will write to her. She must, I collect, find herself at something of a stand, with all her plans tumbled about her ears. I will write and urge her to come back to me. It is, in any case, the best thing for her to do. Mandeville, I apprehend, is by this fled the town, or I do not know you, George. Jennifer shall come back to me and brave it out – she has the spirit for it, I know – and you shall woo her all over again at your leisure.'

He kissed her hand: 'Ma'am, I am speechless . . .'

'Good,' she interrupted him. 'Continue so, while I write.'

CHAPTER XVII

Alone in the room Aunt Foster had now allotted to her, Jennifer paced up and down, facing disaster. Anger with Mainwaring for his unjustified suspicions had carried her through a brief, painful interview with Elizabeth, then, unable to face her sympathy, and infuriated by her criticisms of Mainwaring, she had retreated to face the shipwreck of her plans. Where should she go? What do? Soon, incorrigibly, she was planning again. First, she must use the power she now had over her uncle to force through Elizabeth's marriage with her cousin. Then, she would go home to Denton Hall, make a clean sweep of the Gurnings from her house and settle down to the life of a recluse.

She was considering this prospect, without enthusiasm, when the maid interrupted her with a twisted note that had just been delivered for her by hand. Inevitably, hope sprang up at once. Who but Mainwaring knew where she was? Her hand trembling, she opened the note, considering, as she did so, how best to take his apology. The handwriting was hurried, unrecognisable and, indeed, hard to decipher. 'My dearest life,' she read, 'I find I cannot live without you. You must forgive, you must marry me. I cannot visit you in Holborn. Meet me, I beg, in the Temple Gardens, by the river, as soon as you receive this. I will await you there, your humble servant, all evening.' It was signed with a single initial, 'M'.

How quick, how easy, the transition from despair to rapture. Jennifer was at the glass at once, tidying her hair with hands that shook. It was already evening. He must have been awaiting her for some time, wondering whether she would, in truth, find it in her heart to forgive him. As if she had not done so even while he was speaking. His anger, based on a misunderstanding, had not really referred to her at all. Now, looking back on the scene, she wondered how she could have let it distress her so, for was not his very fury a proof of his love? But she was wasting time. She hurried downstairs, pausing only to tell Elizabeth that she was going out to get a breath of air, to refuse her offer of her company or Edmund's, and to thank her good fortune for Aunt Foster's easy good nature which seemed to see nothing amiss in her going out unattended.

The long, hot afternoon was cooling now, and the city was full of evening cries and evening smells, but she hardly noticed them as she hurried on flying feet down towards the river. The gardens, when she reached them, lay quiet and deserted in late sunshine and she found herself wishing that Mainwaring had given her a more precise rendezvous, found herself thinking, for the first time, that there was something slightly odd about his note. 'My dearest life' – it did not suggest his voice. The unthinking excitement that had brought her so far suddenly ebbed. She stood, alone, at the entrance to the gardens, pulling Elizabeth's hastily borrowed pelisse more closely around her against a chill – was it of apprehension or of the evening air?

But a man's figure was approaching purposefully down one of the alley-ways. She made a hesitant move forward, then stopped and waited. No, this was not Mainwaring, she knew his height and quick stride too well to be deceived. Then, as the man came nearer, she shrank back.

'You?'

'Who else, my dear? And very much at your service,' said Miles Mandeville.

'It was you who wrote to me?'

'My dearest life, of course.'

She should have known. It was his phrase. Why had she not recognised it? But she had been blind, mad, concentrated on Mainwaring. 'Sir,' she pulled herself together with difficulty. 'I owe you an apology if I have raised your hopes by my appearance. But I must tell you that I am come here under a misapprehension. You and I have nothing more to say to each other. I must bid you a very good day.' She turned to leave him, but he had her by the hand.

'No, no,' he said, 'not so fast, my dearest creature. We do not part so easily. But this is rich indeed. I am, I take it, to understand that you are come here in hopes of finding not me, but Mainwaring. What a bitter blow for you; 'tis not the nobleman after all, but plain Miles Mandeville. Well, the die is cast now, you must make shift with me as best you may. We are off, my dear, for France.'

'You are mad, sir.' She tried vainly to disengage herself.

'Why, yes, I rather believe I am. My name, you must recollect, is Mad Mandeville. And I have had cause for madness both from you and from your protector, Mainwaring. Damme, it makes me mad all over again with mere delight to think what a noble revenge fate, and you, my life, have put in my way. He has ordered me out of town like a whipped cur and – to deal plainly with you – I see nothing for it but to go. He is too powerful for me and knows it. But what will become of his triumph when he finds I have taken you with me? You thought it was he who wrote you of forgiveness and marriage? No, no, it was I. If I must go into exile, I will not go alone. But, come, we lose time talking here.' And before she could utter more than a stifled exclamation of protest, he had clapped a hand over her mouth and dragged her by main force to a carriage that was standing at the park gates. Struggling fiercely, she could do no more than deal him one resounding blow in the face before he had thrown her inside, slammed the door on her, and shouted an order to the coachman.

She sank back in the corner of the carriage, amazed to think that she had believed herself in despair before. Then, she had merely quarrelled with Mainwaring and had, perhaps, known in her heart that sooner or later they must come to an understanding . . . But now . . . Even if she should contrive to escape from Mandeville – and she intended to – before he could get her on board ship . . . Even so, she was lost indeed. Who would believe that this new scrape was not of her own choosing, or at least not to some extent her fault? She knew by now all too well how quick Mainwaring was to suspect the worst where she was concerned. What hope had she of explaining away this new misadventure? How could she have let it happen to her? She gave way, for the third time that day, to a tempest of tears, then took herself angrily to task. This was to behave like Elizabeth. She had need of all her strength and all her ingenuity to contrive her escape. Tears would not help her. As for the future, that must take care of itself. The present was problem enough. She leaned cautiously forward to look out of the carriage window. They were passing through Lambeth village. Surely this was not the road for Dover. Where could Mandeville be taking her?

A figure on horseback rode up beside the carriage and Mandeville himself raised his hand in half mocking salutation. She made herself raise her own hand in reply and forced a travesty of a smile to her lips. If she could make him think she had resigned herself to her fate, her chances of escape would be much increased.

Time passed, interminable. The shadows lengthened, the light ebbed from the hills. Were they to drive through the night? If so, she was lost indeed. Then, when she was almost giving way again to despair, she felt the carriage slacken its speed and, leaning forward, saw that they were in the outskirts of a town. They stopped at last in a deserted street, at the entrance of a little inn. The door was opened, the steps let down and Mandeville stood below, all apparent deference, to receive her. She looked quickly round. There was no one in sight but Mandeville and his servants. This was no time to attempt escape. She took his offered arm and alighted, yawning delicately behind her hand.

'My dearest creature,' said Mandeville, 'I beg you ten thousand pardons for bringing you so far, but I wished to reach this inn which is kept, you must know, by good friends of mine. Some supper and a good night's rest.' He eyed her ironically. 'And you will be glad to set forward again for my yacht which lies at Southampton.'

She refused to be aware of his meaning. 'The rest will be most welcome,' she said lightly, 'for in truth I have had a most fatiguing day.'

'I dare swear you have. Well, you shall have time enough for rest when we are safe in Paris. But, come, our host is waiting. He is well used, by the by, to seeing me companioned with a wench. No use squeaking to him, my dear, if you had thought of it.'

Her chin went up. 'It had not occurred to me. I am well aware that you have ruined me by now. What's done is done. And I have no doubt that Paris will prove vastly entertaining.'

He looked at her with puzzled respect. 'Oh, sits the wind in that quarter? You see the game's lost, do you . . . Well, I always liked a good loser. And to be sure you are right. After a night spent here in my infamous company, you would be hard put to it to prove your innocence to a far less difficult judge than Mainwaring. Well, I am delighted; we will pass a happier evening than I had expected.'

Allowing him to guide her indoors, Jennifer recognised his disappointment. He had looked forward to tears and entreaties. This, for him, was anticlimax. Enjoying his chagrin, she found it easier still to play her part. She must convince the host of what she now saw to be a small and secluded inn that she was Mandeville's willing companion.

As the landlord, a short, fat, beery man with a limp, came forward to greet them, she settled her hand more firmly in Mandeville's arm. 'La, my dear Mr Mandeville, where in the world have you brought me? I vow I was never so fatigued in my life.' She sank down, sighing gracefully, into a high wheel-back chair that stood by the fire in the inn's neat little parlour.

Mandeville looked at her with surprise and a sudden touch of suspicion, but was soon busy ordering dinner and beds for the night from the obsequious landlord, who, she could see, was indeed well acquainted with him. When the question of devilled chicken and mutton collops had been settled to Mandeville's satisfaction and he had reassured himself that the landlord still had some of the claret he had recommended, Jennifer put a hand to her head.

'I am all blown to pieces from that draughty carriage of yours, Mr Mandeville. I declare I must be a perfect fright. Take me, pray,' she addressed the host, 'to my chamber.'

'By all means, my dear,' Mandeville flashed her a knowing smile. 'I do not deny that your appearance is somewhat dishevelled. But you may be disappointed to find that this inn has but the one entrance – here.' He gestured to the front door, which he could see from where he sat by the fire.

Jennifer affected disdain: 'And pray, what's that to the question? I want a looking-glass and my dinner, and they are not, I collect, to be found out of doors.'

She flounced upstairs with the landlord in attendance, but dismissed him haughtily when he had shown her to the plain little room that was to be hers. She noted, with a shiver, the connecting door to the next room, observed that there was no lock on either that or the doorway to the hall, and hurried to the window only to see, at once, the reason for Mandeville's self-satisfaction. The inn was built around a central courtyard onto which her window looked. There was no hope of escape this way.

Automatically tidying her hair with the aid of the cracked looking-glass that hung over the fireplace, she took despairing stock of her position. The landlady had not appeared. The landlord was evidently Mandeville's man. She had only herself to rely on. Well, she was not going to spend the night here: that was certain. She looked round the room for a weapon, but could see nothing. Then a thought struck her. Bottles. Bottles of claret. Smiling a little to herself she walked down the steep flight of stairs.

Mandeville came out of the parlour to meet her and hand her with odious ceremony back to the fireside. He was taking no chance of her slipping out of the front door.

'So devoted, Mr Mandeville, you quite overwhelm me.' She seated herself idly by the fire. 'I trust these good people will not be over-long in serving dinner, for I vow I am famished.'

'You are a remarkable young woman, Miss Fairbank.'

'Am I not? Are you disappointed that I am not in strong hysterics? I must confess I never had a turn for them. And they would not particularly avail me, would they?'

'No,' he was glad of the chance to be firm. 'My mind is quite made up.'

'Of course, it is.' She smiled at him. 'Do you know, Mr Mandeville, all these dramatics have made me most unconscionably thirsty. Do you think your friend with the red nose could be prevailed upon to bring me some ratafia?'

He laughed and rang the bell. 'I am sure of it.' He gave the order and stood, smiling down at her, very much too close for her liking. 'Your composure, Miss Fairbank, is admirable. You have not even asked me how I propose to get you to France.'

'Why should I?' She returned his gaze coolly. 'I am sure you have made excellent arrangements. And it is evident enough that you have had a deal of practice in the abduction business.' She regretted the taunt as soon as it was spoken.

He flushed and came a little closer, his hand heavy on her arm. She looked down at it, then exclaimed: 'La, Mr Mandeville, only look at your hands. Why, they are dirty as a stable boy's. I declare, I should blush to sit at table with you. Our red-faced friend will, I am sure, be good enough to keep me company while you make yourself fit to be seen.'

He looked at her in amazement. 'I am sure I do not know what you would be at. But, if you wish it, I will certainly make myself tidy. After all, this is a time to celebrate.' He called the landlord, explained to him that the young lady was liable to nervous fits if left alone and left them together.

The landlord looked in some surprise at Jennifer, sitting composedly in her fireside chair, but complied. While Mandeville was away, she prattled gaily to him about the pleasures she expected in Paris, interlarding her conversation with as many 'las' and 'I vows' as she could get her tongue round. 'And the Rue Rivoli,' she was saying when Mandeville returned, 'and the place where they killed that poor Queen, and the Tull . . .' She hesitated for the word. 'Well, that palace everyone says is so monstrous fine. I shall see it all – and have a new wardrobe too.'

'Are you gone quite mad?' asked Mandeville, when the host had left them.

'Why, no, I am merely practising my part. Do you not like it?'

'I find it ridiculous.' He took an angry turn about the room. 'And I do not understand you.' He came and loomed over her. 'What is going on in that pretty little head of yours?'

She tossed her curls. 'Merely a vast desire for my dinner, and a little philosophy, Mr Mandeville. If I am to end my days as a bit of muslin – I believe that is the phrase? – I must get into the spirit of it. But here, at last, is dinner.' She watched with well-concealed anxiety while the landlord and a scrubby boy of about fourteen brought in the various dishes and bottles that constituted the meal. Would they open all the wine at once? Everything depended on that. At last, hiding her relief, she saw the host open one bottle and economically leave the others on the side table.

Mandeville made a great parade of seating her at the table, but she managed to take the chair furthest from the fire, facing the window and close to the side table. Then, forcing down the food that nearly choked her, she compelled herself to be entertaining, reciting, for her companion's benefit, one after the other of the more lively scandals with which she had been used – how long ago it seemed – to amuse the old Duchess.

The meal passed uneventfully. Mandeville, to her disappointment drank only in moderation. 'This is no night to be bosky,' he told her, giving point to his words with a leer and a tilt of his glass in her direction.

She felt sick, but this, and sundry other insinuations of his, made it easier to go ahead with her plan at which she had found herself almost boggling. The table had been cleared now, and the dessert laid. The host had opened another bottle of claret, but one still remained, unopened, on the table behind her.

'That will do.' Mandeville dismissed the man. 'We can look after ourselves from now on, can we not, my pretty?' He drew his chair closer to hers, and put his hand on her knee.

'Of course we can, Mr Mandeville, and, to begin with, my glass is empty. You may not wish to find yourself bosky, as you so elegantly put it, but, do you know, I rather think I would prefer to be.'

He burst into a guffaw and filled her glass. 'That's a good one, damme if it isn't. Just you wait till I tell them that at the Club. "Prefer to be bosky" . . . Damned if I don't like your spirit, Jennifer.' Absent-mindedly, he emptied and refilled his own glass. Dared she wait until he had drunk a little more?

No. His hand was back on her knee, and beginning to travel. She looked suddenly at the window:

'Lud,' she exclaimed, 'if it isn't Lord Mainwaring!'

'What? Here?' Mandeville turned to the window with an oath.

It was the chance Jennifer had planned for. She picked up the unopened bottle of claret and brought it down as hard as she could on his head. He gave a little grunt and settled down in his chair. She listened. All was quiet. At the back of the house she could hear the landlord's voice raised, haranguing, no doubt, his wife and the scrubby boy. All was well so far. If only she had not hit Mandeville too hard. But he was breathing regularly, if heavily, and his pulse seemed steady enough. At once a different fear shook her. What if he should recover consciousness too soon?

With a shaking hand, she removed the well-lined wallet from his pocket. This went, curiously enough, even more against the grain than knocking him out. But there was no help for it. She must get away as quickly as possible, and that meant money. She tucked the wallet securely into her reticule, put on her bonnet, which she had been careful not to leave upstairs, and took a quick look round the room. She had left nothing that could identify her. Suddenly anxious, she damped a napkin and tied it round Mandeville's head where the lump was beginning to show. That done, she went quickly out into the hall, shot the bolt of the big front door gently back and stepped out into the fresh air of the summer evening.

It had never smelt so good. She took deep breaths of liberty as she looked quickly up and down the village street that lay quiet in evening shadows. It must be very late. Lucky for her that this adventure had happened on one of the longest and lightest nights of the year. Now that she was safe away from Miles Mandeville, she found it impossible to be altogether in despair. Her position was difficult enough, it was true, but she was free, she had money, she would save herself – and her reputation – yet. It was a pity, she thought, starting briskly forward towards the centre of the little town, that she had no idea where she was, but the important thing was to know where

187

she was going. Of that, she was very sure. She was going home. All her troubles had arisen from her folly in running away in the first place. She would go back to Denton Hall, establish herself at last as mistress of her house and defy the world and its gossip. If Mainwaring wanted to seek her out, good. If not – well, it was unfortunate, but must be faced. She would die the most eccentric of old maids. I will breed cats, she decided, or perhaps monkeys, and, entering the central square of the little town, found herself facing the main inn of the place.

A few people were still stirring in the square and she was aware of being the target of some curious glances. She should have been considering what story to tell at the inn to account for her unattended and baggageless state. Then she squared her shoulders and threw back her head in a gesture that Mainwaring would have found oddly reminiscent of her older brother. Why should she have to explain herself to these people? She had money and a clear conscience. What more could anyone want?

She swept into the inn with a very passable imitation of the Duchess's manner when irritated and demanded the landlord in imperious tones. He came, somewhat reluctantly, from the toasted cheese he had been enjoying by the kitchen fire, and asked her with scant civility what she required at this time of night.

'A hack chaise and four of your best horses at once,' was her uncompromising answer.

'A hack chaise? Four horses?' He had never heard of such a thing. A young lady – he used the term with much implication of doubt – a *very* young lady. And all on her own ... What could she be wanting with a chaise and four?'

'That,' said Jennifer, 'is none of your business, my good man. I am late already. I will pay well if the chaise is ready in ten minutes.' Casually, she withdrew Mandeville's wallet from her reticule.

'Oh?' The landlord raised his eyebrows, begged her pardon and gave the necessary orders.

After an anxious quarter of an hour, in the course of which she learned by discreet questioning that she was in Epsom, and,

188

in return, unbent so far as to favour the now mollified landlord with a few casual references to death and catastrophe in her family, she set forward, at last, for Denton Hall.

The sun had set long since. The moon rose. Jennifer slept fitfully, tossed this way and that as the carriage rumbled on. When she woke at last, stiff and tired, she recognised the walls of Petworth Park on her right. She was nearly home. The coachman stopped in Petworth Square for directions, then they lumbered on again. It seemed no time before they were in Denton Park. A deer galloped away, startled by the sound of the carriage. Cool dawn lay kindly on the old house. Jennifer alighted with a lump in her throat and a suspicion of tears in her eyes. Wiping them briskly away, she paid off the coachman and turned, with a strange lightening of her heart, to the steps of her house. She was safe; she was home; she was herself again.

She climbed the steps and played a lively tattoo on the knocker. So, years ago, her brothers used to announce an unexpected return. Oddly, she found, for the first time, that she could think of them without pain. I am grown up, she told herself; how strange.

But a light had sprung up in the still-dark house and now the big door swung slowly open to reveal Soames, the butler, in his greatcoat and nightcap, a candle in one hand, his old face a mask of anxiety.

It thawed at sight of her. 'Miss Jennifer,' he said, 'oh, happy day. You are home at last.'

'Yes, Soames,' she stepped into the quiet hall and he shut the big door behind her. 'I am come home to take charge, as I should have long since.'

He wiped an incongruous tear from the side of his nose. 'This is good news indeed. But, Miss Jenny, are you all alone? No boxes? No abigail?'

She smiled at him ruefully. 'Is it not shocking, Soames? What a fortunate thing there is no one but you here to see. Now, I am going direct to bed, and, I think, Soames, that I have been here, indisposed, for some time.'

He smiled at her in affectionate comprehension. 'Ah, Miss

Jenny, you were ever a wild one. It broke our hearts in the servants' hall, indeed it did, to see you knuckle under to that . . .'

'Hush, Soames,' she interrupted him, 'enough of that. It is all over now. And back to bed with you before you catch pneumonia. I am going to my room. You may call me at noon, and please arrange for Hobson the agent to see me at one o'clock.'

He was so delighted at this fresh proof that she meant to take charge of the estate that he did little more than mutter unavailingly about aired sheets and warming-pans as he led her up the stairs to her room. She dismissed him with a summary, 'Nonsense, Soames,' climbed into the familiar bed, and was asleep.

CHAPTER XVIII

In London, Lord Mainwaring paced up and down, up and down, this way and that, in his grandmother's boudoir, while she sat, very upright, in her big chair and watched him with sympathetic, malicious eyes.

'George, you make me giddy,' she said at last, 'it is worse than the beasts at Exeter 'Change. Can you not sit down and possess your soul in patience, like a Christian?'

'No, ma'am.' He paused beside her. 'If it was not all my own fault, I could bear it. But I have done so much to affront her. How can she forgive me?' He resumed his pacing, but in a different direction which allowed him to look, as if casually, out of the window for sight of his grandmother's footman, returning from his message to Jennifer.

'How she forgives you, I collect, is her problem,' said the old lady, 'but forgiveness, you know, comes more easily to a female. The times I have forgiven your grandfather ... Oh, dear me ...'

'But you were married to him, ma'am.'

'You think that makes it easier? I wonder, George, I wonder.'

But he was no longer listening to her. 'At last,' he said. 'What can the fellow have been doing all this time? But here he comes, I think.'

He made as if to leave the room and go to meet the footman, but his grandmother held up a restraining hand. 'Patience, George, patience a little, and remember that the note will be addressed to me.'

But there was no note. After what seemed to Mainwaring a quite intolerable delay, the footman appeared in all the splendour of his indoor livery and reported to the Duchess that he had received no answer to her message.

'No answer?' She raised her eyebrows. 'No, stay, George, do

not go to the devil yet. I find this hard to believe. Miss Fairbank – I beg her pardon, Miss Purchas – is proud, but she was never discourteous.' She turned to the footman. 'You delivered the note into Miss Fairbank's own hands as I bade you?'

He quailed under her penetrating eye. 'No, I could not, your grace, she was not there.'

'Not there? Then why did you not await her return?'

The man reddened and wriggled his neck as if the collar of his livery jacket was too tight: 'If your grace would bear with me . . . I know you do not like to listen to servants' gossip . . . I waited as long as I could . . . They were all at sixes and sevens, your grace. There seemed no sense in staying longer.'

'No sense? Or do you mean that it was your dinner hour? Plague take you for a faithless featherheaded fop of a worthless servant. But what is this about sixes and sevens and servants' gossip?'

'Why, your grace, not to put too fine a point upon it, they were saying in the servants' hall – if you can call it such, with but three maids, the cook and the butler, and him out of livery, too.' He shrank at his mistress's impatient exclamation and continued: 'Well, to be short with your grace, they were saying in the servants' hall that Miss Fairbank is run off.'

'What, again?' said the Duchess. 'Impossible. No, George. I will not have you fly off before I have sifted this further. I am tired of your tantrums. Behave yourself and listen.'

No one had spoken to Mainwaring like that for a long time. Surprised at himself, he subsided into a chair and listened to his grandmother's cross-examination of the footman. He had arrived, it seemed, to find the house in great commotion. Mr Gurning had come in to speak to Miss Fairbank; had found she had gone out unattended, and had flown at once into a passion – not, the footman had gathered from a sympathetic maid, a rare occurrence with him. Miss Gurning had done her best to soothe him, explaining that her cousin had only stepped out for a breath of fresh air and that her other cousin Edmund, anxious at the impropriety of her being out alone, had gone after her. As all this had taken place in the front hall of the house, the footman, comfortably ensconced below-stairs, had heard everything that took place and had waited, contentedly enough, it was clear, for Miss Fairbank to return. 'I shall never remember to call her Miss Purchas,' sighed the Duchess at this point.

But instead, Edmund had arrived, slamming the door, white of face, shouting out to all who cared to hear that his cousin Jennifer had been carried off by a man in a maroon travelling carriage. Mr Gurning had flown into a new passion, his sister had burst into tears, and his daughter had threatened to do likewise, but had refused to believe Miss Fairbank was gone off of her own free-will. By now, of course, the servants were unashamedly listening. They had heard Miss Gurning run upstairs and come back with a note addressed to Miss Fairbank, which she had found on the floor of her room. It made an assignation in the Temple Gardens. Going innocently to keep it, Miss Fairbank must have been abducted. At this point, Mrs Foster's tears turned to hysteria and Miss Gurning had finally collapsed, dropping the note as she did so.

'And what happened to it?' asked the Duchess shrewdly.

'Well, your grace.' The man's collar was too tight again. 'I don't know whether I done right and that's a fact. I only hope your grace won't be angry with me, but knowing what an interest you take in the young lady, and happening to have an opportunity.' He pulled a crumpled piece of paper out of his pocket and handed it to her. 'I picked it up and here it is.'

'Good,' said the Duchess. 'You have done better than I thought. Now you may go to your dinner.'

Alone with Mainwaring, she smoothed out the crumpled note and read it aloud: '"My dearest life, I find I cannot live without you. You must forgive, you must marry me. I cannot visit you in Holborn. Meet me, I beg, in the Temple Gardens, by the river, as soon as you receive this. I will await you there, your humble servant, all evening." Hmm,' she considered it, 'fustian, but to the point. And signed, George, with an "M". You are not, I take it, responsible?'

'I? Responsible? This is no time for jesting, ma'am. She is run off, it seems, with Mandeville. I know that maroon carriage of his. Well, I wish them joy of each other.'

'George, you try my patience beyond bearing. Have you no sense whatever? Or are you so blind and deaf in your own passions that you did not hear what the man said? Miss Fairbank was carried off, George, in that maroon carriage, which, you say, belongs to Mandeville. This note, of course, is from him. I recognise the style. He has taken a fine revenge on you indeed. I wonder if he intended Jennifer to think the note was from you or whether that was merely a piece of luck for him.'

'From me? What do you mean?'

'God give me patience! Have you not twigged it yet? Jennifer, distracted, no doubt, from her scene with you, receives this note, with its talk of forgiveness and marriage, its initial "M". Of course she jumps at once to the conclusion that it is from you and hurries off to the rendezvous to forgive and be forgiven.'

He jumped up. 'And finds Mandeville instead. I shall never forgive myself. If I had only gone back to her instead of coming here and talking of my pride and my despair and a parcel of other trash . . . But we waste time. I thank you from my heart, ma'am, for making me see reason. Now, will you add to your kindness by lending me your fastest carriage and my grandfather's pistols?'

'Of course.' She rang and gave the necessary orders. 'But can you guess where he will have taken her?'

'I hope so. I must stake all on that. His yacht, I know, lies at Southampton. And I recollect Harriette Wilson's telling me of a night she once spent with him at a little inn at Epsom where he brags of being lord of the roast. He will take her there, for the night, to make her ruin complete, then on to France, to escape my vengeance.'

'And what will you do, George?'

'Kill him, if necessary. And marry Jennifer tomorrow whatever has happened. You might ask your cousin the Bishop to put things in train for a special licence, ma'am.'

'Certainly. But I hear the carriage. Do not do more shooting than you must. And, George,' she called him back. 'Whatever has happened to her, do, I beg, remember not to bully Jennifer. We never like being taken for granted.'

He hurried back to kiss her hand. 'Oh, ma'am, if I can but find her . . .'

The Duchess's coachman was not used to letting anyone else drive his team of greys, but one look at Mainwaring's face sent him meekly to their heads. He was grateful enough to be taken up and allowed to go too. As they swept headlong into Park Lane he closed his eyes in silent prayer. A blind beggar, on the other hand, who was laboriously tapping his way across the road, opened his eyes and, his sight miraculously restored, leapt for the gutter and safety. In Whitehall, a young ladies' seminary, out for its afternoon walk in demure crocodile, scattered like leaves before a hurricane. The coachman settled his hat more firmly on his head and grinned at Mainwaring's man. 'It seems we are in a hurry,' he said.

The greys were badly winded when Mainwaring drew up outside the little inn Harriette Wilson had described to him, but the coachman had not even ventured a protest. Now, Mainwaring flung the reins to him and hurried inside. It was late. But was it too late? The question had been ringing in his mind all the way.

There seemed to be no one about. He hammered angrily on the door with the butt of his whip and shouted: 'House, there, house!'

An old woman came tottering out from what smelled to be the kitchen and looked at him in quavering alarm. 'Lawk-a-mussy,' she said, 'more quality. As if we had not had enough trouble tonight.' Then, raising her voice, 'John,' she called up the stairs, 'John, here's another on 'em.'

'Coming, ma,' said a man's voice. There was a sound of conversation above and then a short, fat, red-faced man came downstairs holding a basin which he handed to the old woman. 'The sawbones says more cold compresses and look sharp about it. And the spirits of ammonia, too, for fear he goes off again.' Then he turned civilly enough to Mainwaring. 'I beg your pardon, sir, for keeping you, but we are all to pieces here tonight. And I who have always kept as respectable a house as any in Surrey.'

'I am sorry to trouble you at such an awkward time,' said Mainwaring, wishing he had considered more carefully what he was to say, 'but I am searching for a young lady who I believe may have been brought here.'

'Young lady,' the landlord bristled up at the phrase, 'young vixen, more like. Young lady, you call it! You should have heard what Mr Mandeville called her when he came to his senses. And him the most generous, open-handed gentleman that ever drew breath. To treat him so; why prison's too good for the likes of her. Young lady, indeed, young besom, I should call her . . .'

Mainwaring was too much delighted at the implications of this speech to care for the man's vehemence: 'Call her what you will, my good man, only tell me where she is.'

'I can tell you where she ought to be, right enough, and that's in the lockup for manslaughter, robbery with violence and I don't know what else, but Mr Mandeville will never bring a charge, so good as he is, and him lying there dead to the world for some half-hour or more before we found him. For he had given orders, you see, after I put the dessert on the table, that he was not to be disturbed. And natural enough, saving your honour's presence, with such a prime handful for his companion. Too prime and a half for him, was what she proved . . . But how was I to know, when she sat there prattling away about Paris, and new bonnets and I don't know what kick-shawses . . . How was I to know, I ask you, that all the time she had murder in her heart?'

'And had she?' Mainwaring was feeling better. The quick pulse that had beat out its refrain of 'too late, too late' in his head all the way from London had slowed to a steadier beat. Jennifer was safe.

'Had she not, sir? No sooner is my back turned than she ups with a bottle of claret – a full bottle, sir, of my best claret that set me in I don't know what the dozen, and cracked the poor gentleman over the head with it as cool as you please. *And* picks his pocket too, sir, and then has the effrontery to bandage up his poor head for him before she walks out of the house as cool as a cucumber. And he will not even have the constable after her, sir. You never saw the likes of it, just lies in bed and groans when I urge it.'

'Well,' it was hard to conceal his relief. 'You can hardly be surprised at that. He would look a pretty fool letting himself be robbed by a young lady.'

'Young lady.' It started the landlord off again. 'Young termagent if you ask me. He should have known better than to take up with a red-head wench; there never was but trouble come from them, and so I could have told him . . .'

But Mainwaring had heard all he needed to know. Jennifer had got safe away and had already dealt so roundly with Mandeville that there was no room for his intervention. You can hardly shoot a man who is in bed with concussion. So much, he thought rather ruefully, for his knight errantry. But it was still urgent that he catch up with her as soon as possible. Besides, a cold thought struck him, had the blow which felled Mandeville been self-defence, or revenge?

Spurred on by this thought, he bade a curt farewell to the landlord, returned to the carriage, jumped inside and ordered the Duchess's coachman to drive him to the centre of the town as fast as possible. Here, too, he found that Jennifer had left her mark. Questioned, the landlord of the coaching inn was voluble in his detcription of her high-handed ways. 'But free of her purse.' He pocketed Mainwaring's tip. 'A very free-handed young lady. And nicely spoken, too, once she had got her own way.' Yes, she had taken his best team of horses; she was going Petworth way . . . driving through the night . . . a death in the family, perhaps a couple of them, he was sure he did not know . . . Mainwaring cut short his wonderings, thanked him for the information, hired his second best team of horses and set out in his turn for Denton Hall.

Jennifer, meanwhile, had waked, dealt kindly but firmly with her aunt's hysterical amazement at sight of her, discussed with her father's delighted agent her uncle's depredations on the estate and found them little worse than she had expected, and sent off a messenger post-haste to London with letters for the Duchess, her uncle and Elizabeth. The gist of all of them was the same. She was at home; she did not explain how or why; she proposed to stay there, and, so far as the world was concerned, she had, in fact, never left. Writing her gratitude once again to the Duchess, she could not banish from her mind the possibility that Mainwaring, too, might read what she said. It made the task doubly difficult and the note rather shorter than she would have liked. To Elizabeth, she was soothing; to her uncle, firm. She had talked to her agent, she told him, and knew exactly how matters stood. She awaited the news of Elizabeth's engagement to Edmund. The wedding, she suggested, should take place at Denton Hall, where she hoped to see them all shortly.

So much for the past. At least, she had got much of it tidy. As for the present, it seemed to consist mainly of her lachrymose Aunt Gurning, who appeared equally in despair at the idea of her husband's returning or of his staying away. In either case, it seemed, she was bound to suffer from his fury at the thwarting of his plans.

'Never fret, Aunt,' said Jennifer at last. 'I will protect you.'

'You, Jenny?' Her scepticism was all too evident.

'Who else? I am the head of the family now. I cannot think why I had not realised it long since. I will see to it that my uncle treats you properly.' She rang the bell. Already she was tired of the present and longed to be alone to face the future. 'Soames,' she said, when he appeared, 'what horses have we in the stables?'

'None fit for you to ride, I fear, Miss Jenny. There is only your brother's Black Prince and you know you were never allowed to ride him.'

'No more I was, Soames.' She smiled at him brilliantly. 'Order him saddled at once.'

Soames protested, old Thomas the groom threw up his hands in horror. But she was Miss Purchas of Denton Hall and she intended to be obeyed. When she came downstairs twenty minutes later, Black Prince was jigging about on the carriage sweep, held by a stable boy, while Thomas waited in attendance on his own cob, disapproval in every inch of him.

'He's mortal fresh, Miss Jenny,' said the stable boy as he helped her to mount.

'Good,' said Jenny. 'So am I. I have wanted a real gallop this age. No use looking such a death's head, Thomas, but I suppose I must let you come too if you wish.'

She had her gallop, all out, on the Downs above her house, then paused to let Thomas catch up with her and to look with a prodigal's affection at the prospect of park and woodland below her. Then, as Thomas rode up, puffing and reproachful, she stiffened. 'Is not that a carriage, turning off the Chichester road towards the Hall?'

He looked but shook his head: 'Indeed, I cannot say, Miss Jenny, my eyesight is failing sadly these days.'

But she was sure of it now. A carriage and four horses. Her parsimonious uncle only travelled with a pair. Who could it be? She would not let herself hope. But she dug her heels into Black Prince's sides and said: 'I'll race you home.'

Mainwaring was there before her. Asking if Miss Purchas had yet returned to her home, he did not miss the look of surprise and anxiety on Soames' face.

'Returned, my lord?' asked the butler, at his stateliest. 'Miss Purchas has not been away. But she is out at the moment. Riding, I believe.'

And in confirmation of his words, a figure appeared, taking, at speed, a hazardous curve of the Downs, vanishing for an instant, then reappearing, riding more sedately through the outlying trees of the park. Mainwaring stayed where he was on the graceful steps of the house, with Soames, unheeded, behind him. She rode up, her colour high, her curls dishevelled, smiled a greeting to the Duchess's coachman, who was walking his horses, dismounted, and came, leisurely it seemed, towards Mainwaring, drawing off York tan gloves as she came.

'You were seeking me, my lord? Soames, refreshments in the office, if you please.' She led the way indoors. 'I will be with you in a moment, Aunt.' A fretful voice had called her from the head of the stairs. 'This way, my lord,' She led him into a plain, work-a-day room he had not seen before, motioned him to an upright chair and settled, herself, at her uncle's desk. She was glad to do so. Her knees were shaking.

For a moment, both were silent. Outside, Thomas and the stable boy discussed racing form as they led the horses round to the stables. In the room, rose petals, falling from a vase on the chimney-piece, sounded loud in the tense quietness.

Mainwaring spoke first. 'Your butler tells me you have never been away.'

She smiled. 'Good Soames. He does so hate to lie; but he will do anything for the Family, as he calls us.'

Another silence. She was not going to speak. He stood up and prowled over to the window. 'It is not enough,' he said, 'you do not understand the force of scandal. Jennifer – Miss Fairbank, devil take it, I mean Miss Purchas, you must see there is no help for it but to marry me.'

She looked up at him, dark eyebrows raised. 'Must I, my lord?'

'I tell you, it is the only way. Too many people remember Miss Fairbank, who made, you must recollect, a considerable sensation. Return to town as Miss Purchas – can you not imagine the talk?'

'Easily, my lord. But I do not propose returning to London. Miss Fairbank is dead and gone. We will forget her, and her follies, if you please. As for Miss Purchas, she has had enough of London. She will live in the country, a paragon of good works. You have no need to have me on your conscience, my lord. I can take care of myself.'

For the first time he smiled. 'No need to tell me that. I am but now come from Epsom.'

'Oh,' her hand flew to her mouth, 'you know, then? How is Mr Mandeville?'

'As angry as concussion and a country doctor can make a man. But that is why I am come to you so fast. Tell me nothing. I do not want to know what happened between you and Mandeville, but you must see that it leaves you no course but to marry me. The landlord will talk, even Mandeville himself may, though I doubt it after the floorer you gave him. And what of your silly cousin and your uncle who were, by all accounts, canvassing the whole affair in front of the servants. Everything else – Miss Fairbank and her follies, if you must call them so – all that might pass, but this . . . Believe me, I speak as your friend. Marriage is your only hope.'

'You are too good.' She had herself well in hand now. 'But I do not need such forced friendship. I have told you already that your promise to my brothers must be forgotten. Now, I beg you to leave me. We have no more to say to each other, you and I.'

He was angry now; angry because she had not needed his help; angry because he loved her. He turned from the window and stood over her: 'Very well then. Stay here and rot in your country retreat. Devote yourself to good works, bully your servants, breed dogs – I beg your pardon?'

'I said, not dogs. Cats, perhaps, or monkeys . . .'

Suddenly he was laughing. 'Jenny, have I lost my temper again? Have I been bullying you? My grandmother told me not to. Why do I never remember her advice in time? Do you not understand that I love you, have loved you this age, have fought it, have tormented myself with scruples? Do you not see that that is why I want you to marry me? To the devil with promises, brothers, uncles, the whole pack of them. Who cares for them, or your name? Have half a dozen, if you like, if you will only take mine as well. Take me, Jenny; forgive me. I am but a poor hand at a speech. I have made a mull of things from start to finish, but, believe me, I love you. I think I always have.'

She looked up at him. 'Even when I stole your horse? Confess you thought me a complete hoyden.'

'Yes, but then you looked at me with those fierce eyes of yours and gave me such a setdown. You, a governess, a little chit of a thing . . . You made me *see* you. I shall never want to look at another woman. Marry me, Jenny. You would not condemn me to becoming a bad-tempered gouty old bachelor – Oh, damme, I know what that smile means. I am quite bad-tempered enough already. It is true, Jenny, I am a spoiled, cross-grained wretch, who does not deserve you, but you could tame me, I promise you could.'

'And suppose I fail?'

'You *fail*? When did you fail at anything you set your hand to? You have made a friend of my grandmother and an enemy (God bless you) of my Aunt Beresford. You have defeated Mandeville and outgeneraled your uncle. Surely, after that, you are heroine enough to try your hand with me? I shall be a brute, Jenny. I shall sit up to all hours drinking with my political friends. I shall come home in a rage when things go ill at the House and expect you to be waiting there to soothe me. Indeed, I shall always want you to be there. I shall love you very much, Jenny. My grandmother says forgiveness is easy for a woman. Can you find it in your heart to forgive and love me a little?'

'Your grandmother,' said Jennifer, 'is a very wise woman. I shall like being her granddaughter.'

He took her in his arms. More rose petals fell on the chimney-piece. It was very quiet in the little room. At last, he moved his head to look down at her: 'And no more running away, my love.'

She smiled up at him. 'Run away?' she asked. 'Why should I?'

WATCH THE WALL, MY DARLING

JANE AIKEN HODGE

Christina Tretton came home from the wilds of America to the stranger, solitary world of Romney Marsh. There she met her tyrannical grandfather and her two cousins, one whom he has decreed she must marry. Richard proves to be a selfish fop, Ross overbearing and heartless — and moreover, somehow mixed up with dark deeds on the marsh. Whom can she trust? Where does Ross disappear to, and what is he doing? And why should she obey him when his whims mean danger for herself?

'Smuggling and suspicion keep the pot on the boil'
The Daily Telegraph

'Entertaining'

The Evening Standard

'Jane Aiken Hodge takes her rightful place alongside Helen MacInnes and Mary Stewart'

Bestsellers

CORONET BOOKS

ALSO AVAILABLE IN CORONET BOOKS

JANE AIKEN HODGE

☐	02892 0	Watch the Wall, My Darling	75p
☐	10759 6	The Adventures	80p
☐	16465 4	Maulever Hall	75p
☐	15029 7	Marry in Haste	60p
☐	18806 5	Strangers in Company	70p

NORAH LOFTS

☐	16950 8	A Rose For Virtue	50p
☐	16216 3	Lovers All Untrue	50p
☐	19352 2	Crown Of Aloes	50p
☐	17826 4	Charlotte	50p
☐	18403 5	Nethergate	50p

All these books are available at your local bookshop or newsagent, or can be ordered direct from the publisher. Just tick the titles you want and fill in the form below.

Prices and availability subject to change without notice.

CORONET BOOKS P.O. Box 11, Falmouth, Cornwall.

Please send cheque or postal order, and allow the following for postage and packing:

U.K. – One book 22p plus 10p per copy for each additional book ordered, up to a maximum of 82p.

B.F.P.O. and EIRE – 22p for the first book plus 10p per copy for the next 6 books, thereafter 4p per book.

OTHER OVERSEAS CUSTOMERS – 30p for the first book and 10p per copy for each additional book.

Name ....

Address ....

....